NEVER
COMING
HOME

BOOKS BY KATE WILLIAMS

Never Coming Home

THE BABYSITTERS COVEN SERIES

The Babysitters Coven

For Better or Cursed

Spells Like Teen Spirit

NEVER COMING HOME

KATE WILLIAMS

DELACORTE PRESS

All rights reserved. Published in the United States by Delacorte Press, an imprint of Random House Children's Books, a division of Penguin Random House LLC, New York.

Delacorte Press is a registered trademark and the colophon is a trademark of Penguin Random House LLC.

Visit us on the Web! GetUnderlined.com

Educators and librarians, for a variety of teaching tools, visit us at RHTeachersLibrarians.com

Library of Congress Cataloging-in-Publication Data
Names: Williams, Kate, author.
Title: Never coming home / Kate Williams.
Description: First edition. | New York : Delacorte Press, 2022. | Audience: Ages 14+. |
Summary: Ten teen influencers arrive on Unknown Island expecting to find a tropical paradise, but instead they discover a deserted resort, poisonous snakes, and secrets worth killing for.
Identifiers: LCCN 2021038354 (print) | LCCN 2021038355 (ebook) |
ISBN 978-0-593-30486-0 (hardcover) | ISBN 978-0-593-30487-7 (ebook)
Subjects: CYAC: Internet personalities—Fiction. | Murder—Fiction. |
Social media—Fiction. | Revenge—Fiction. | LCGFT: Novels. | Thrillers (Fiction)
Classification: LCC PZ7.1.W5465 Ne 2022 (print) | LCC PZ7.1.W5465 (ebook) |
DDC [Fic]—dc23

The text of this book is set in 11.65-point Baskerville MT Pro.
Interior design by Ken Crossland
Jacket art used under license from Shutterstock.com.

Printed in the United States of America
10 9 8 7 6 5 4 3 2 1
First Edition

For my parents, who love a good mystery

THE FIRST TEN

☉ **Margot Bryant (643k followers)** .... **The CEO**
Founder and CEO. @forbes 20 under 20. The future is @SHEmail

☉ **Manuel de La Cruz (1.3m followers)** .... **The DJ**
Miami Nice streaming now. Get at me.

🐦 **Graham Hoffman (121k followers)** .... **The Politician**
Former Minneapolis city council member. Current Princeton '24.
#njyoungdems

♪ **Xander Lee (22.4m followers)** .... **The Athlete**
I'm just happy 2b here. Jeremiah 29:11.

☉ **Emma Jane Ohana (6.6m followers)** ....**The Rich Girl**
✌ plannedparenthood.org/donate

▶ **Chelsea Quinn (12.8m followers)** .... **The Beauty Blogger**
Long lashes, high standards. Subscribe for tutorials, demos & MORE!

♪ **Frankie Russh (130.6m followers)** ....**The Superstar**
Nothin but 💜 for ya, bb. linktree.com/frankierussh

▶ **Robby Wade (8.6m followers)** ....**The Chef**
Chef/owner @hock_and_jowl. Host @yungcheffintv

☉ **Justice Wilson (236k followers)** .... **The Environmentalist**
There is no planet B. 🌍 #climatestrike2022 #classof2023

🎮 **Celia Young (13.6m followers)** ....**The Gamer**
info@cy.net

NEVER
COMING
HOME

CHAPTER ONE

You're not in Kansas anymore. It was the kind of one-liner that immediately made Justice Wilson write people off as boring and unoriginal, but now she couldn't help but say it to herself. She was halfway around the world, and she liked it.

The tropics swarmed in as soon as the plane doors opened. Wet, humid air that turned walking into swimming, and palm trees whipping in the wind like they were trying to lure customers in to buy a used car. When she'd left Kansas City this morning, or last night, or whenever it was that she'd gotten on the first plane, the hue of the sky matched the concrete, the people were pale, and everything was cold. Now, she was surrounded by heat and a riot of color. Turquoise sky, emerald leaves, people with golden-brown skin, airline employees dressed in bright florals with flowers tucked behind their ears or pinned to their shirts. It was the kind of placed Justice had always dreamed of, but dang, was it hot.

She reached up and readjusted her scarf and then fanned the back of her neck. It was barely six a.m. here, but the sun was already blazing, and the people in front of her were moving like they were still asleep. Justice was too excited to be annoyed or tired. It had taken her three planes and almost twenty-four hours to get here. When she first saw the agenda, she'd shuddered at the carbon footprint of such a flight, but they had assured her that everything was offset. More than offset, even, which was just one of the reasons she knew this trip was going to be worth it. Honestly, she would have taken the trip even if there wasn't a carbon offset. She needed this trip. This was the farthest from home she'd ever been, and that was what Justice wanted more than anything right now. To be far from home.

She had at least a few hours before her parents realized where she'd gone. By then, her father could threaten to ground her or take away her car, or demand she come home, and all for naught, because she'd be safely out of reach, on a private island where there were no flights in or out. It was easier to ask for forgiveness than permission, and when Justice returned after her week in paradise, even her uptight parents would see that traveling to Unknown Island was the best thing she could have done for her future.

The line was finally moving, and Justice made her way down the stairs and onto the runway, heat radiating off the pavement in waves. She stepped to the side, set her suitcase down, and pulled out the handle, then headed into the airport. She'd expected it to be air-conditioned, and was surprised when she walked through the doors and found the inside even wetter, and stickier, than outside. This realization made her smile, and laugh at herself a little. She could be such an American sometimes, thinking that everything should be comfortable and convenient, a Starbucks on every corner and a UPS truck on every street.

She was going to have to get used to this. If she was going to be an environmentalist like she wanted, she would be spending a lot of time in the third world. Wait, *was* this the third world? Probably not, because even with the lack of air-conditioning, the airport was pretty nice.

Justice forced herself to ignore her phone, which was tucked in the pocket of her carry-on bag. She'd kept it off all through her last layover, resisting the urge to check it while going through customs and passport control. Looking at her phone was exciting but also kind of scary.

She found the bathroom, peed, washed her hands, and soaked her red headscarf before retying it, which made her feel a little cooler. She'd managed to sleep a little on the flight, so she wasn't too exhausted, but she could still tell that her body was confused by the time change and wasn't sure if it wanted to eat, go for a run, or pass out. Back out of the bathroom, she wheeled her suitcase over to an empty chair in a waiting area, plopped down, took a big drink of water from her Hydro Flask, and then, only then, did she allow herself to check her phone.

The invitation had come a couple of months ago: an all-expenses-paid trip to Unknown Island, a high-profile, exclusive tropical resort. Rachel, the publicist Justice had talked to, had explained that Unknown Island represented a new kind of travel, one that let travelers avoid crowds and meet and mingle with curated strangers instead. Justice was invited to be part of the inaugural group, a tight selection of ten next-generation influencers. The tagline was grandiose and bold—*The future of humanity meets the future of travel*—and Justice hated to admit it, but she felt pretty honored to be included.

Unknown Island had picked her because they thought that she, especially, could help demonstrate how serious they were about sustainability and ecotourism. Justice had sent Rachel a list of content ideas, and the publicist had loved all of them, even telling her that they hoped this would be the start of a long-term partnership. Justice hoped so too, because that might be the exact kind of thing to get her off Harvard's waitlist.

And then, of course, her parents said no.

"You're seventeen," her mother said. "There's no way you're flying three-quarters of the way around the world by yourself to go to some island with a bunch of strangers." Justice had tried to be mature about it and hadn't pointed out that if she was flying three-quarters of the way around the world, then she was only one-quarter of the world away.

But her parents wouldn't hear her out. They refused to discuss it after that, refused to listen to her arguments, refused to get on the phone with Rachel to get all the details about what an incredible opportunity this was for Justice. She could feel Harvard slipping even further away, so when Rachel sent the waiver for her parents to sign, Justice signed it herself and sent it back. No doubt her parents had forgotten about the whole thing weeks ago, but she still held her breath as she turned her phone back on, waited for it to come to life, and then connected to the airport's free Wi-Fi.

She relaxed when she saw she had nothing from her parents, who thought she was at Nicole's for the weekend. But then her phone started buzzing and didn't stop. The notifications came fast and furious, and Justice watched, amazed, each new one making her heart pound a little faster.

Though it hadn't even opened yet, Unknown Island already had millions of followers. It had followed no one on its social media accounts until the day before this first trip, when it started following its first ten guests. In the short amount of time since, Justice had gained more followers than she could count, and the last two things she did before getting on the plane to come was post a video about Unknown Island, just as she had been instructed. And block her parents.

People were loving it. The video had already gotten more comments than anything Justice had ever posted before. There was a fair amount of hate, of course—people calling her a hypocrite, saying that this kind of travel was wasteful and environmentally disrespectful—but there were also a ton of people cheering her on, saying she deserved this trip, or that they were jealous. That was the majority of the comments, people saying they were jealous. Everyone knew Unknown Island, because who in the world didn't want a free vacation? And part of what had gotten the world's attention about Unknown Island was that it was always going to be free. That was one of its biggest hooks. Exclusive, curated groups of guests, all picked because they had something to offer the other guests, and the world. No one knew who owned Unknown Island, and when Justice had asked Rachel about it, she refused to answer. "A billionaire philanthropist who wishes to remain anonymous," she had said. Maybe Bill Gates or Mark Zuckerberg, Justice thought, but she hadn't pressed the issue for fear she might cross a line and get herself uninvited.

Justice stood up, looked around, and tucked her phone back into her pocket. This was a life-changing opportunity, and she needed a life change. She went to go find her ride.

Manny de la Cruz had been hoping for a private jet. He'd only been on a PJ once, and he was about one #tbt post away from looking like a loser desperately mining the past. But it wasn't that big a deal, and who was he kidding? First class was still first class.

He had friends who'd never even been on a plane. Plus, he'd taken a good pic of his Air Max 90s peeking out from underneath a first-class comforter. It wasn't too braggy, he thought. It just looked like he was trying to document his new kicks, and no one but the old man sitting next to him knew that Manny had spent five minutes arranging the comforter to make sure the airline logo was visible.

But a helicopter, *that* was cool. Probably even cooler than a Gulfstream. When the car turned in the gate, he saw the chopper sitting on the landing pad and felt a wave of excitement wash over him. The whole thing made him feel like a kingpin or an action hero. The driver got out and opened the door for him, then got his bag out of the trunk and set it on the ground next to his feet.

"Thanks, man," Manny said. "Appreciate it." He held out a crisp ten-dollar bill, folded in half lengthwise, and the driver smiled as he took it.

"Thank you, sir," he said. "Have a good trip."

Within seconds of getting out of the car, Manny started to

sweat. He took a bandanna out of his back pocket and lifted his ball cap to wipe the sweat from his forehead. Coming from Miami, Manny was used to the heat, but he was still dressed for the plane in socks and jeans and a hoodie. He quickly pulled the hoodie off and stuffed it in his backpack. The heat reminded him of trips to visit his mom's family on the islands, even though this was like no island he'd ever been to before.

He started to walk across the helipad, and with each step, he felt some of the adrenaline leave his body. He'd spent the past twenty hours looking over his shoulder, scoping everyone out, expecting, at any second, for someone to come up behind him, grab his arm, and say, "Sir, you need to come with us." Fuck. The stress of this trip alone had probably taken three years off his life, but it was going to be worth it. He hoped this trip would put him over the edge, be the thing that made it so that he could leave all that other shit behind for good.

The Unknown Island rep he'd talked to had never explicitly told him what to do, but the hints she'd dropped were hard and heavy. "Listen," Lindsey had said, "I've got a lot of friends in Miami, and everyone says you're a good guy to have around. We need someone like you on this trip to make sure everyone has everything they need to have a good time." Of course. It had all made sense then.

Lindsey assured him, several times, that security and customs weren't going to be a problem, and she'd been right. Manny thought he might throw up in front of the TSA agents, but they'd been too busy talking about someone who took extra-long lunch breaks to give him more than a glance. As for customs, he hadn't even seen any agents. He'd only talked to Lindsey on the phone, but she'd been crisp and competent, and it wasn't until Manny was on his way here that he realized he'd never asked who her friends in Miami were.

From the beginning, he found it kind of weird that he was given one of only ten slots on this high-profile trip, but he guessed it made sense enough from the outside. Manny had built up a decent following over the years, between his music and the people he knew, even though being publicly famous meant nothing when he wanted to be a producer. For a producer, he always told himself, it was all about how many followers your followers had, and the comments section on Manny's posts were always littered with blue check marks.

True, none of those people had asked him for a beat or to collab, but he knew that these things took time. And after it had been announced that he was coming on this trip, his DMs had filled up with people wanting to book him to play parties, or telling Manny to hit them up when he got back. He planned to do just that, and more. Forget waiting for people to ask for a track. He was going to start sending them.

If he was being honest, the Unknown Island guest list had been a real disappointment, a bigger letdown than the lack of a Gulfstream. He was the only musician. But that was all part of Unknown's deal, apparently: it was designed to get you mixing with people you wouldn't otherwise meet. And he did like the ratio: four guys, six girls, two of whom were definitely hot. One was a rich party girl from LA, and the other was Frankie Russh. Maybe she counted as a musician?

Frankie was a dancer with a massive following, and there'd been rumors of her working on an album, but Manny didn't hold out hope that she would be anyone he wanted to collab with. Girls like that were always working on an album, even though he had no idea how you "worked on an album" when you didn't write songs, sing, play an instrument, or make music.

Manny made his way to the only shade in sight, a few sheltered picnic tables on the other side of the blazing concrete. There were already four people sitting there: a tan, blond girl in heels and a short dress who was fanning herself with two magazines; another girl, who appeared to be asleep; and two others—also girls—who were staring at their phones. There was no one else in the vicinity. As Manny walked toward them, he noted that there was no place for him to duck behind and change out of his jeans. He should have done it at the airport, taken a few minutes to clean himself up, but he'd been so anxious to get out of there he hadn't even stopped to use the bathroom.

As he walked by the helicopter, he decided he couldn't let the opportunity go to waste. Sure, he might not have been here for the best reasons, but he was still here and he might as well make the most out of it. He held out his phone, making sure he got the chopper in the background as he cheesed and snapped a few selfies. When he finished, he looked up to see that the three girls who were awake were watching him. One set her phone down, then stood up and started walking toward him, her arm outstretched.

"Here," she said, motioning for him to hand her his phone, "let me do it, and you can get your suitcase in, too." Manny hesitated for a moment. "Trust me," she said, "I'm practically a professional."

Manny handed his phone to her, and she took a few steps back. "Now walk that way and don't look at me," she said. "Never acknowledge the paparazzi."

He laughed, and followed her directions. She took several pics from a few different angles, then handed his phone to him when she was finished. "Thanks," Manny said, slipping the phone back into his pocket.

"Aren't you going to look at them?" she teased, smiling. "They could be total crap. I could have cut your head off, or gotten an angle that gave you three chins."

Manny laughed. "Nah, later," he said. "I'm sure they're good."

"Ooh," she said, "that confident, huh?"

"Yeah, I am that confident," he said. "Not in my skills as a model, in yours as a photographer." Normally, Manny would have looked at the pics immediately, but he wasn't going to blow his first meeting with a girl like this by spending the whole time messing with his phone. This was Frankie Russh, after all, and Manny was kind of surprised. In her photos, she was internet hot. In person, she was humanly gorgeous.

"So," he said as they started walking toward the shade, "where'd you fly in from?"

Five minutes in and there was already a love connection forming. Manny had introduced himself to all the girls, even though it was a given that they already recognized each other from their socials, but it was clear he only had eyes for Frankie Russh. Now they were playing a serious game of getting-to-know-you and talking about their favorite airports. Chelsea Quinn had to give it to them: they would make an attractive couple, and they had that whole opposites-attract thing going for them, Frankie being the kind of girl who wasn't lying when she said "I don't really wear makeup" and him being a bad-boy, hip-hop type. A few minutes ago, Manny had taken his shirt off, revealing Justin Bieber–level tattoos, a Ken-doll physique, and a Calvin Klein waistband, but Chelsea didn't think he was trying to show off. It really was that hot out here.

Hell, she'd take her dress off if she could. Tie it around her head like a scarf and climb aboard that helicopter in her panties. Instead, she settled for spritzing her face with her Evian atomizer. There was no breeze, and Chelsea felt like pudding in the sun. No amount of loose powder was going to keep her under-eye concealer anywhere near under her eyes, and sweat had turned her dewy foundation into sludge. She scanned the horizon for someone, anyone, who might be coming to save her from this hellfire on concrete.

There was no one, of course, and this whole thing again struck Chelsea as rather weird. She'd been on several sponsored trips before, and lots of launches when she still had her CoverGirl contract, and on those trips she hadn't been left alone for a minute. There was always an advertising director and a PR director and a marketing director and a thousand assistants running around taking care of everything. She could have dropped a used Kleenex and someone would have grabbed it before it hit the ground.

But there was no one from Unknown Island in sight. Just a hired driver who had met Chelsea at the airport and then dropped her off here, where there wasn't so much as a bottle of water or a place to charge her phone. She did some quick calculations in her head. Between the five of them, across platforms they had close to two hundred million followers. Granted, most of that came from Frankie Russh, but Chelsea herself still had almost thirty million when she added them up, which she did frequently, and no matter what, that was still a lot. So WTF? Who flies five influencers around the world just to let them slowly die of thirst in the blazing heat? They'd been sitting here forever. It seemed like they were waiting for something, but there was no one to ask what for.

Emma Jane had fallen asleep immediately after introducing herself and had barely stirred since. With Frankie and Manny well on their way to becoming #franny, or whatever dumb nickname people would give them, Margot Bryant was the only one Chelsea could talk to, and in the space of just a few minutes, Chelsea had decided that Margot Bryant might be one of the most annoying people she'd met in her entire life.

She kept talking to Chelsea like they had a lot in common, name-dropping makeup and skin care brands even though she looked like she'd applied her eyeliner with a trowel. Margot also kept referring to herself as a CEO and trying to bring every topic of conversation back to her company, which was apparently email for women. Like, seriously? Just use Gmail like everyone else! And then there was the name: SHEmail. The first time Chelsea had heard it, she'd choked and swallowed her gum. Surely, she had thought, Margot was joking. Margot was not.

Chelsea found herself too tired to call Margot out, and as the girl nattered on about herself and her company, Chelsea tuned her out and tried to stay positive. Sure, there was something off about this whole thing, but it was also the first time in ages, the first time *since*, that Chelsea had been invited to a big event. She used to dream about someday attending the Met Ball, or sitting front row at Paris Fashion Week, but now she was lucky to go to the opening of a brow boutique in the Valley. At least she still had her followers, and she'd actually gained a lot since it was announced that she was coming here. That had to count for something. It felt like ages since she had done anything for the "exposure," but here she was. Might as well make the most of it.

Still, it was hard to totally block her out, and Margot's incessant chatter made Chelsea want to take off her heels and drive them into her own eyes, but thankfully Emma Jane woke up.

"Look," she said, stretching and pointing at a golf cart in the distance with two people in it. "Maybe someone's coming to rescue us." They all watched in silence as the cart approached and came to a stop in front of the picnic table. A man in a polo shirt got out and walked toward them.

"Hello," he said, "I'm Mario. I'll be your pilot over to the island. We are so sorry to have kept you waiting, but we have one guest who is unaccounted for."

"What does that mean?" Chelsea asked, shading her eyes.

"Well," Mario continued, "we can't find her. We know she was on her flight, but it was late and we haven't been able to locate her since the plane landed."

"Can't you just take us and come back for her?" Chelsea asked.

"I wish I could," the pilot said, "but the helicopter was only reserved for one trip."

Okay, more proof that this was weird. All the expense to set this whole thing up, and then they were cheaping out on transportation for the last leg of the trip?

"Maybe that's her now?" Margot said. The others followed

her gaze across the helipad, heat radiating off the concrete in waves, to a white car that was turning in through the gates.

"Jesus, I hope so," Chelsea said, and everyone nodded in agreement. They all watched as the car drove over to them, and then the rear door opened and a small girl got out. The driver didn't move to help her, so she fumbled her own massive suitcase out of the trunk by herself. Then she stood there, looking at them. They all looked back at her.

The girl started to drag her suitcase toward them. "Hi, um, is this the helicopter for Unknown Island?" she asked.

"It is," Mario answered.

"Okay," the girl said. "My name is Celia Young, and I'm supposed to be on it." Chelsea did a double take at hearing Celia's name. So this was the famous gamer? The teenage girl known for making grown men cry? She looked about twelve.

Mario clapped his hands. "Fantastic!" he said. He grabbed a walkie-talkie from his belt and spoke into it. A few minutes later, the helicopter's blades started to spin. Chelsea held her arms out from her sides, *Titanic*-style, and let her sweat dry in the gusts. Paradise was waiting for them. No breeze had ever felt so good.

Never be the most famous person in the room. That was one of the first pieces of advice Roger had given Frankie Russh when they started working together, and in the two years since, it had become part of their gospel. Roger was more than just Frankie's manager. He'd become the dad she never had, her forty-six-year-old gay best friend, and the only person she trusted anymore.

So why was she here? The whir of the helicopter blades was deafening and any hair that was not tied back whipped into eyes and lip gloss, but everyone was grinning as they rose off the ground and into the sky. Frankie forced herself to grin, too. She didn't want to seem like she was anything less than thrilled to be here, but . . . she was less than thrilled to be here. Something was off. Where was everyone? Where were the publicists, the marketing directors, security?

There had been no one but a driver to meet her at the airport. He'd helped with her bags but done nothing to keep people from taking her picture, to keep that red-faced American man from hugging her without asking. "My daughter loves you!" the man had said, but Frankie could tell he was lying. She knew he didn't have a daughter, and his arm had brushed the side of her boob.

She peered out the window at the clear blue South Pacific below, rippling and stretching in every direction like frosting, then glanced quickly at her fellow passengers. The lack of a warm welcome she could deal with, but these people were really bothering her. They just didn't make sense.

All eyes were on Unknown Island this week. It was one of the most anticipated hospitality launches in recent history, and there had been an insane amount of buzz about who would be invited first. Roger had started negotiating Frankie's invite months ago. Unknown Island was paying her a huge sum of money, and there was a strict NDA, part of which was that she wouldn't know who the other guests were until she was already on her way.

It had been intriguing, and Frankie had spent a fair amount of time imagining who the other guests might be. Greta

Thunberg maybe? Or Billie Eilish? But Greta Thunberg and Billie Eilish weren't on this trip. Not even close. Instead, it was an odd mix of people, most of whom Frankie had never heard of. She got that Unknown's whole thing was about carefully curated groups from different walks of life, but this group was hardly . . . exclusive.

Frankie hadn't done research on anyone, of course; she'd just looked at their numbers. Working with Roger, she had learned it was possible to tell where someone was in their career by which of their platforms had the most engagement. If they were blowing up on a newer platform, they were someone to watch. If they had their biggest following on Instagram, their career was leveling off, and if the bulk of their following was on Twitter or Facebook, then forget it. They were pretty much dead.

Frankie had made her career on TikTok and lived in fear of some new app that would take its place, leaving TikTok a wasteland for parents making jokes about wine or barbecues. Frankie needed a new thing so that she could leave social media behind before it left her, but that new thing was slow in coming. Even though she had a makeup line and a clothing collection and had cohosted and produced her own reality show, most people still thought of her as a girl who posted dance videos. She had one of the biggest followings in the world, but it was hard to get excited about that anymore. Because what did one hundred and thirty million people want on TikTok, especially when most of them were tweens? Dance videos. They wanted dance videos.

Frankie had hoped the people on this trip would signal that she had jumped up a level. But, no. These people definitely still used hashtags. Roger had said he was pretty sure she was the only one getting paid and that everyone else was just doing it for the exposure. Ha, exposure! Frankie could barely remember those days, they were so far behind her. Now, she didn't even drink coffee without getting paid for it.

Roger had assured Frankie she could cancel, and she knew he meant it. But her bank account had taken a serious hit last year, and Frankie needed to make that money back while she still could. Plus, when she got paid, Roger got paid. She owed him that much, considering she could never truly repay him for all that he'd done for her, for cleaning up her messes.

Frankie was glad she was wearing sunglasses so that no one could read her eyes. Their headsets were wired so they could talk to each other, and when Margot yelped, "Oh my god, dolphins!" they all craned their necks to get a look. Manny caught Frankie's eye and smiled, and she smiled back.

At least Manny was cute, and Chelsea Quinn didn't seem like a total idiot. Frankie had already met Celia Young, of course, but she wasn't going to bring that up unless Celia did. Frankie could get through this trip; she just needed to lie low and try to relax. It was only a week. Nothing could be that bad when it was just a week.

Xander Lee took one look at the palm trees as he got into the van and knew he was never playing football again. He owed a lot to the game, but it had never taken him halfway around the world on a free vacation. Dancing had done that. Specifically, videos of him dancing. And if Xander really drilled down, it was videos of him dancing with his shirt off. People loved it, girls loved it, and this trip was the tipping point. Xander wasn't an athlete anymore. He was an influencer. He already had almost as many followers as Tom Brady on Instagram and he'd never even won a Super Bowl.

When the Unknown Island rep had reached out (Monica? Michelle? He couldn't remember her name), her invite felt like an offer from heaven. It wasn't exactly what he'd been praying for, but it was proof that God was still watching out for him.

Xander had needed a vacation. He needed time to think and get his head in order. Everything had happened so fast that he hadn't had time to sort any of it out, to untangle all the threads knotted in his brain. To figure out what had happened. Whether it was going to happen again. Xander forced himself to put it out of his head. He thought about it all the time. He didn't need to think about it here, now.

The colors around him were so bright they looked artificial, and Xander watched the fields and coastline as the van zoomed past them. Aside from a family trip to Hawaii a few years ago, he'd never been anyplace tropical, and certainly never this far away. It was just a few minutes' drive to the dock, and as soon as they arrived, Xander grabbed his bag and hopped out of the van, thanking the driver and shutting the door before the man could hurry around to help him.

A small white motorboat was parked at the dock, and an old man in swim trunks, a polo shirt, and bare feet was loading a backpack into it. The backpack belonged to a tall, pretty Black girl Xander recognized from his flight, and from her profile. She was wearing jean shorts and a yellow tank top and was chugging from a blue water bottle. She smiled as he approached. "Hey," she said, brightly, "I'm Justice. I think we were on the same flight."

Xander smiled back and held out his hand. She shook it, then wiped her hand on her shorts. "Sorry," she said. "It's not you. I'm just sweaty."

Xander laughed. "I'm from Texas," he said. "I'm used to humidity."

"Oh, cool," she said. "I'm from Kansas City." When you were this far from home, being two states away pretty much made you neighbors.

Xander resisted the urge to say she wasn't in Kansas anymore. "You a swimmer?" he asked instead, taking in her ripped arms and broad shoulders. She looked at him and ran a hand over her left biceps. Xander immediately regretted saying anything. He never knew what girls were going to be insecure about. But then, to his relief, she grinned.

"Individual medley and four-hundred-meter freestyle," she said. "I'm missing a meet to be here. My coach will not be happy."

"You didn't give 'em a heads-up?" he asked. Xander had spent his life clearing practically everything with a coach and couldn't imagine just not showing up to a game. Justice's expression seemed to shift at his question. He couldn't see her eyes behind her sunglasses, but a crease had formed between her eyebrows.

"Long story," she said, looking away and taking another drink from her bottle. Then she glanced at her phone, which she'd done about fifteen times already in the short time they'd been talking. Xander couldn't help but think that she seemed nervous about something.

"Did they offer to take you by helicopter?" she asked. "I just felt like that would be too wasteful," she added when he nodded. Xander thought it was a weird thing to say. He doubted she was paying for this, so what was she worried about wasting?

"I don't do helicopters," he said, even though this was the one and only opportunity he'd ever had to turn one down. "RIP, Kobe," he added.

Justice gave a rueful little laugh. "Yeah," she said. "Makes sense. RIP."

The man in the polo shirt climbed out of the boat and walked toward them. "We leave now," he said, in a way that Xander couldn't tell if it was a question or a command.

Xander glanced at Justice, who smiled and shrugged, then looked at her phone again before tucking it into her backpack. "We're ready," Xander said. He walked down the dock and then hopped into the boat, sending it rocking in the water. He turned to help Justice, but the man already had his arm out for her. She sat down on one of the benches, nestled her backpack between her feet, and then unwrapped her headscarf and tucked it into her bag.

"Are there life jackets?" Justice asked, yelling over the motor as it roared to life.

"No," the man called back, pulling out into the open water. "But I get you there safe. I drive these waters for fifty years. You are not going to drown today." Just then, the boat hit a wave, rising into the air and then slapping back down with a jolt.

Xander laughed, but Justice yelped. "I thought you were a swimmer?" he teased.

"In a pool," she said. "Not a lot of waves in Kansas!" They both grinned as the boat zoomed away from shore. Xander took a deep breath and felt all the stress in his body start to evaporate as the ocean air filled his lungs. He could taste salt on his lips. The water that flew past below them was bright and clear, and Xander looked around in amazement. It felt like a dream, to be this far away, someplace where no one knew him and no one had any expectations of who he should be. Except the twenty-two million people who followed him on TikTok, of course.

When Xander had started posting to TikTok the summer before last, his teammates had chided him. "Dude," they said, laughing, "that's so gay." Then he'd hit one million, two million, three million followers, and it just kept going. His teammates sure as hell weren't laughing now; they were always trying to get him to be in their own posts.

Xander was going to shoot a ton of content this week, take advantage of the tropical backdrop, and then, as soon as he got home, he was quitting the team. If he lost his scholarship, he'd deal. College athlete had been part of his brand, but not anymore. It was time to pivot.

He turned back toward the driver. "How long's our ride?" he asked.

"Should take about a half hour," the man replied, scanning the horizon. "Only a couple of miles straight shot, but we have to go around."

"Why is that?" Xander had to shout above the wind.

"The island is very remote!" the driver shouted back. "Lots of coral reefs surrounding it. Good for surfing, not so good for boats. One way in, one way out."

"I'm hoping to do some of that this week," Xander said. "Surfing."

The man nodded. "Big waves here," he said. "Some of the biggest in the world. Not so good for beginners."

Xander turned and scanned the water. It was flat as an ice rink. The man seemed to read his mind. "Storm is coming this week," he said. "You just wait. Biggest waves you've ever seen."

"Maybe I'll stick to paddleboarding," Xander said. He meant it as a joke, but the man nodded seriously. There was something curious about his demeanor. He was almost stand-offish.

"So, what's the island like?" Xander asked him.

"I don't know," he answered. "I have never been on it."

"Don't you work for Unknown Island?" Xander asked, and the man shook his head.

"I just drive the boat. I was hired to take you there and drop you off, that's it," he said.

"But your shirt," Xander said, and the man looked down at his white polo with the Unknown Island logo embroidered on the chest.

"A free shirt is a free shirt," he said with a shrug. Xander decided to drop it, but to his surprise, the man kept going. "Only a foreigner would want to open a hotel on that island," he said. "The locals know better. It is too remote, too many ghosts."

"Ghosts?" Xander asked.

"It was a prison," the man said, "where people were sent to die. Without a boat, one way in, no way out. Ghosts can't swim."

"Oh my god!" Justice's scream made Xander turn. She was pointing at something, so excited her finger was shaking.

"Look, dolphins! A whole pod of them!" Right then, as if on cue, one leaped out of the water and did a full backflip before slapping the surface with a splash. Then another, and another. Justice was so excited she was clapping her hands like a little kid. Xander glanced back at the driver, whose mouth was set in a grim line and who seemed completely unmoved by the dolphins.

Xander decided the man was crazy. This place was obviously paradise. And anyway, Xander didn't believe in ghosts.

CHAPTER TWO

Graham Hoffman took off his glasses and rubbed his eyes. He hadn't been able to sleep at all on the flight over, and he had no idea how long he'd been awake. He was so tired that words were starting to blur and swim before his eyes. He read Sharon's text message again to make sure he was getting it right. The text was so long that it came through in three blocks, each one taking up almost the whole screen.

Graham!!! I am so, so sorry, and I will explain when I get there, but all I can say is you are a lifesaver and I am so glad we have someone like you on this trip. We have a major fire with our investors—huge!!!— and the marketing and PR teams and I are stuck here doing serious damage control. We won't get to the island until after breakfast. It's a nightmare. I need you to step in for me. You're the only one with the right experience.

Just welcome everyone to the island and take a group shot as soon as everyone is here. Text it to me right away so I can at least post that on schedule. If people complain about their rooms, remind them that this is a SOFT OPENING and WE ARE STILL WORKING OUT THE KINKS!!

Go in my office. There is a stack of welcome letters on my desk. Please distribute these to everyone after breakfast. NOT BEFORE! After breakfast. You are a lifesaver—did I already say that?! Lol, it's true—and the only one who can help me out here. We will make this worth your while and will discuss additional compensation as soon as I get there. YOU ARE THE BEST! I CANNOT THANK YOU ENOUGH.

It was a good thing that Sharon was always so complimentary, and so clearly impressed with his prior work, because every time Graham talked to her, Unknown Island's marketing director was incredibly flaky. So flaky, in fact, that he had never actually talked to her. They always communicated via text and emails, because Sharon seemed to have as many technical difficulties as she did investor fires. Bad connections, Zoom glitches, you name it. He guessed he could understand that. Getting internet to a remote island couldn't be easy. Case in point: right now. He had tried to text Sharon back, asking if she could hop on a quick call to discuss, and the text wasn't going through. It just hung there, undelivered.

Sharon's text had popped up almost the second Graham

landed on the island, and by the time he'd read it in its entirety, the boat that had dropped him and Robby Wade off was already disappearing back out to sea. Graham was now sitting in Sharon's office, at what he assumed was her desk, and sure enough, there was a stack of envelopes, the paper thick and textured and expensive-looking, each one addressed to a different guest in elegant curlicue calligraphy.

One of them had his name on it, and he would have opened it right then to see what the fuss was all about, but it was sealed with black wax embossed with the letters *UI*. If he opened it, he wouldn't be able to seal it again. Regardless, distributing the envelopes after breakfast was going to be easy. It was the "soft opening" part that was going to be hard. This opening was so soft it was raw. From what Graham had seen so far, the hotel was totally unfinished.

There was a swimming pool and a hot tub that both looked okay, but there was nowhere to sit by them. Not a single lounge chair. The sea was cerulean blue and the sand was soft and white, but the beach had clearly never been raked. It was littered with branches, and when Graham had walked down to the water, a dead snake nearly washed up on his feet. It was a big snake, too, at least a yard long, with thick black-and-white stripes. Graham was glad no one had been around to hear him scream. But also, no one was around.

He'd gone in search of a hotel employee to tell them about the snake, but he'd only been able to find two. One was a woman working in the kitchen who seemed so busy helping Robby prepare breakfast that Graham didn't want to bother her; the other was a man who was literally still putting doors on the bungalows. That also seemed more important than the snake, as people usually expected their hotel rooms to have doors, but Graham had tried to explain anyway. He wasn't sure what language the man spoke, but it was definitely not English, and all he seemed to understand was "snake."

"Bad! Stay away!" the man said, hooking two of his fingers into fangs and then hissing to mimic a snake. Graham just smiled and walked away.

The dining room table was set, but the furniture was cheap and mismatched. The same with the lobby. One of the couches had a stain on it, and the floor looked like it had never been swept. Fly carcasses piled up in the corners. There were holes in the walls where wires sprouted out like vines, connecting to nothing, and the fluorescent lighting flickered, illuminating the raw edges of the drywall. Anything with fabric smelled faintly of mildew. Unknown Island wasn't a resort, it was a motel, and it looked nothing like the pictures.

The promo video that Unknown Island had posted to launch its campaign was gorgeous and sophisticated. Models jumping off boats, running down beaches, splashing in waves. Sex and glamour, that sort of thing, and all of the pictures that Unknown had posted to its accounts had been dripping in luxury. Soft white linens, clusters of frangipani flowers, glowing candles, polished mahogany, roasted shrimp, and drinks garnished with orchids. Even at his age, Graham had enough marketing experience to know that everything required a little spin, but this much spin was dizzying. He could already tell the other guests were going to be pissed off when they arrived, and he hadn't even seen inside the rooms yet.

And then there was breakfast.

Robby Wade was one of the guests, but he was also in

charge of breakfast. Robby was only seventeen and already a high-profile chef with a huge YouTube channel and a buzzy restaurant in Atlanta. It made sense to have the first meal on the island prepared by a big name, but on the boat ride over, Graham had asked Robby what he was cooking, and Robby said, "Biscuits and gravy." It was over ninety degrees. Who wanted to eat biscuits and gravy in a swimsuit and then go sit on the beach? Graham must have made a face, because Robby got all huffy. "It's my signature dish," he'd said. "They requested it specifically."

The office was, of course, not air-conditioned, and the heat made it hard for Graham to think straight. He was from Minneapolis, and when the temps dropped to the twenties, all he needed was a windbreaker. He'd already soaked through two T-shirts in the short time he'd been here; at this rate, he was going to have to do laundry. He grabbed a tissue and wiped his forehead, then looked around for someplace to throw it. There was no trash can, of course. The office was sparse, and there was nothing personal in it, like Sharon had never even been here.

Aside from the desk, computer, and uncomfortable chair, the only other thing in the office was a safe, a big hunk of gray metal that seemed oddly threatening. No doubt a resort like this needed a safe, but why not hide it in the wall? Or at least find some other way to disguise it. It made the place look like a bail bondsman's office or a pawnshop, two places Graham only knew about from TV. He looked at his phone and saw that the text to Sharon still hadn't gone through. He figured he had two options when the other guests got here: He could throw up his hands and tell them all the truth, that he had nothing to do with this and he had no idea what was going on. Or he could do his best to follow Sharon's instructions.

When she had first approached Graham about being the youth liaison for this whole thing, he was psyched and flattered. It was a big job, and he was pretty impressed that his reputation had filtered all the way up to the people at Unknown Island, whoever they were. That was the thing, he had no idea who was behind Unknown Island. Yeah, maybe the execution was a little janky, but they clearly had money, lots of it, and the marketing campaign had been insanely successful. They'd worked with NothingBurger Media on it, and those guys were huge. The more Graham thought about it, the more it seemed like this was a bridge he did not want to burn, because he still had no idea where it was going to lead. He'd always thought of himself as a problem solver, so now he just needed to solve some problems.

He would do what Sharon had asked, but at the same time try his best to make sure that no one blamed him for the situation. He'd let the guests know that, if he had been in charge, this place would have air-conditioning.

Robby Wade knew that no one wanted to eat biscuits and gravy on the beach. He should have been preparing fruit platters and yogurt parfaits, but biscuits and gravy were what Suzanne from Unknown Island had requested. Maybe it made sense?

Biscuits and gravy were his most famous dish, featured in the first video of his that had gone viral, when he was just fifteen. The internet had loved it, a Black teenager with a Southern accent and a Gordon Ramsay personality, cooking up food that looked like it had been lifted straight from the pages of *Bon Appétit*. So, he'd made another video, and another. At the time, Robby had been playing a character, an exaggerated version of himself, but that wasn't so true anymore. Now that he owned his own restaurant, YouTube Robby and real-life Robby were one and the same. He wasn't sure he liked it, but he had a business to run and not a lot of time to self-analyze. That's why Unknown Island's offer had been so appealing. All he had to do was cook breakfast, and then he was on vacation. Robby needed that right now.

Not that Hock & Jowl wasn't doing well. It was. When Robby had opened his restaurant at age sixteen, he had just planned to do a pop-up to capitalize on his YouTube fame. Then it became one of Atlanta's hottest restaurants and sold out every seating for a year. The next thing he knew, he had investors and an architect drawing up blueprints, and Hock & Jowl was pop-up no more. He was the head chef and restaurateur of his very own dining establishment, and most of his customers had never even seen the biscuits-and-gravy video.

This was all a dream come true. Sometimes, when Robby was in the shower, planning menus in his head, or even more so, when a former classmate came in the restaurant with their family, it would hit him just how strange it was to have your dream come true when you were only seventeen. He was grateful that his mother hadn't forced him to finish high school just to make a moot point about the importance of an education.

Now, every time he walked through the door of the restaurant, he thought about how he never wanted to see the place again. That was why he was here, standing over a cast-iron skillet in ninety-degree heat, trying to explain to a woman who was clearly uninterested, that they would have to plate everything at the very last second or the gravy would congeal.

"When you go to plate and serve it," he said, "make sure you wipe down the rim of the plate so that there are no drips."

"Oh, I'm not serving this," the woman said. Her words felt like a slap and Robby bit his tongue. No one in his restaurant would ever talk to him like that.

"What's wrong with biscuits and gravy?" he asked. Besides the obvious, he thought.

"Oh, nothing," she said with a shrug. "But my shift will be done in fifteen minutes. I will not be here to serve the"—she peered into the skillet—"gravy."

"Who is going to help me serve it, then?" he asked.

"I do not know," she said. "I did not make the schedule."

Robby sighed. "Okay, well, when will whoever it is get here?" he asked.

"When they get here," she said. Robby paused and gave her a look. He was going to have to ask Suzanne about Unknown Island's hiring. Certainly, this woman did not seem like someone who should be working in high-end hospitality.

"How long have you been working here?" he asked her.

"I got here at eight p.m. last night," she said, before going back to washing dishes. Maybe there was something lost in translation in his question or her answer. Surely Unknown Island wouldn't have such a green employee working a big launch?

Then again, what he had seen of the island in the hour or so that he'd been here was not exactly impressive. As soon as the boat had pulled in, Robby had headed straight to the kitchen to start cooking. It was stocked with everything he had requested, but other than that, there was just a bunch of junk food and snacks. It wasn't like the island was going to let anyone starve, so he assumed they just hadn't stocked the fridge beyond breakfast, but still, he was glad the rest of the week's meals weren't his problem. All the kitchen equipment was cheap and flimsy, like it came from the dollar store, and Robby hated plastic colanders. At least he had brought his chef's knives from home.

Robby was stirring the gravy when Graham appeared in the doorway of the kitchen. "Hey, man," he said, wiping his brow. "I need you to come take a picture really quick." Graham was sweating so much that he looked like he'd been dipped in baby oil, and he seemed to shrink back from the heat of the stove.

"What?" Robby said. "I have to get breakfast ready! And as you've probably noticed, there's no one to help me."

"It'll be quick," Graham said. "I promise. The helicopter just landed, and I can see the boat pulling in. Sharon really wants to get a picture of everyone right when they get here so they can post it."

Robby stirred the gravy even more furiously. "I don't have time for photos right now," he said, but when he looked back, there was a hardness in Graham's face.

"They're paying you for this, aren't they?" Graham said. "So, if Sharon wants a photo, she's going to get a photo." Then he smiled. "It'll take two seconds, for real."

Robby turned the heat off under the gravy and moved the pan off the burner. They *were* paying him, and a lot, so he wiped his hands and followed Graham out of the kitchen and down to the beach. Graham was pretty smug for someone so sweaty and, Robby noticed, this was the third time he'd referred to Suzanne as Sharon. I bet they're paying you, too, Robby thought, so at least get her name right.

As the helicopter descended, Emma Jane Ohana felt like she might throw up. She'd messed up and taken an Ambien too late on the flight over, and now she felt like a bag of wet sand. The pill was starting to wear off, but she felt nauseous and had a headache. She needed a shower, some real sleep, and about a gallon of water.

She had told herself no pills on this trip, but the plane ride over had been so hellacious. She couldn't get comfortable, and there was turbulence, drops so sudden that drinks spilled and even the flight attendants looked nervous.

This flight hadn't been much better. As her fellow passengers chatted through their headsets, Emma Jane tried to concentrate on her breathing and staying calm so she didn't yak in somebody's lap. Inhaling through her nose and doing a long exhale through her mouth, she leaned over and looked out the window. The helicopter blades sent ripples across the surface of the water, and the green palm fronds thrashed around like crazy. Another week, another island.

Emma Jane couldn't remember if she'd been to this part of the world before. After a while, all azure seas and powdery beaches start to blend together. A yacht in the Mediterranean melts into a sailboat in the Caribbean into a catamaran in the Adriatic, and paradise is oppressive when you're seasick.

Emma Jane wasn't super excited about this trip, but it wasn't like she had anything else to do. This trip was business, and she had to think more about business. She was eighteen now, and in two months, she would officially be done with high school and be an adult, as her dad never stopped reminding her. She didn't think he was really going to cut her off—like Noah Ohana was going to let his daughter go live in a one-bedroom apartment in Highland Park or something—but lately he seemed more serious than he had in the past.

Emma Jane had always been her daddy's little girl, the apple of his eye. He loved her fiercely and she returned the feelings. When Emma Jane was a little kid, Noah, not her mother, was the one she'd run to when she skinned her knee, and he—worth approximately seven billion dollars in recent estimates—would sleep on the floor of her room when she was sick. Lately, though, the love between her and her father had felt different, like it had frozen over. Emma Jane suspected it was because her father, the person who knew her best in the entire world, was the only one who didn't believe her.

As soon as Unknown Island had started following Emma Jane, her own following had skyrocketed. She had to figure out a way to leverage all those likes and turn them into a real opportunity. For what, though, she didn't know. She loved photography, but she'd stopped posting the pics she really liked online. They were of light and shadows, fleeting moments captured before they were gone forever, but they never got any likes. The only thing her 6.6 million Instagram followers appreciated, apparently, was her in a bikini.

When she got back, she was going to figure her shit out. No more pills, no more parties, no more paying anyone to secretly do her homeschool coursework. She'd find a therapist, be totally honest with them, and have them help her figure out where to start. She wanted to do something to make her dad proud. And Sergio, too. Ugh. She didn't want to think about him. Not here. Not now.

The helicopter settled onto the landing pad with a thump, and Emma Jane relaxed, just a little bit. She'd made it through the ride, at least. Now she just needed to go to her room and lie down for a bit. As soon as the blades stopped whirring, the pilot jumped out and started unloading their bags. Manny got out first and then helped all the girls down. Emma Jane smiled and mumbled thanks, stumbling a bit as her feet hit the concrete. She looked over to see the pilot unceremoniously piling their bags off to one side, and she sucked her lip at seeing her Goyard tossed into the sand.

She glanced around. The island was tiny, with a narrow strip of white sand between the water and a dense grove of palm trees that obscured any buildings from sight, except for a boathouse at the end of a long, narrow dock. Everyone milled around on the helipad, not sure where to go, and then the pilot motioned them off to the side so that he could start the blades up again. The passengers moved to stand by their luggage and were blasted by the wind. Sand blew into Emma Jane's eyes and mouth, and then the helicopter took off again, buzzing back out across the water. It had all happened so fast that it was already a speck in the sky before Emma Jane realized the six of them were alone.

Shouldn't there have been some hotel employees there to take their bags and welcome them with a cool, refreshing beverage? Emma Jane would have paid a hundred dollars right now for a glass of hibiscus iced tea or a pineapple juice or even just a bottle of water. She swallowed, and her tongue stuck to the roof of her mouth.

Manny started picking up the bags and setting them in a row back on the concrete. Celia and Frankie joined him, but Chelsea just stood there. "What the fuck?" she said to Emma Jane. "I feel like an Amazon package that just got tossed on a porch."

Emma Jane laughed. "That's accurate," she said. "I definitely arrived damaged." Chelsea sighed, and bent down to take off her shoes. She was wearing strappy gold heels that couldn't be comfortable. Emma Jane slipped out of her slides, and then the sound of a motor made her turn around. A boat was pulling up to the dock, and everyone watched as it stopped so two people could climb out. The driver of the boat dropped their bags onto the dock and then jumped back into the boat. The two people picked up their bags and started walking toward the beach. Emma Jane noticed they were both carrying backpacks, the kind used by people who brag about staying in hostels.

"Hey," the girl said when they were close enough to not have to shout. "I guess this is where we're supposed to be?" She was glancing around, looking confused.

"We know as much as you do," Chelsea said. "Which is jack shit."

Just then, two guys came crashing through the palm trees. One was pale and wearing glasses and a very sweaty button-down shirt; the other was tall and skinny and wearing an apron. He might have been cute, Emma Jane thought, if he wasn't scowling and wearing clogs.

"Welcome to Unknown Island!" the guy with glasses yelled. "How was everyone's trip?"

"You've got to be kidding me," Chelsea muttered under

her breath. Emma Jane was kind of taken aback too, and judging by how everyone else stayed quiet, she didn't think she was the only one. This was the welcome wagon?

"Thanks, man," Manny said finally. "Happy to be here."

"Looks like everyone's here!" glasses guy said, clapping his hands like a kid about to eat cake. "So, I'll give you all the rundown whenever you're ready."

"Sure thing," Manny said.

"We've been ready," Chelsea said, her voice dripping with saccharine sarcasm. As Emma Jane got her bearings, she recognized everyone from their profiles. Glasses guy was Graham Hoffman, and clog guy was Robby Wade. The girl who'd just gotten off the boat was Justice Wilson, and the guy who looked like an underwear model was Xander Lee. He was shirtless, a walking thirst trap, and she was nothing if not thirsty. Emma Jane straightened up a little, and then she remembered all the Bible quotes in his captions and let herself slouch again.

Graham cleared his throat. "So, uh, first I want to thank you all for coming," he said, "on behalf of Unknown Island, of course. This is a special place for a special group of people, and I, for one, am super honored to be here."

"Do you work for them?" Margot asked.

"Not really," Graham said. "I just got here this morning, but I have a relationship with Sharon—business relationship, of course—and she asked me to welcome you guys and let you know she will be here just as soon as she can. She got held up with some investor stuff—"

"Wait," Margot interrupted. "Who is Sharon?"

"He means Suzanne," Robby said, growing more annoyed by the second.

"No, I don't," Graham said, "I mean Sharon, Unknown's marketing director."

"I talked to someone named Lindsey," Manny said. Emma Jane tried to remember the name of the person she had talked to. It wasn't Sharon, Suzanne, or Lindsey.

"Doesn't matter," Graham said, moving on brusquely. "I'm sure Unknown has a large marketing staff, all of whom will be here just as soon as they can. This is a soft opening, after all, and we all know how soft openings can go. Kinks need to be worked out, everyone's just doing their best, yada yada. In the meantime, we need to get a group photo and then everyone can go relax in their rooms until breakfast."

"When is breakfast?" Xander asked. "I'm starving."

Graham turned to Robby. "Hey, chef," he said, grinning, but Robby didn't smile back, "when will breakfast be ready?"

"The longer I'm standing here," Robby replied, his voice dripping with Southern snark, "the longer y'all are gonna wait."

Graham looked at Robby like he hated him, but smiled. "Of course," he said. "So let's just take this photo like they want us to, and get on with it."

"Wait, you want us to take a photo now?" Chelsea asked. "Don't we get to freshen up or anything first?"

Emma Jane had wondered the same thing, but she was focused on the part of Graham's speech where he had said they could all go to their rooms and relax.

"Where's the photo going?" Frankie asked.

"They're not going to post it anywhere," Graham assured her. "They're in a big investor meeting right now and they want to show the money people that everyone has arrived. We're all guests here, so let's just give 'em what they want, okay?" He turned around like he was looking at something, and waved at a man and a woman in white shirts walking down the dock to the boat that had dropped off Xander and Justice.

"Excuse me," he called. "Could one of you come take our picture really quick?" The man started walking toward them, and as he got closer, Emma Jane realized he was wearing an Unknown Island polo shirt. So there *were* hotel employees, they just weren't welcoming the guests?

But before she could think about it too much, Graham was herding everyone into a group, and they were all scrambling to get ready for photos. Chelsea, Frankie, and Margot had compacts out and were frantically touching up their makeup. Manny was trying to straighten out the wrinkles in his shirt, and Justice was tying a red scarf around her head. Celia was just standing there awkwardly, watching everyone else.

The next thing Emma Jane knew, Xander was lying down in the sand in front of the group and everyone was throwing their arms out and smiling and yelling and posing and then, just like that, the man was handing the phone back to Graham and the photos were done.

Robby took off back through the trees, while everyone else crowded around Graham to look at the photos. Chelsea made him delete a few. Emma Jane didn't care about the photos. She didn't even know if she had smiled, and she could feel the nausea rising again. She looked back toward the water and saw the boat with the hotel employees pulling away from the dock.

Celia Young hated having her picture taken. Hated, hated it. She never knew what do with her face or her hands, and it wasn't until all of the pictures had been taken and she saw them on Graham's phone that she realized she was the only one who hadn't put her bag off to the side. There she was, front row, gripping her rolling suitcase like it was a security blanket. Her awkwardness knew no bounds.

She shouldn't have come. Everything was going wrong already. First, her flight out of San Francisco was delayed. Then, she missed her connection in Hong Kong. Mark, the publicist for Unknown Island who'd set this trip up for her, had told her to look for a guy with a sign with her name on it when she landed. But by the time she landed, the guy was long gone and she couldn't get ahold of Mark. She'd finally gotten a cab, but she had no cash in the local currency, so the driver had taken her to a bank, and for the entire ride, Celia couldn't stop thinking that this was exactly how people go on vacation and get murdered.

Celia was only sixteen. She was the youngest on this trip, but her parents had signed the waiver without even reading it. "It's a great opportunity, sweetie," her mom had said when Celia protested. "You should be honored you were invited. It's a really high-profile activation for someone like you. You could really grow your audience."

Celia was a gamer, and while her parents understood a lot of things about fame and money and exposure, they didn't understand gaming. And they especially didn't understand that the only way to really grow your audience as a gamer was to play video games, not spend a week on an island with a bunch of people who filled out their swimsuits in a way Celia was pretty sure she never would. What her parents hadn't said, even though Celia knew it, was that with Caroline gone, Celia was their only child, and their only hope. So, here she was.

Halfway around the world, standing on a beach with a bunch of influencers, squinting into the sun while holding on to her suitcase for dear life. It was in that moment she realized yet another way she'd messed up: she had come to a tropical island for a week and hadn't brought a single pair of sunglasses.

"Okay, okay!" Graham shouted, tucking his phone back into his pocket. "I'm going to send them all to Sharon and I'm sure—if they were going to post any someplace, which they are not—that they will Photoshop them so that everyone looks good! Now, go check out your rooms."

"Where are the rooms?" Justice asked.

"On the other side of these trees," Graham said, then started walking and motioned for everyone to follow him. So they did.

Justice and Xander had backpacks, but everyone else had suitcases. Celia noticed that she wasn't the only one having trouble dragging hers through the sand. Manny picked his up and carried it. Margot, Emma Jane, and Chelsea looked like they had all packed for a month in Russia, with suitcases the size of Mini Coopers, but Frankie Russh's suitcase, Celia was surprised to see, was of a reasonable size, and after a few yards, Frankie picked it up and carried it, too.

Celia's parents had been very excited about Frankie Russh. "Make sure you take lots of pics with her," Celia's mother had said before giving her a hug and sending her through security at SFO. "Get lots of pics with everyone!"

"Ta-dah!" Graham shouted. They had rounded a curve in the beach and into view of their accommodations, which were little thatched bungalows standing on stilts over the water.

"Oh my god, cute!" squealed Margot.

"How do we know which one is ours?" Justice asked. Celia watched as the smile faded from Graham's face. Everyone was looking at him.

"I have no idea," he said, finally. "Just pick one, and if there's a problem, we can sort it out when Sharon gets here."

A couple of people were upset about this, and Celia tuned out their arguing as she looked around at everyone. She was used to being an observer, and here, there was plenty to observe. So far, only Manny and Chelsea had spoken to her directly. Chelsea had just made small talk, but Manny knew who Celia was, which was kind of impressive. Emma Jane seemed like she was asleep and had barely spoken to anyone, and Margot was clearly not interested in Celia at all, which Celia found kind of amusing, since Margot had one of the smallest followings of anyone on the trip.

Frankie was a different story. Frankie was huge. Celia had always thought of Frankie as cutthroat and ambitious, but here, she seemed almost nice if distracted. She had smiled at Celia once, in the helicopter, and Celia had smiled back. She was pretty sure Frankie didn't remember her, which made her stomach feel hot and empty.

The other guests started walking down the boardwalk to the bungalows, and Celia hurried after them. She had this weird feeling, like she always did in a restaurant when she worried that the waiter would forget her food. What if there were only nine bungalows and everyone got one but her? Even though, deep down, she knew that wasn't going to be the case, she still thought it.

"You have every right to be here with the pretty people,"

Celia told herself. She turned toward a bungalow and opened the door. She paused as soon as she stepped inside.

It wasn't that there was anything wrong with the room. It was just unimpressive. There was no art on the walls or knick-knacks on the table or dresser. In fact, there wasn't even a table or dresser. Just a queen-size bed with two pillows, a nightstand, and a wooden chair in one corner. Celia walked over and ran her hands over the sheets. They were not the softest sheets she'd ever felt. She went into the bathroom. She didn't know what she was looking for. The bathroom had all the normal things that were found in bathrooms: a shower, a bathtub, a toilet, and a sink. But there were no fancy amenities, just a bar of soap and a couple of washcloths, and the bathtub was smaller than the one in her parents' house.

Celia walked out of the bathroom and sighed as she sat down on the bed. Of course she'd picked the worst bunga-low. It was just her luck. She pulled out her phone to text her parents, then remembered she didn't have service and wasn't connected to the Wi-Fi. Her phone was almost dead anyway, so she unzipped and opened her suitcase to get her charger, but what she saw on top made her stop.

She pulled out the dress that was carefully folded in a plas-tic bag. She held it up in front of her so that she could look at it. The dress was a pale cornflower blue with bright red tropical flowers on it, and it was so not Celia. It was the kind of thing that would have made Caroline look like a dream, but Celia was not Caroline. A fact that her parents sometimes seemed to forget. As soon as she thought that, though, she felt guilty. Her parents had been through hell these past two years,

43

ever since Caroline's death, and that was why Celia was on this trip. The look in her mother's eyes when she'd found out that Celia had been invited was the first time she had seen her mother look happy in ages.

Her mother had taken the invite as a sign. "Someone is still watching out for us," she'd said, which was why Celia had let her buy the dress and then pack it. Celia hung the dress up on the bathroom doorknob since there was nowhere else to hang it. She couldn't go home early, she'd have to stick it out, play the part for a week, even take some pictures with Frankie Russh. That was the least she could do. Maybe, before the week was over, she'd put the dress on in here, alone in her unimpressive room, and take some stupid selfies in the mirror.

Margot Bryant was pissed about the whole no-assigned-rooms thing. She, like everyone else, had picked one at random, and she'd ended up in a bungalow that must have been meant for one of the employees, Graham or Robby. It might as well have been a Holiday Inn; there wasn't even any shampoo or conditioner. She always brought her own, since she only used products from women-owned brands, but still, that was beside the point. Luxury hotels should have shampoo. So far, though, Unknown Island didn't seem all that luxurious, and her suitcase had sand in the wheels to prove it.

Margot washed her face, then changed clothes and redid her makeup. She wanted to make a good impression at breakfast. She'd had a nice talk with Chelsea when they were waiting for the helicopter, and while she was thinking about it, Margot grabbed her phone, opened the Notes app, and made a few notes about their convo. She liked to do that when she met important people, because then she could impress them later on with how much she remembered. She checked herself in the mirror and decided that, even though she hated to do it, she was going to have to wear a ponytail. This humidity wasn't doing anything for her hair. She smoothed it back and then grabbed her phone and headed out to dominate the breakfast table.

Even though she was only twenty, Margot was the founder and CEO of a technology start-up, SHEmail. It was email for women, and the tagline was "Fight the patriarchy with every send." Margot was proud of that. She'd come up with it herself. Well, technically, one of her copywriters had, but Margot was the one who had tweaked it to get it perfect.

Margot had conceived of SHEmail her freshman year at NYU, and when a friend of the family offered to invest, she'd dropped out to make the dream a reality. She'd hired a team, gotten a flurry of press, and even made it onto the *Forbes* list. But the truth was, it had been over a year since their first round of investment, and SHEmail was still struggling to get off the ground. Their user base wasn't growing, their tech was riddled with bugs, and market research kept turning in reports that most people saw SHEmail as a novelty. They liked the idea of "email for women, by women," but they also liked email that came with calendars and cloud storage and that could be used to log into other accounts. People were really demanding when it came to email.

When Margot had told everyone at SHEmail that she was going on this trip, one of her managers had wondered if it sent the right message to the employees, considering last week's layoffs, and Margot had had to remind her, in front of everyone, that what was good for the CEO was good for the company. Besides, this wasn't a vacation. It was a networking opportunity.

Waiting for her flight out of New York, Margot had taken advantage of the free Wi-Fi in the first-class lounge and done a deep dive on all of the other people who had been invited. She'd made a list, ranking them in order of who had the most potential to benefit SHEmail, and another list of conversation topics tailored to each person. This way, she'd come across as informed no matter who she was talking to.

But aside from Chelsea, she'd failed to connect so far. Frankie Russh and Manny de La Cruz had been talking like no one else existed, which was fine, because neither of them were right for the SHEmail brand anyway. Manny was some sort of DJ who seemed to spend a lot of time in strip clubs, and Frankie was one of those people who'd gotten famous just for being attractive. Margot doubted that she was very smart. Neither of them were important.

Emma Jane had been asleep practically the whole time, and Margot was very unimpressed with her so far. Margot wasn't totally writing Emma Jane off yet, though, because she had rich parents. Her father was a billionaire financier, and maybe if Emma Jane got involved in SHEmail, her dad might want to invest. This was an example of why Margot was a good CEO. She looked at all the angles and had decided that Emma Jane might be important.

Celia Young had a huge following on Twitch, but the SHEmail demo didn't care about gaming and Margot didn't think she needed to waste her time with someone who was involved in such a sexist industry. Not important, though much younger, so it was still good to be nice.

The two people on the trip that Margot was most interested in meeting were Justice Wilson and, of course, Chelsea Quinn. Justice was still a senior in high school, but she'd made a name for herself as an environmental activist. Her following wasn't huge, but she had a very serious platform and it seemed that people really respected her. Margot was impressed that Justice had pics of herself with Kamala Harris. Also, Justice was Black. Jeremy, SHEmail's main investor, was always telling Margot that SHEmail needed to capitalize on the diversity trend or risk getting left behind. Involving Justice would be a great way to do that.

Chelsea Quinn was a beauty YouTuber, which wasn't that special, but she was trans, and that would be a great look for SHEmail. Margot could double down on her message that SHEmail was "email for all women." There was, of course, some nasty business about Chelsea and a car accident, where Chelsea had literally run over an old woman in the street. So Chelsea wasn't necessarily a shoo-in, but Margot was going to give her the benefit of the doubt. After all, if anyone understood bad press and rumors, it was Margot. She figured she'd see how the week went, and if she and Chelsea were besties by the end of it, she'd talk to her about coming on as an advisor.

Of course, some people always made a fuss about SHEmail's name, but surely Chelsea was more sophisticated than that and would totally get that it was a play on "email" and nothing more. Margot started to get annoyed just thinking about all the time her employees had to waste deleting comments that complained about the name, and she sighed.

Graham Hoffman had potential to be important, as he was the only other person here who'd made the "20 Under 20" list. He'd won some local election when he was still in high school, and now he went to Princeton and did a lot of "get out the vote" work for the Democrats. It was too bad that Graham was kind of chubby and not cute at all, but if Margot played her cards right, Graham might be able to introduce her to some important women.

Robby Wade would be good for the diversity angle. Margot could see maybe hiring him to cater a SHEmail event, but that would be a hard sell, him not being a woman. Margot categorized him as not important, but she'd have to give him as much attention as she gave to the others, lest she come across as racist.

There was only one guy on the trip who Margot was really interested in, and when she got to the dining room, she was quite pleased to find Xander Lee there alone. She put on her best smile. She wasn't normally into Asian guys, but Xander was very attractive and tall. Plus, she liked guys with big followings. These days, who wouldn't?

The room had been the kicker. Frankie had been feeling uneasy about this whole thing, and then when she saw the bathroom, with one towel that looked like it had come from the sale rack at HomeGoods and a bar of Dial soap, she had decided she was done.

She splashed some water on her face and then unzipped her suitcase. She was planning on being on the first boat, helicopter, or paddleboard out of here, so she wasn't going to unpack or even change clothes for breakfast. But she was going to take her supplements: turmeric, vitamin B6, vitamin D (though maybe she wouldn't need that on a tropical island), ashwagandha, reishi, vitamin C, a vegan omega-3. No matter what was going on in her life, supplements always made her feel better, made her feel healthy, in control. She dispensed a couple of drops of jet lag tincture onto her tongue, and then tucked everything back into her bag and went to find a way off the island.

Halfway down the boardwalk, she paused to take in her surroundings. It really was beautiful, though there was also something harsh about it, the glaring sun and the way the far side of the island rose up in a rocky mountain. She wondered if maybe it had been a volcano at some point. The island certainly had a volcanic vibe, like it might erupt at any minute.

When Frankie walked into the dining room, she was surprised to see she was one of the last to arrive. Everyone must be hungry or, like her, plotting their escape. She noted that she was the only one who hadn't changed her clothes, and the realization made her feel suddenly ashamed. Maybe she was a spoiled brat for not appreciating this, for thinking the resort was raggedy, but still, she had a career to think about. It was so strange that Roger had booked her on this trip. He was normally so diligent about everything, and she wondered briefly if he'd been bamboozled by Unknown's fancy photos, which were all clearly fake.

More likely, though, it had been the check that dazzled him. When Frankie thought about the amount of money, she felt torn again. She was about to go tell Graham she wanted to leave, when Manny caught her eye.

Something about the way he was looking at her made her breath catch a little. He'd changed into board shorts and a tank top that showed off his shoulders. Frankie had to admit she liked all his tattoos. They looked piecemeal, like they'd been added one by one, rather than a sleeve he'd gotten all at once because he'd decided he wanted a sleeve. She and Manny had talked a bit while they were waiting for the helicopter, and when he dropped hints about his upbringing and childhood friends who thought he'd made it already, she found herself wanting to tell him how similar they were. She found herself wanting to tell him about Hannah.

Just thinking about Hannah made Frankie feel like the room was tilting, and she sank into the nearest chair at the table. She grabbed a glass of water and chugged it, fighting the urge to hold the sweating glass to her forehead. If she couldn't leave immediately after breakfast, then she was going to get in the pool. When it came to temperature, Unknown Island could go toe-to-toe with hell.

In the chair next to Frankie, Chelsea was fanning herself with a napkin. "I'm sweating my fucking tits off here," she said. "I didn't know it could be this hot. How do you build a hotel with no AC in a place where it doesn't dip below eighty at night?"

Frankie nodded in agreement and was about to respond when something on the other side of the dining room caught her eye. Mounted right in the middle of the wall was a large screen, like a monitor, that displayed Unknown Island's Instagram account. Frankie stared at it. The account was a total lie, she realized. None of the pictures that had been posted were of this island, she could see now. The coastline was a totally different shape.

"Odd, isn't it?" Frankie turned. Celia had sat down on the other side of her and motioned toward the screen.

"Yeah . . . ," Frankie said.

"I looked at it a minute ago," Celia continued. "It's set into the wall and behind glass. It seems like the one thing here where they spared no expense."

"No joke," Frankie said, and then all conversation died as Graham walked into the room and took one of the last two remaining chairs.

"Hey, Graham," Justice said, picking up her phone, "what's the Wi-Fi password?" Everyone nodded eagerly and pulled out their phones. Everyone but Graham. Instead, he cleared his throat.

"I'm sorry to say that the Wi-Fi appears to be out," he said.

"What do you mean?" Margot asked.

"I mean the wireless internet is not working," he said.

Frankie swallowed.

"How is the Wi-Fi out?" Justice said. She sounded genuinely, on-the-verge-of-tears upset.

"I have no idea," Graham said. "I was connected to it one minute and sending texts, and then all of a sudden, it was out. I'm sure that Sharon and her team will fix it as soon as they get here."

Frankie felt anger rise in her throat. "Sharon is going to have a lot to answer for," she said. The others nodded in agreement. Then Robby appeared in the doorway, balancing a giant tray. He took a few steps toward the table and the tray wobbled. Someone, maybe Margot, gasped.

Xander was up in a second, his chair scraping against the floor. "You need help?" he asked, but Robby shook his head.

"Nope," he said. "Cooked it all myself. Might as well serve it all myself too." He walked to the end of the table, set the tray down, and then deposited a plate in front of Margot with a *thunk*.

"Smells great, man," Manny said. "What is it?"

"Biscuits and gravy," Robby said.

Frankie balked. She couldn't think of anything less appealing right now.

Celia was the only one to speak. "I love biscuits and gravy!" she said. Robby sat a plate in front of Frankie and she peered down at it. Big, buttery chunks of doughy biscuit smothered in rich, creamy gravy with flecks of pepper and chunks of sausage. The smell and heat wafting up from the plate made Frankie's stomach turn.

"Do you think I could get a smoothie?" Emma Jane asked. Robby didn't even look at her.

"I'm sure there's a Jamba Juice around here somewhere," he said, turning to walk out of the dining room. "I'll be right back with the bacon."

Justice felt herself getting more and more nervous with each passing minute. There was no way that her parents hadn't tried to get ahold of her by now. Even if they still didn't know that she wasn't just at Nicole's grandma's for the weekend so they could go to the outlet mall after the swim meet, they would have texted her about something. Her mom would want to know what Justice wanted for dinner on Sunday night, or her dad would be asking what setting the TV needed to be on for Netflix. What if they thought she'd been kidnapped? Or worse? By coming on this trip, she'd opted for forgiveness over permission, but going completely MIA had never been part of her plan.

Justice tried to eat her biscuits and gravy—her stomach had been growling since she got off the plane—but she couldn't get it down. Emma Jane might be a privileged little rich girl, but she was right on the smoothie front. Justice took a drink of water to wash down the flaky biscuit and looked around the table. Only Celia and Xander had cleared their plates. "Do you know when Sharon is going to get here?" Justice asked Graham.

"I do not," he said, "because I have not been able to get ahold of her since the Wi-Fi went down."

"So we are alone on an island with no way to get in contact with anyone?" Justice said. Her words brought everything in the room to a halt. Chelsea paused with a glass halfway to her mouth, and Xander coughed.

"I don't think it's that serious," Graham said, his tone patronizing. "It's a soft opening. There are bound to be glitches. The people from Unknown will be here any minute, I'm sure, and then this will all be sorted out."

"Do you think they're bringing shampoo and conditioner with them?" Chelsea asked. Frankie was taking a drink of water and choked. Justice was pretty sure it was because she had started to laugh. To Justice's surprise, Graham laughed too.

"Look," he said, "I'm just as shocked as you guys are. This

place is not what I . . . expected. But whatever. It is what it is, and it's a free vacation at a very high-profile resort. Aside from us, no one has to know that this place is . . ."

"Motel 6 on the beach?" Chelsea offered.

"Exactly," Graham said. "But hey, when I got here this morning, they were still putting doors on the bungalows. Now we at least have the luxury of locking up our stuff." Suddenly, Frankie was standing and sprinting across the room to the screen.

"I thought you said the Wi-Fi was down," she said, turning accusingly to Graham.

"It is," he said.

"Then how the hell?" She moved from in front of the screen, and Justice saw what Frankie was talking about. Unknown Island had just posted a new pic, the one of all of them on the beach, taken just an hour ago.

"No, I swear," Graham said, as everyone joined Frankie and crowded around the screen. "I texted those pics to Sharon and then two seconds after they went through, the Wi-Fi went out. I haven't had service since."

"Then how is this connected?" Justice asked. She pulled her phone out and clicked into Settings, but it still showed no Wi-Fi available.

"It must be connected via Ethernet," Celia said, looking up from her own phone. "With the wires running through the walls or something."

"So this island skimps on everything except a monitor to broadcast their own profile?" Manny asked. No one answered him as they were all absorbed by the screen. Below the picture of them was a caption. "The guests are here, let's have some fun, counting backward ten to one," Manny read out loud. "Their futures are bright, their pasts untold, three cheers for never growing old." He looked at the others. "What the hell is that supposed to mean?" he asked.

"Why are they posting captions in rhyming couplets?" Justice asked.

"Obviously, they're trying to be disruptive," Margot said. Behind her, Justice saw Graham roll his eyes and she felt a strange moment of kinship with this sweaty guy who seemed to be just as clueless as the rest of them.

"This isn't disruptive," Frankie said, "it's stupid. Captions mean nothing. The only people who read captions are doing it because they're hoping you'll say something wrong so they can tear you apart in the comments."

"I'm with you," Graham said. "It's strange."

The caption made Justice uneasy. It wasn't just strange, it was eerie, and on a whim, she stepped forward and tapped the screen. She could hear a few gasps behind her when it responded, and the picture blew up to fill the glass.

"At least they picked one with my good side," Chelsea said, but Justice wasn't looking at the picture. In the few seconds since it had been posted, it had already gotten thousands of likes and the comments were rolling in.

Justice flicked the screen with a fingertip, scrolling up, and the comments ran by. She stopped and read one at the top, which nailed it. Someone with the username Travelwh0re called out the exact reason Justice found the caption so unsettling: *Unknown you're tripping with this weirdness. Never growing old just sounds like they're going to die.*

Justice tapped the screen again to close the window.

Graham had lost the room. He could feel people looking at him, and the anger bubbling up his way. He no longer cared about Sharon and Unknown Island, but he did care about himself. He didn't want these people to hate him for no reason. These were all people who had been picked specifically to come on this trip. That meant they were people worth knowing. He had to do something to regain control and their respect.

"Look, why don't I go look for the router?" he said. "If this screen is live, then we know there's an internet connection on the island. Maybe it's just a matter of resetting something."

"I'll help," Frankie said.

"Me too," Manny said.

"I'm in," Xander added. The next thing Graham knew, everyone was standing up. There went his chance to be the hero.

"Okay, great," he said, "always good to have so much enthusiasm." He wasn't quite sure how to go about finding the router, though.

"So, um, I guess we look," he said, and he started walking out of the room.

"We really only need to search the main buildings," Manny said. "If this one is wired, there are probably underground cables, and they're not going to bother to run them to all the bungalows. If we can at least find an Ethernet cable, I can hook up my laptop." Everybody nodded, and then the internet search party set out.

Graham left Manny and Frankie to check out the reception area. They would look along floorboards and examine any wires that came out of the walls. Celia, Chelsea, and Margot took the dining room, while Robby, Xander, and Justice took the kitchen, the laundry room, and the gardener's shed out back.

Graham went into Sharon's office, where he made a big show of getting down on his hands and knees under the desk, should anyone happen to walk by the open door. The thing was, Graham knew they weren't going to find any internet because he'd already looked for it. It had been out for a couple of hours already. He'd been standing by the pool, sending Sharon the pictures, as requested, and he'd almost pumped his fist in the air when he saw that they'd actually gone through. Then, not a second later, while he was still staring at his phone, he lost service.

The only place in the office Graham hadn't looked was the closet and that was because it was locked. He decided that he no longer respected Sharon's right to privacy and they should break down the door. Not that *he* could break down the door, but he would get Xander and Manny to do it. Graham was about to go out to reconvene with the others when he pulled open the one drawer in the desk for a last look and saw a set of keys. He inhaled sharply, because he was pretty sure they hadn't been there earlier. Then he picked them up and went to the closet. One of the keys fit in the lock, so he turned it and opened the door.

There was no router, but there was a mini fridge. Briefly, he wondered why anyone would keep a mini fridge locked up, but then he opened its door and answered his own question. The fridge was stocked with bottles of champagne. Nice champagne, too, he figured, since the yellow labels were in French.

He grabbed as many bottles as he could carry and started to head back to the dining room. As he turned, something on the corner of the desk caught his eye: the envelopes addressed to each guest.

In his mounting panic at everything going wrong, Graham had forgotten about Sharon's other request, that he deliver the envelopes after breakfast. He shifted the champagne bottles to one arm and picked up the envelopes. They looked fancy and expensive, so maybe between whatever was in them and a few drinks, he could turn this party around and be the hero after all. He tucked them into his back pocket.

When he returned to the dining room, all the girls were there. Xander and Robby came walking in right after Graham.

"We got the shed door open," Robby said to no one in particular, "but there were just a bunch of rakes and gardening equipment. The shed's not even wired for electricity."

Frankie moaned, and Justice put her head down on the table.

Graham cleared his throat, and everyone shifted to look at him. "Who wants a mimosa?" he sang. Chelsea looked up from the compact she had been holding in front of her face.

"Thank fucking god," she said, snapping the compact shut. "Hit me. Give me a mimosa, hold the orange juice."

"Are we supposed to drink that?" Celia asked. "I'm underage."

"We all are," Graham said, setting the bottles down on the table. "And I think we are definitely not supposed to be drinking this. It was locked up, but I figure Unknown Island owes us this much. No peer pressure here, though. Do not partake if you don't want to." Everyone but Frankie held out a glass, even Celia.

Graham hadn't been invited to many parties in high school. Even now, as a sophomore in college, he wasn't invited to parties, but in that moment, he got an idea of what it must be like to be a jock with access to a keg. He picked up one of the bottles, pulled off the foil top, and then pulled out the cork with a loud *pop*. The champagne started bubbling over. Graham had never opened a bottle of champagne before, so he hoped this was what was supposed to happen.

He filled everyone's glass, and as they waited for the bubbles to settle, Manny raised his in the air. "I know this is turning out to be kind of shitty," he said. "But I'm still happy to be here, and to have met all of you."

Sheesh, Graham thought, the guy's acting like he's the best man at a wedding. But as he looked around the table, all the girls were beaming at Manny, especially Frankie. Everyone took a drink, and Chelsea, Emma Jane, and Robby drained their glasses and held them out for more. Graham filled them, then set the empty bottle down on the table. Then he remembered something.

"Wait," he said, practically shouting, "I have something else." He pulled out the stack of envelopes and started distributing them.

"Ooh, what's this?" Chelsea asked, taking the one that he held out in her direction.

"Just a little welcome from the island," Graham said. He didn't know what was in the envelopes, but judging from the luxe paper and wax seals, it was something nice. A gift certificate, maybe. But one by one, as everyone opened their envelope, they fell silent, champagne-induced smiles melting off their faces. Justice seemed frozen in place. Xander looked confused. Celia sniffed, and Robby shook his head slightly, looking at the paper in his hands like he wanted to rip it to shreds and burn the pieces.

What the hell? Fumbling, Graham tore open his own envelope, the wax seal crumbling, and pulled out a thick, cream-colored piece of paper that looked like a wedding invitation. Then he read the words:

Welcome to Unknown Island.
You have been invited here because you are all murderers.

Chelsea Quinn, you killed Margaret Harrington.
Manuel de La Cruz, you killed nine people.
Graham Hoffman, you killed Tommy Bledsoe.
Frankie Russh, you killed Hannah Carrington.
Emma Jane Ohana, you killed Sergio Ramirez.
Xander Lee, you killed Damien Richards.
Celia Young, you killed Stacia Lindstrom.
Robby Wade, you killed Braxton Ross.
Margot Bryant, you killed Sarah Riley.
Justice Wilson, you killed Tyler Pritchard.

Gotcha. Murder follows back.

CHAPTER THREE

Manny stared at the piece of paper in his hand. It didn't make sense. No, it did make sense; it was some sort of cruel joke. A game that he would refuse to play. Fuck it and fuck this stupid island. He crumpled the paper into a ball and threw it on the table. Then he took a sip of champagne and gagged almost immediately. Too many bad memories. He grabbed his water and took a few gulps to try to get the taste of champagne out of his mouth.

He looked around the table, at the nine faces all staring silently at the missive they had just received. Margot looked like someone about to ask to speak to the manager. Graham looked like he might cry. Only Chelsea looked composed, a slight smirk on her face. Next to him, Celia stood up. "I'm going to go back to my room," she started. "I don't feel very . . ." Then she collapsed, her body going liquid from the toes up.

"Shit!" Manny scrambled out of his chair and managed to catch Celia just before her head would have smacked the table. She hung in his arms like a rag doll, limp and unmoving.

"Oh my god," Margot shrieked. "Is she dead?" The only other person who moved was Justice. She jumped up, ran around the table, and took Celia's wrist in her hand. Manny felt relieved when he realized Justice was checking her pulse.

"No, you—" Justice started to snap at Margot, and then stopped herself. "She fainted. Here," she said, looking at Manny, "let's get her lying down."

Celia couldn't have weighed more than a hundred and ten pounds, but Manny was grateful for Justice's assistance in getting her to the floor without cracking her skull. "We need something to put under her head," Justice said, but there wasn't a cushion or a pillow or anything soft in the room.

"Here," Emma Jane said, offering her Chanel bag, "you can use my purse." Justice took it, and Manny carefully lifted Celia's head so that Justice could slide the bag underneath.

"What else do we do?" he asked, looking at Justice.

"We need to elevate her feet above her head," she said. "And then we just wait for her to come out of it." Manny nodded, then stood up, grabbed a chair, and turned it on its side. He lifted Celia's feet and propped them on the chair's back. Looking at the tiny girl, unconscious, with a Chanel bag under her head and a chair under her feet, the absurdity of it all hit him. A strange game on a bare-bones island, all of them lured here by the promise of luxury and a whole lot of likes. He felt like an idiot.

Frankie came over with a napkin soaked in water and kneeled down next to Celia, holding the napkin to her forehead.

Celia stirred, and her eyes opened. A strand of Frankie's hair fell across Celia's face and she sneezed, causing everyone who had gathered around her to jump back. "Oh!" she said, struggling to push herself up. "I'm sorry!"

"No, it's okay," Justice said, leaning in. "Just rest. Don't get up."

Celia nodded. "I fainted, didn't I?" she asked.

"Yeah, it's not surprising," Frankie said. "This heat is brutal, and . . ." Her voice trailed off as she looked away. Her gaze settled on Manny, and he was surprised when she didn't look away immediately. He smiled at her, knowing it probably looked more like a grimace, because that was how it felt, and she gave a little nod. Manny was struck once again by how real and natural she looked in person, but this time he noticed something different in her eyes. They were cold and hard. She was pissed. Really, really pissed.

Manny looked at Celia and thought about how fitting her last name was. She looked so young, which was crazy. She probably made the most money out of all of them, except for Frankie, and right now, she looked like she wanted to disappear. He stepped forward and lightly touched Frankie's shoulder. "We should give her some space," he said, directing his words at Graham and Xander and all the others who were doing nothing but crowding around. They nodded and returned to their seats. Frankie stood up and took a few steps back. Justice stayed on the floor next to Celia, though, and Chelsea took a step toward them.

"Sweetie, can I get you anything? Orange juice, coffee?" Chelsea paused. "Jesus, I sound like a flight attendant." To everyone's relief, Celia giggled. She pushed herself up to sitting, waving away Justice's concern.

"Yeah," Celia said, blinking. "I've fainted before, so I know I'll be okay in just a minute. But I would like a cup of tea."

"Tea?" Chelsea said, seeming relieved to have an ask. Celia nodded. "Like, iced tea?" Celia shook her head.

"No, hot tea." Chelsea's eyebrows shot up, no doubt surprised at the request for a hot drink in hot weather, but she nodded. "Sure thing. I'll see what I can find in the kitchen." She walked out, and after she left, something shifted. All the action that could be taken had been taken, and now it was time to address the elephant in the room. Manny felt his anger rise. It had been years since he had been in a fight, but right now he felt ready to throw a punch if someone so much as breathed wrong.

"What the fuck are you trying to do?" he asked, fixing his gaze on Graham. His anger seethed, but Manny unclenched his fists as soon as he saw the look on Graham's face. The guy looked like he was about to shit himself. He was no mastermind, just a stooge.

"I swear to god, man," Graham said, his face growing red and blotchy and his eyes brimming with tears, "I didn't know what was in those letters. I was just told to hand them out. I thought there was going to be a gift card in there, something good. . . ."

"You thought that someone lured us to this shitty island under false pretenses to just give us a Starbucks card?" Emma Jane asked.

"I swear," Graham said again, "I haven't talked to Sharon . . . I mean, I've *never* talked to her, and I haven't gotten a text from her since before you all got here. I just did what I was told. It wasn't supposed to be like this. I was supposed to be a liaison between you guys and the island. I wasn't supposed to have any responsibility. I wasn't supposed to be in charge. I didn't know anyone was being lured, that the island was shitty, or that . . ." He paused, then held up a letter. "I have one too. I really don't know what is going on here."

"Wait," Manny said, "you never actually talked to Sharon?"

Graham shook his head. "We were supposed to talk, but something always came up," he said, "so we just texted and emailed. Until today, she was always super responsive."

"I never actually talked to anyone either," Margot said. "But the emails I got were from someone named Peter. If we had Wi-Fi, I could pull them up on my phone."

"Madison," Xander said. "I remember now. Her name was Madison. We only talked once, at the very beginning."

"My manager did all of my negotiations," Frankie said. "And I don't know who he talked to."

"I didn't talk to anyone either," Robby said, "I just emailed with someone named Suzanne."

"I talked to someone," Manny said. "Her name was Lindsey. What'd Madison sound like?" he asked, turning to Xander.

Xander shrugged. "I don't know," he said. "Like a girl. Young."

Manny nodded. Lindsey had also sounded young over the phone. He didn't add that she had also sounded hot. That seemed so embarrassing to admit now. "Lindsey was young too," he said. "Anybody else have an actual conversation?"

"Email," Emma Jane said.

"Email," Justice said.

"Email," Celia said.

"Huh." It almost made Manny laugh. "So we all traveled

thousands of miles to this remote island because someone we never met invited us."

"When you put it that way, it sounds so stupid," Celia said.

"It is stupid," Robby said, his voice flat.

"Everyone knows Unknown Island," Margot said. "People have been talking about it for months. Their marketing campaign was huge. Everyone I know wants to come here. It all seemed very official, especially when they sent that huge contract."

Justice was crying. "I lied to my parents so that I could come here," she said, wiping her eyes with the heel of her hand. "I forged their signatures on the contract and the release. They don't even know where I am right now." Manny could feel his heart start to race. Some of these people were underage. This wasn't just wrong. It was evil. He looked around the room, waiting for one of them to start laughing, or for someone to come in the door and yell "Surprise!" Something needed to happen, right now, for Manny to continue to think that maybe this was all just a misunderstanding, a joke gone wrong. But nothing. Just the roar of silence in his ears.

"Did you read the contract before you signed your parents' names?" he asked Justice. She gulped and shook her head.

"It was really long," she said. "And they said they needed it back right away."

"Fuck," Manny said. He hadn't read it either. If Justice had gotten the same contract he had, it was a beast. When it had arrived, for a brief moment, he thought he should have a lawyer look it over. But it had come through late at night, when he was headed out the door to the club, and Lindsey had said she needed it back by the morning. So Manny had glanced over the first few paragraphs, then signed and sent it. "Maybe there was something about this in the contract," he asked. "Did anybody actually read it?"

The only one who nodded was Frankie. "I read every word," she said. "I always do. There was nothing about"—she picked up one of the letters and waved it—"whatever this is."

Manny nodded, then turned to Graham. "Why did they tell you no one from the island was coming?" he asked.

"Sharon didn't say they weren't coming," Graham said. "Just that they were going to be late. There was a fire with the investors."

"Yeah, if I was an investor, I'd have problems with this too," Margot said. "It's awful and it's mean." Her face had gone red, her neck splotchy, and she sputtered a bit. "You can't just accuse people of murder! That's not even legal!"

"I don't think Sharon has a fire with the investors," Manny said. "I don't think there's a Sharon. For whatever reason, we were tricked." His words sank in, and the others nodded glumly.

"This is unbelievable," Frankie said. "They're going to pay us all this money just so they can get us here and try to embarrass us? Who does that?"

"Who's getting paid? I'm not getting paid. You're getting paid?" Chelsea asked. All heads swiveled to the doorway, where she stood holding a teacup.

Frankie groaned. "Not very much," she said. "It was part of a package deal with a couple of other activations." Manny got the sense that she was lying, but only Chelsea seemed worried about the money right now.

"There are easier ways to do this if they're trying to get

something out of us," Xander said. "It's like blackmail, but if someone's blackmailing you, don't they normally tell you what they want?"

"Yeah, extortion doesn't have to be this complicated," Emma Jane said. "This took months of planning. This is clearly the work of a psycho, someone who is completely crazy."

"You're not supposed to call people crazy," Margot said. "It's ableist."

Emma Jane looked at her. "Oh, shut the fuck up, you crazy bitch," she said.

Margot's mouth fell open in shock. Justice bit her lip, but Manny could see a grin pull at the corners of her mouth.

"You do not talk to me like that," Margot spat at Emma Jane. "I'm a fucking CEO. I built my company and my following from the ground up, and the only reason anyone knows who you are at all is because you have a rich dad and fake tits."

"Ha!" Emma Jane threw her head back and laughed. "My dad is rich, and maybe he'll buy me your company for my birthday. And guess what?" Emma Jane grabbed her boobs. "These are real. Unlike your nose."

Justice burst out laughing, and it was the first time Manny had seen her look happy. Chelsea applauded. Manny smiled too. He'd underestimated Emma Jane. Still, he was in no mood to break up a girl fight right now, so he stepped in.

"I think we need to calm down and remain focused," he said. "That letter. Do any of you—"

Margot cut him off. "I have never killed anyone," Margot said. "It's just awful. It's libelous, and I'll sue."

"Of course you will," Emma Jane said.

"I've never even heard of that person," Celia said.

"How did they get that information? How did they get those names?" Justice was no longer laughing. Her voice shook, and several people were nodding in agreement.

"It's all a bunch of lies," Graham said. "All of those were lies!"

Manny had a knot in his stomach. For the past couple of years, it had pretty much always been there, and he'd gotten used to living with it. It was a knot woven of guilt and shame that grew tighter with every day of living a lie. Except, that wasn't true exactly.

Manny hadn't lied about it. If anyone had bothered to ask, he would have told them the truth. But no one asked, at least not anymore, and so Manny never talked about it, and that had started to feel like a lie. When he'd read the words on that piece of paper, they came as a shock. But also a relief, almost. It was an opening, the kind that he waited for in every conversation, the kind that never actually came up. He took a deep breath.

"It was true about me," Manny said, sending a wave of silence through the room.

"What are you talking about?" Robby asked finally.

"What the letter said is true," Manny said. His voice was flat, no hint of emotion.

"You didn't kill nine people," Frankie said. "If you did, you'd be in jail."

"No," Manny said, "I did kill nine people, and though this island feels like a prison right now, I am not in jail."

All eyes were on Manny. The only sound in the dining room was the waves softly tumbling onto the beach. The air moved in what could barely be considered a breeze. Frankie stared at him; she could see the rise and fall of his chest underneath his tank top, his breathing shallow and rapid.

"What the hell are you talking about?" Xander said.

"I used to throw warehouse parties in Miami," Manny said. "Not by myself, with a group of people. A couple of years ago, a fire broke out at one of them, and a crowd got trapped in the warehouse. Nine people died." Silence again, broken only by a small sniff from Margot. "Most died of smoke inhalation, but a couple actually burned to death," Manny went on. "One girl was only fourteen, and one of the guys had two little kids at home." Frankie said nothing; her heart was beating like a frog trying to escape her rib cage.

Emma Jane was the first to speak. "But it was an accident, right?" she said. "It wasn't like you killed them yourself."

"Maybe not," Manny said. "But it was still my fault. We didn't have permits, insurance, anything. The whole thing was illegal. We knew the warehouse was barely standing, but we didn't care. We packed thousands of people in there that night, and then the whole thing caught fire."

"Then why are you here and not in jail?" Justice asked, and Manny shrugged.

"Everyone else got locked up, but I was only sixteen," he said. "I did some time in juvie, but got let out early for good behavior. I got my GED while I was in there, and even graduated early. Since I turned eighteen, none of this is on my record anymore."

Frankie swallowed and finally found her voice. "So, people know this about you?"

Manny shrugged. He wasn't looking at her, or anybody, just drawing patterns in the condensation on his glass.

"Some do," he said, "some don't. The scene I'm in isn't really about deep conversations, you know? People come and go. I started using my mom's last name a couple of years ago, so even people who know the story might not know it's me." He looked up from the glass and around the table. "I guess what I'm trying to say is that I'm not hiding it, but I'm not advertising it either. It's not a secret. It would have taken two Googles to find."

The palm leaves rustled, and then Justice took a deep breath and sniffed. "This whole thing is really messed up," she said, tears running down her cheeks. "I have no idea why anyone would accuse me of . . ." She paused like she couldn't even say the word, and her mouth twisted. She took a deep breath and continued. "But I do know him. The name in that thing. Tyler Pritchard was my neighbor's little boy. He died last year because he got into some poison and ate it. In the backyard, or the garage, or something, they don't know how. I hardly knew him, but it was awful for our whole town! Why would anyone bring that up? Trying to put that on me . . ." Her voice shook. "I had nothing to do with it." She grabbed a napkin from the table to wipe her eyes, but the tears just kept coming.

When Frankie had first opened the letter and read the words, she felt like she'd been slapped. Shock was quickly replaced by anger. Someone, anyone, was going to pay. But now the anger was draining away and fear was creeping in. This was a nightmare, someone dragging the worst of her life out into the open for these people to see. Frankie had to keep it together, not let anyone else know how bad this was. *Don't lose control of the narrative,* she thought, repeating another bit of Roger's sage advice. *Once you lose the narrative, you don't get it back.* She was having trouble breathing, like she was allergic to air, and she kept swallowing, trying to keep the tears at bay. If the tears came, then the sobs would come and she wouldn't be able to stop. She would fall apart right here, in the dining room, on this weird island, and the others wouldn't be able to do anything for her. They'd have to pick up her bits and pieces and carry them out to the beach to be washed away by the waves. This was how she had felt since Hannah died, like she was made of glass and one crack would make all of her spill out. She took a deep breath. She wasn't going to let this be that crack.

She had to get in front of this, come as clean as she could. "I knew Hannah Carrington. She was my best friend," Frankie said. "We grew up together. She was the person I loved more than anyone in the world, and after I started to get . . ." She paused. Frankie hated to call herself famous. "Successful," she continued, "I hired her to be my assistant so she could make some money. Hannah was a party girl, though. I mean, we both were at one point, but then I grew out of it, and Hannah . . . she OD'd in her hotel room one night. She took a whole bunch of pills and just never woke up. . . . Fuck this!" Frankie stopped and looked at the ceiling to calm herself down. She went on, picking her words carefully. "I was just down the hall, a few rooms away. There is not a day that goes by that I don't miss Hannah or that I don't kick myself for not intervening in her addiction." Frankie picked a letter up off the table and waved it. "I do blame myself for her death, but I didn't kill her."

"Of course you didn't kill your best friend," Graham said. He stepped forward and put one hand on Frankie's shoulder. His hand felt like a rotten banana, and she shrugged it off as quickly as she could. Graham didn't seem to notice. "It's a preposterous suggestion," he went on. "They're all preposterous suggestions. I knew Tommy Bledsoe, but barely. I hired him to photograph this fundraiser I put together, and he fell down the stairs and broke his neck. It was awful. Ruined the whole campaign, but it wasn't anyone's fault." Graham stopped and swallowed. "I mean, I guess it could have been his fault, because he wasn't watching where he was going, but that's it. Everything was up to code, and we had tons of insurance. The congressman we were raising money for even sent flowers to the funeral."

Watching Graham speak, Frankie couldn't help but notice that his eyes shifted in Manny's direction on the word "insurance," as if he thought a policy was all it took to make the loss of a life okay.

But still, if everything had happened the way Graham said it did, then it wasn't anyone's fault. Accidents happened all the time. But something gave Frankie an odd feeling that things had not, in fact, happened the way Graham said they did.

Xander cleared his throat. "I, uh, feel like I ought to say something, too," he said. "Damien Richards was a kid I went to high school with. We weren't friends or anything. Totally different crowds. He was into drama and art and stuff."

"So he was gay," Justice said.

Xander sputtered. "I didn't say that," he said.

"No, you didn't," Justice said. "But when someone like you

says that someone else is into 'drama and art and stuff,' what they mean is 'gay.'"

"I don't know," Xander said, and he sounded legitimately pained. "Like I said, we weren't friends. I only knew him because he was my calc tutor for a while." Xander stopped and swallowed. "He committed suicide right before graduation."

Justice seemed to regret what she had said. "Sorry," she muttered. Xander looked hurt, and maybe right after they had been accused of murder was not the best time to call someone out on their homophobia. Still, Frankie thought that Xander seemed too upset over the death of someone he wouldn't even call a friend. The silence settled again, and they all looked at each other, wondering who would go next.

It was Celia. "That name that was associated with me," she said, "I don't recognize at all. Stacia Lindstrom? I don't know her."

"It's kind of a famous true crime case. I listened to a podcast about it." Emma Jane said, and everyone turned to look at her. "Her ex was stalking her. He found her and killed her in the parking lot outside of her job."

"Jesus," Graham said.

"She worked at a flower shop," Emma Jane added. "Apparently, she had a restraining order against him and had moved to Phoenix to get away from him, but he broke into her email to find out where she lived."

Celia listened raptly. "Oh," she said, after a few seconds of silence, "that's awful. I went to Arizona once for a convention, but I think it might have been in Tucson." Celia looked even paler and frailer than before.

Emma Jane seemed to realize then that everyone had

turned their attention to her. "I knew Sergio Ramirez," she said. "But I don't really want to talk about it."

"I don't think that's an option right now," Manny said.

"And why isn't it?" she snapped. "I don't know you people, and as soon as I can, I am getting out of here and going home and never seeing any of you again."

"That's a nice thing to say," Frankie said.

"Oh, come on," Emma Jane said. "You are all thinking the exact same thing. Be honest. It's not like we're going to leave here and start a group text. 'Remember that time someone lured us all to an island and accused us of murder? LOL, amirite?'"

Everyone was silent, looking at Emma Jane, and she stared back, the defiance in her eyes dimming. "Okay, fine," she said. "Sergio was our housekeeper's son. I guess you could say we grew up together. One night he convinced me to take him to this party in Beverly Hills. I knew it wasn't his scene, but I agreed because I didn't want to seem like a bitch. But while we were there, he stole a whole bunch of jewelry. It shouldn't have been a big deal, because he was only seventeen, but for some reason they decided to try him as an adult."

"Some reason being 'racism,'" Justice said.

"Maybe," Emma Jane said, her voice quieter than before, "but he got sent to prison, and got killed there. I guess someone thought he was someone else, or something like that. I don't know. Trust me, I feel super guilty about it. I should have stopped him, you know? But people make their own decisions." From where Frankie was sitting, she could see that Emma Jane was shaking.

"I feel like I should say something," Robby said, "because

this kind of accusation, this kind of rumor, could kill my career. At Hock and Jowl, we take food allergies very seriously." Everyone looked at him.

"Food allergies?" Frankie asked.

Robby nodded, and realized he needed to start from the beginning. "Braxton Ross was a teenager who died from anaphylaxis due to an allergic reaction to sesame seeds," he said. "He and his family had eaten at my restaurant earlier that day, but we're Southern food. We don't have anything with sesame on the menu. We have a lot of things with peanuts, but anyone who eats there knows that."

"I didn't know that people could die from food allergies," Xander said.

"It's rare," Robby said. "Really, really, really rare."

"It's not actually that rare," Celia said. "My sister was allergic to shrimp. The only way my parents found out was because she ate some when she was little and blew up like a blimp. She could have stopped breathing, but someone in the restaurant knew what to do."

"It's still rare," Robby said, though he seemed less sure of what he was saying now, and more like it was wishful thinking. He shook his head. "What a bunch of bullshit. Someone drags people out here just to throw awful things in—"

Chelsea had been uncharacteristically quiet, and everyone turned to look at her when she interrupted Robby. "So this doesn't bother me at all," she said.

"You're kidding, right?" Frankie said.

"No, I'm not. I killed Margaret Harrington," Chelsea said matter-of-factly. "I thought everyone knew that."

"How would we know that?" Robby said.

"It was on all the websites," Chelsea said. Everyone continued to stare at her, and Frankie thought that this was the first time she had seen Chelsea look horrified. "You mean none of you read about it?" It was almost like she was upset that they didn't know her dirty laundry.

"She ran over a woman with her car," Margot interjected, like she was trying to come to Chelsea's defense. "The woman died, but she was really old."

"Wait," Justice said, holding one hand up while she worked something out in her head. "I remember reading about it!" The look on her face changed from the elation of piecing it together to disgust. "It was a hit and run! You were trying to upload a selfie, and you didn't even notice you'd hit someone. A bystander had to chase you down and you didn't stop for several blocks."

Chelsea frowned. "Well, it wasn't exactly like that," she said, her voice icy. "I'm not a monster. Margaret Harrington was a really old woman who stepped out from between two cars at night. But no one had to chase me down, and I stopped as soon as I realized what had happened."

"How old was she?" Graham asked.

Chelsea had to think for a second. "Sixty-four," she said.

"What?" Robby said, his voice rising to a screech. "That's not even that old! My mom is fifty-seven! Why aren't you in jail?"

"Did you not hear me?" Chelsea said, her voice rising. "She came out of nowhere. The judge ruled that it wasn't my fault, but I still paid her family forty-three thousand dollars of *my own money*!" Frankie bit her lip to keep from sneering, because the way Chelsea emphasized "my own money" made it sound like she was affronted that someone hadn't offered to pay for her.

"So forty-three thousand dollars is how much someone's life is worth?" Robby asked.

"Look, biscuit boy," Chelsea said, her brow furrowing as she pointed a finger tipped with a teal, almond-shaped nail at Robby, "it was an accident. No one told me I had to give her family any money, but I did anyway. I lost all of my major contracts because of it, and a lot of my followers. So I paid for it, and I will continue to pay for it every day for the rest of my—"

"You can't just run somebody over—" Robby was almost yelling now, but Chelsea interrupted him, yelling back.

"Well, you'd better make sure you don't step out in front of my car, then—"

"Stop!" Graham bellowed. "Sharon, or whoever she is, should be here soon, and we need to be a united front."

Robby swallowed and nodded. "Sorry," he said, looking back at Chelsea. She shrugged.

"Fine," she said. In the silence that followed, everyone shifted, looking at different places, biting nails, cleaning glasses, picking at invisible pieces of fuzz, every single one of them in the most beautiful place they had ever been and desperately wishing they were somewhere else.

"Whoever is behind this," Justice said, "I hate them."

"We don't know them," Celia said, "but they sure know us."

"What do you mean?" Manny asked.

"They found people we knew who died. I mean, I thought, I don't know Stacia Lindstrom . . . But maybe I do? What if they know something about me that I don't even know myself?"

The thought sent a chill through Frankie, and it was then

that she noticed she wasn't as hot as she had been earlier. There was air moving through the dining room now, and outside, the sky had grown dark with clouds.

"Is it going to rain?" she asked. "The sky was totally clear just a while ago."

"It feels like it," Manny said. "Tropical storms do that. They just show up."

Frankie shivered and rubbed her arms. The clouds felt like a sign that the weather had picked sides, and it wasn't on theirs.

Graham cleared his throat. "So none of us knew each other before this, right?" he said. Everyone shook their heads except Frankie, who nodded.

"Celia and I knew each other," she said, and Celia looked over at her, surprise in her eyes. "I don't know if you remember," Frankie went on, "but I was friends with Caroline. We used to hang out quite a bit."

"I remember," Celia said, and the pain clearly visible on her face made Frankie feel like she needed to apologize.

"I didn't bring it up earlier," she went on, "because I wasn't sure what to say. I didn't want to say anything if it was something you tried not to think about."

"It's okay," Celia said.

"Who's Caroline and what happened to her?" Graham said. He had about as much tact as a city bus, Frankie thought, but before she could say anything, Celia answered him.

"She was, I mean is, my sister," Celia said. "She died a couple of years ago." Graham winced. At least he realized his mistake.

"I'm sorry," he said.

"It's okay," Celia said. "I mean, it's not really, but I don't mind talking about it." She looked at Frankie when she said this, and Frankie wished they were alone so they could really talk about it. Frankie felt like she might know what it was like to lose a sister.

When nobody else spoke, Graham started again. "Okay," he went on, "but aside from the two of you, none of us knows each other. We're all from different places, and we all do different things. But what do we have in common?"

"The internet," Celia said.

"Exactly!" Graham said. "All of us are successful on the internet! I mean, we're all successful in real life, too, but . . ."

"The internet is real life," Frankie said, weary of all the talking. She'd had this conversation a million times, weathered the same tired barbs from people who didn't understand social media. "Yes, but what do you do?" they would ask, somehow unable to wrap their brains around the fact that social media was what she did.

"Yeah, I know," Graham said in a way that made her think he didn't, not really. "But we have what millions of people want. Whoever is doing this is someone who's jealous."

"Yeah!' Xander seemed invigorated by the idea and leaned forward in his chair. "Haters gonna hate. I can't even post a selfie without some fat dude who plays football from his couch telling me I throw like a girl."

"Girls can throw," Justice said. "And kick."

"I know," Xander groaned. "His words, not mine. But Graham's right. What if whoever is doing this is trying to take us down because they can't stand to see other people succeed?"

Everyone nodded. It was a flimsy explanation, but it was the only thing that could possibly make sense. Frankie was used to people being jealous of her. She'd seen it over and over in the comments. The same user who just last week had written "OMG I want to be u!" was now calling Frankie a slut and telling her she deserved to die. "Don't read the comments" was the first rule of the internet, and it was also the rule that everyone broke. But what did Unknown Island have to be jealous of? Aside from her, it had more followers than anyone here.

Margot cleared her throat, and the others shifted to look at her, waiting for her to say something. After a few seconds of silence, it became clear that she really had just been clearing her throat. "What about you?" Manny asked her. "How do you know the name in your letter?"

Margot sat up a little straighter. "I don't wish to discuss it," she said.

"That's BS," Emma Jane said, as if she had been designated the official Margot tamer. "The rest of us *did* discuss it, even if we didn't want to." Heads nodded vigorously.

Margot was not allowed to sit this one out, but she plastered a fake smile on her face. "I'm not saying anything until I talk to my lawyer," she said. Margot was unbelievable. She was the poster girl for privilege, secure in her assumption that no one would make her do something she didn't want to do and that authority would come to her rescue.

Robby wasn't having it. He grabbed the nearest letter and read from it. "Sarah Riley," he said. "That name doesn't mean anything to you?"

"Of course it does," Margot snapped. "But I have no obligation to tell any of you anything!"

A light bulb went on in Frankie's head. She reached over and picked up the letter, staring at it while the connection formed in her mind. "Wait," she said. "The name doesn't mean anything to me, but I think I know what this is about. One of SHEmail's publicists reached out to me a while back, wanting to do a partnership."

Margot's head snapped in Frankie's direction. "I doubt that anyone from my team ever contacted you," she said. Her mouth was smiling, but the rest of her face looked like it might crack. "No offense, but I don't really think you're a fit for the SHEmail brand."

"I'm not," Frankie said. "Which is why we said no. I also remember that my manager said something about how you didn't give your employees health insurance, and one of them got cancer and died." It was obvious from the flush creeping up Margot's face and the anger in her eyes that Frankie had hit the nail on the head.

"Why are you doing this to me?" Margot whined.

"Wait," Graham said, snapping his fingers, "I remember this too! I read about it. The girl was working sixty hours a week or something but was still classified as part-time."

Margot exploded. "I challenge any of you to build your own business from scratch and not make a few mistakes along the way," she hissed.

"Like a transphobic name," Chelsea suggested under her breath, but Margot went on. "We are a start-up, which means we run lean! Everyone who works for SHEmail does it because they believe in what we are trying to accomplish, and if health insurance is something that is important to them, then they should go work for Facebook!" Her outburst drained her, literally. The red in her face had faded away, and now she looked like a pale ghost that was about to cry. "I don't understand why everyone is trying to bully me!"

"No one here is trying to bully you," Justice said. "We're all getting bullied. We should stop fighting and stick together. I think we should leave as soon as we can, even if it looks really bad."

Frankie slapped the table. Justice's words had given her an idea. "We can write a statement, and we'll all post it on our own accounts at the same time," she said. "Unknown Island is a scam and worse, a bully, and none of us stand for that. We don't have to go into details about what happened, but we can hint at it, and it will be stronger if we all have the same story. No matter how crazy this gets online, we have to stick together."

Graham was excited. "That's a great idea," he said. "If we spin this right, it could be even better for us than if everything had gone according to plan."

Margot was nodding so fast that her blond ponytail shook. "Graham's right," she said. "Everyone loves a victim narrative. And there could be a ton of press since everyone is going to want the inside story. . . ."

Frankie leaned forward and pointed a finger in Margot's face. She took the tone she used to take with her mother. "No talking to the press," she said. "This isn't about any of our individual stories. We leave the island as a group, post one statement as a group, and then we move on. Strength in numbers."

"Sure, sure, of course," Margot said, though Frankie didn't believe her for a second. "Just remember," she added, "there's no such thing as bad press."

"Wrong," Frankie said. "There is." She pulled out her

phone. "I'll start drafting a statement and then we can workshop it together."

"Fantastic," Graham said.

"Whatever we write, I'm going to need my attorney to look it over first," Margot said.

"Does LegalZoom vet Instagram statements?" Emma Jane asked, but before Margot could answer, a pop made everyone jump.

Chelsea hadn't meant to open the champagne so dramatically, but the cork had practically shot out of the bottle, and now everyone turned to stare at her as it foamed over in her hand. She licked her lips, tasting the citrusy tang of her lipstick, and stared back. Whatever was happening, she wasn't going to panic. She'd panicked enough.

That night in LA, she'd been on her way home from a party in West Hollywood to celebrate the launch of a new curling iron. She hadn't worn her contacts because they made her eyes water and her eyeliner run, but she'd been running late and forgotten her glasses. Fine on the way there. Not so fine on the way home, after the sun had set. She'd been fumbling with her phone, looking for a playlist on Spotify, when she hit something. For a split second, she thought it was a speed bump. When she realized it wasn't, she froze. She had no idea how long she sat there, car stopped, hands on the wheel, staring straight ahead. She'd hit someone, yes, but she hadn't run, because in that moment, Chelsea couldn't even move. Somehow, somewhere deep inside of her, she just knew: she'd killed someone. And her career.

People gathered. The police came. An ambulance. There

was an investigation, and Chelsea entered her plea and paid her fine, and prayed that maybe no one would find out. Her prayers weren't answered. There were the comments, the un-follows, the loss of her contracts. The way they were all so nice about it—apologetic, even—assuring her they understood that it was all out of her control, but this was business, and killing someone, even by accident, wasn't aspirational.

After mistakenly thinking that a comment that called her "the Gen Z Noxzema girl" was a compliment, Chelsea went dark on social. She went dark in her life. Moved back in with her parents. She didn't leave the house, didn't get dressed, didn't put on makeup, didn't shower for weeks. The one day, her dad knocked on the door to her room and walked in anyway when she didn't answer. She was in bed, of course, and when he stood above her, she pulled the comforter up over her head.

"Get up," he said, "You're not going to let this ruin you and destroy everything you've worked for." She pulled the comforter down and glared at him. "I mean, look at you!" he went on. "Your eyebrows aren't even on fleek anymore!" She groaned and threw a pillow at him, but then she got out of bed and took a shower. That was the beginning of her comeback.

So maybe it was the worst moment of her life that had gotten Chelsea here, but she was still here, and this was still an opportunity, even if it wasn't the one she had thought she was signing up for. Deep down, Chelsea had always known she would be a household name someday, and if this was how she was going to get there, so be it. She was sure, looking at the faces of the nine people looking back at her, that she was not like them. They were terrified, but she wasn't scared. She had nothing more to hide.

"This is fabulous theater," she said, pouring the champagne into her glass, "but I think we're taking this way too seriously."

"Accusations of murder are supposed to be taken lightly?" Graham said.

"Come on," she said, using the bottle to gesture around the room. "There are probably hidden cameras all over the place recording our every move, and I have to say, we are all doing a banger job at playing our parts. He's the bad boy with a heart of gold," she said, pointing at Manny. "She's the girl next door—literally, in this case." Here, she pointed at Justice. "Xander's the jock, Frankie's the princess, Graham's the dweeb, and Robby's the hot asshole." Graham looked hurt and Robby sneered.

"Is that supposed to be a compliment?" he asked, but Chelsea ignored him.

"Emma Jane's the villain that we all secretly root for, and Celia's the nerd. No offense, sweetie."

"None taken," the girl said. "That's how I would have cast myself."

"I'm the comic relief and Margot's the white privilege," Chelsea finished. Margot started to protest, and Chelsea happily ignored her, too. "This is what happens when you don't read your contracts because you're so excited about a whole bunch of new followers and a free vacation."

"I read every word of the contract," Frankie said, "and there was nothing—"

With two fingers holding the stem of her champagne glass, Chelsea pointed at her and Frankie shut up.

"This is clearly a reality show," Chelsea said, almost unable to believe that no one else was figuring this out. The more she thought about it, the more obvious it became. "Like a cross between *Survivor* and a murder mystery party. The fact that we're all caught off guard just makes it that much more intriguing. It makes no sense to accuse people of stuff they didn't do, but something they maybe *could have* done? Pure genius. Right now, the producers are somewhere watching us bite each other's heads off and high-fiving themselves on their next hit show. I, for one, am thrilled."

"How on earth could you be thrilled about any of this?" Frankie said, her voice almost a whine.

"Because isn't this giving us what we really want?" Chelsea said. "After this, we are all going to be very, very famous." She paused and smiled at everyone. All eyes were on her, and she imagined that the cameras were, too. Whatever this game was, she had no doubt she could play it, and no doubt she could win. One hell of a comeback indeed. Sephora was probably going to always be out of the question, but maybe, if she played this right, she could still have a shot with Ulta. "Cheers," she said.

With that, she raised her glass, then put it to her lips and drained it in one gulp. She drank so quickly that she started to cough. Something tasted off in the champagne. Acrid, chemical. She set her empty glass on the table, and it tipped over and fell on its side. Chelsea was starting to feel like she couldn't breathe. She couldn't control her lungs. She wasn't getting any air. The room started to spin. Now she was panicking. Holding a hand to her chest, she looked out, trying to signal to someone, anyone, what was happening. They just looked back, and those eighteen eyes were the last things she saw before the world went black.

She fell forward and lay there, completely still.

CHAPTER FOUR

For a few seconds, everything stopped, and then the first drops of rain started to fall. "Oh my god!" Margot screamed. "Is she dead?" Justice wanted to throttle her, but this time, it was a valid question. Margot's words were like a shock, jolting Justice into action. She dashed across the room to where Chelsea lay slumped in her chair, her head on the table and her champagne glass rolling back and forth from the fall.

Manny was standing next to her chair, his dark eyes wide with panic, and he bent down to talk directly in her ear. "Chelsea, Chelsea," he said, his voice soft but urgent, "are you okay? Can you hear me?" He stood back up and looked at Justice. She was sure the look on her face mirrored his, and then, without saying anything, they reached out and each took hold of one of Chelsea's shoulders and leaned her back in her chair. Justice could tell from the way Chelsea's head hung forward, her ombré beachy waves obscuring her face, that the answer to Margot's question was yes.

"Wow," Robby sneered, "and the Academy Award for Best

Inappropriate Performance in an Already Horrible Situation goes to . . ." Justice swiveled in his direction, giving him the same look her father gave people when he was about to throw them out of court. Robby shut up.

"Is she . . . ?" Manny started, and Justice looked up at him. They were still holding Chelsea by the shoulders, and when Justice looked down, she saw that the champagne had spilled on Chelsea's hair and down the front of her dress.

"I don't know," Justice said. She and Manny lowered Chelsea out of her chair and onto the floor. Then she took a deep breath and reached down to find Chelsea's wrist. Justice had gotten CPR certified as part of her lifeguard training when she was fifteen. She was aware of the irony that this now made her the resident medical expert, and she didn't relish it. In her job at the country club pool, the most first aid she'd ever had to administer was to a four-year-old who stepped on a bee.

Chelsea didn't have a pulse, and Justice felt her own heart start to pound. "Help me get her down on the floor," she said to Manny, "Lay her flat." They scrambled, and as soon as Chelsea was on the floor, Justice straightened her arms, placed her right hand on top of her left, and then situated her hands in the center of Chelsea's chest and started compressions. She counted out loud, her voice the only sound in the room. It was thirty compressions, and then two breaths, but after thirty, she felt herself freeze. She'd only done CPR on a dummy before, but now, she knew, she just knew, that Chelsea wasn't dying.

"She's dead," Justice said. "I don't know what else to do—" A crack of thunder made everyone jump.

Seconds, minutes, maybe an hour passed in silence, and all Justice could think about was her dad's voice when he was angry. Judge Harold Wilson had a deep, booming voice that made lawyers shake in their leather shoes and defendants wish they were already in prison. It was a voice Justice had spent most of her seventeen years trying to avoid at all costs, and now it was the only thing in the world she wanted to hear. Her dad's voice on the phone, yelling, threatening, telling her she had to quit swimming, give up her car, that she was grounded until she was thirty. She'd take any of it, and willingly, just to hear him tell her that he was coming to get her, that he was coming to take her away from this tiny tropical island and this dead girl's body. She gulped back a sob.

Emma Jane was hugging herself, her arms crossed over her chest and her hands rubbing her arms like she was trying to warm them. Margot looked shocked, her mouth hanging slightly open. Robby's mouth was set in a grim line, and Graham kept pulling at his hair, making his black curls stand out in every direction. Finally, Frankie spoke.

"We have to go for help," she said. "This isn't funny anymore."

"It was never funny," Robby said.

"I know," Frankie said, "but whoever planned this cruel joke, or whatever they think it is, didn't plan on someone dying on this island."

"What happened to her?" Celia asked. "She seemed so . . . alive." Around the room, heads nodded in agreement. Justice thought that as long as she lived, she would have that image of Chelsea in her mind, smiling as she made a toast and then, two seconds later, crumpling. The weight of it was crushing, that death could be that instantaneous, so quick and yet so permanent. She didn't like to think about death.

The lights in the room flickered and it took Justice a second to realize it was lightning. "If anyone was coming over," Xander said, "I don't think they are now. I talked to the guy who brought us over here. He said there's one way in and one way out, and that these waters can get pretty dangerous. And there's no way you can fly a helicopter in this weather. So even if someone is coming, they won't be here for a while."

Graham stepped forward. "We have to put her in the freezer," he said, his voice quiet and calm. Justice swiveled toward him, ready to lay in, but she saw that his expression was serious. "No, really," he said, "look." Justice looked back down and saw what he was pointing at. Trails of ants were already running up and down Chelsea's body, swarming the sweet champagne. Justice tried to brush a couple of them away, but they squashed under her fingers. "With the bugs, and the heat and humidity here, she'll . . . uh . . ." Graham seemed like he wasn't quite sure how to explain it. "She won't be in good shape for her family," he said finally. "Especially if we don't know how long we'll have to wait to get her out of here." Justice had to give it to him. It was a thoughtful idea, and if not a good one, then the best one they had.

Manny stepped forward. "Somebody want to help me out?" he asked. Xander took a gulp of water and then moved toward him.

"I can get her head," Xander said, "and you take her legs."

"I can show you where the freezer is," Robby offered. Justice nodded. She felt like she should come, too, that she now had some custodianship of Chelsea by virtue of being the one who had pronounced her dead.

"How could she just die like that?" Celia asked.

"I don't know," Justice said. "Maybe a heart attack? Or a brain aneurysm?"

"What if there was something in her drink?" Celia asked. "Like, poison?"

Justice felt totally defeated. It seemed incredible that Chelsea had died like that, right in front of them, instantaneously, from natural causes. But it seemed more incredible that it could have been anything else. An eerie accident. Or worse . . . murder.

"She opened the bottle and poured it herself," Manny said. "We all watched her do it. I don't know how anyone could poison a sealed bottle of champagne."

Justice nodded and felt something in her chest loosen a bit. Chelsea had to have died of something natural. Strange, yes, but still natural. There was no other option.

There was another flash of lightning. The rain was really coming down now.

"We should get her into the freezer before it starts raining any harder," Graham said. Manny and Xander were moving into position, when Emma Jane ran up.

"Wait!" she said. She had her phone out, and before anyone could stop her, she took a picture of Chelsea's dead body. Then another, and another.

"Are you serious?" Frankie asked, staring at Emma Jane in disbelief. Emma Jane kept snapping away, and Frankie took a step toward her, like she was about to slap the phone out of her hand.

"Show some respect," Robby said, a note of incredulity in his voice. Emma Jane stopped and looked at both of them, her eyes bright with defiance.

"On every crime show ever, the first thing the investigators do when they find a body is take a million pictures and don't touch anything," she said. "You're right that we can't leave her to be ant food, but when the cops or whoever gets here, they're going to want to know what happened, and this way we can show them."

Justice was impressed. This was smart.

"It's a good idea," Graham said, in a way that almost sounded like he had thought of it. He whipped out his own phone and began taking pictures from different angles. "If they show up and there's a dead girl in the freezer, they need to know there was no foul play." Then Graham pocketed his phone and stepped back. Manny and Xander exchanged a look and got ready a second time.

Picking Chelsea up wasn't easy. She didn't weigh much, but she was limp, and the only way Xander could keep her head from rolling all over the place was to grip her under the arms and hug her to his chest. Justice saw him gag a little, probably from Chelsea's lifeless face being just inches from his own, and then they started toward the kitchen.

It was like a small funeral procession. Manny and Xander were the ushers, Robby, Justice, and Graham trailing after them like mourners. Celia stood up and swayed a little. She thought about death all the time. The whole point of video games was to kill or be killed, but this was different. She'd never seen someone die before in real life. "I think I'm going to go back to my room and lie down," she said, looking around at the three other girls.

Emma Jane sat with her knees up, hunched over into a ball,

while Frankie just stared out the window. Only Margot, who was still sitting up very straight, like she was about to be graded on her posture, acknowledged Celia. She nodded a little, but nobody said anything. Celia stepped out of the dining room and into the rain.

She'd done research on tropical storms before coming here and knew that they were mercurial beasts. One minute the sky would be dark and thunderous; later that same hour there wouldn't be so much as a cloud. She looked out over the water and saw waves swelling on the horizon. She walked past the pool, where a dark shape lay on the bottom, far beneath the rippled surface. She peered at it and saw that it was a palm frond, then jumped back when it moved.

A snake came slithering out from underneath. A black-and-white-banded sea snake, highly venomous, but docile unless provoked. Celia had done research on snakes, too, and had long ago decided to steer clear of the beach. Now she knew she wouldn't be swimming at all this trip, not even in the pool.

By the time she got to her bungalow, Celia was soaked. She slid off her shoes and left a trail of wet footprints across the wood floor as she walked to the bathroom. She pulled her wet T-shirt off, and then started to dry her hair with the one towel, which turned out to be about as absorbent as a plastic bag. She was hanging it up when there was a knock on her door.

Celia froze. Maybe it was just something that had sounded like a knock. But then she heard it again, and someone calling her name. "Just a minute," she said, and hurried to pull on a new T-shirt. Then she crossed the room and opened the door.

Frankie Russh was standing there, wet hair plastered to her

forehead and rain dripping off her nose. Celia was surprised. "Hi," she said.

"Hi," Frankie said. "Um, can I come in?"

"Oh, shoot," Celia said, jumping back. "Of course." It hadn't crossed her mind to invite Frankie in out of the rain. Frankie stepped into the room, and Celia shut the door behind her. She could tell Frankie was assessing the room.

"Looks just like mine," Frankie said, crossing the room and sitting on the bed since there was no place else to sit. Celia felt like maybe she should offer Frankie something—that was what one was supposed to do with guests, but there wasn't anything to offer, not even a dry towel. Frankie pushed her hair off her forehead.

"How are you?" she asked. "Are you okay?"

Celia walked over to the chair in the corner, moved her suitcase to the floor, then carried the chair to the bed so she could sit closer to Frankie. "I mean, I guess," Celia said. "I don't know. As okay as I can be, but I want to go home." She paused, then added, "Are you okay?"

Frankie started to nod, then, mid-nod, shook her head. "No," she said, "I'm really freaked out. I don't know what's going on and I don't know . . ." Celia waited for Frankie to finish her thought, but she stared at the wall.

"I don't think anyone knows what's going on," Celia said. Frankie's gaze snapped back to Celia, and her eyes were burning.

"Do you think we can trust them?" she asked.

"Trust who?" Celia asked.

"The rest of them," Frankie said. "Graham and Robby

and Justice and Manny . . . all of them. We don't know any of them, really."

"But we know each other?" Celia said. She meant it as a question; it struck her as odd that she and Frankie were now a "we." Frankie took it as a statement and nodded.

"It's weird, isn't it?" Frankie said. "That you and I would end up on this trip together. I would never have thought this was your kind of thing."

"It's not," Celia said. "I'm only here because my parents thought it would be good for me. It's the kind of thing that Caroline would have loved. In theory, of course, before all this went down."

The air was still and heavy. It sounded like the rain was letting up, and the only sound in the room was the squeak of the bed as Frankie shifted. Her fingers were adorned with rings, thin strands of gold and a chunky ring embossed with an *F*, and she twisted them around and around. She stopped and looked up at Celia.

"I am very sorry," she said. "About what happened to Caroline. I know how close you were. I wanted to come to the funeral, but I was in Japan. I sent flowers."

After Caroline died, the house had overflowed with flowers. Over-the-top, overpowering arrangements of lilies and roses and orchids. They covered every available surface, and there were so many bouquets that Celia's mom had started putting them on the back porch. Celia could smell the flowers as soon as she walked through the door, a sickly-sweet scent that grew even stronger as the flowers started to decay. When it became clear that her mom was just going to let the flowers rot, Celia threw them out, tossing the bouquets and vases into the garbage. She could still hear the glass breaking as the vases piled on top of each other. Celia had hated flowers ever since. But Frankie didn't have to know that.

"I know," Celia said, sensing that Frankie wanted her to say something. "They were really pretty."

Frankie nodded. Her eyes filled with tears, and she tried to sniff them back. Celia had never seen Frankie cry before, so she was surprised to see that Frankie, who seemed perfect in every way, was an ugly crier. Her face got red and blotchy, her eyes became puffy slits, and snot trailed out of her nose.

"I should have done a better job of being there for her," Frankie said. "It's just . . . I was so busy. Everything happened so fast, and it wasn't just Caroline. I lost touch with all of my friends. And then, when that video went viral . . ."

Mention of the video made Celia feel like she'd been punched in the gut. Caroline's excitement at first, when she saw how well it was doing, then panic when she realized most of the comments were negative, her frenzy to delete it only to discover it had already been posted several other places. That was the end for Caroline.

"I should have called," Frankie said. "Done something so she knew I was still there for her." Celia nodded.

"It's okay," she said, even though it wasn't. Frankie hadn't just not called Caroline. She had unfollowed her.

Frankie stood up, sniffed again, and wiped her nose with the back of her wrist. She walked over to the door and paused, her hand on the doorknob. "I'm sorry if I interrupted you, if you want to take a nap or something," she said. "I just wanted to say that, and I wanted to say that I think we should stick together."

"Yeah," Celia said. "Of course."

Frankie opened the door to leave and Celia saw that the sky was starting to clear, blue showing through in patches.

"Hey, Frankie," she said, and Frankie turned back toward her. "How's your mom?" The look came and went from Frankie's face in a fraction of the second, but Celia still saw it. A grimace of anger.

"She's fine," Frankie said, flashing a bright smile. Celia nodded.

"Her videos are . . . cute," she said. Frankie didn't say anything, just smiled another fake smile and shut the door behind her.

Celia's heart was racing.

CHAPTER FIVE

For a second after Frankie left the dining room, Emma Jane wondered if she should leave, too. She didn't want to, but she also didn't want to be alone with Margot. Then, to her relief, Margot stood up and left without a word.

Emma Jane waited a few seconds to make sure no one was coming back. The she got up and walked over to the screen, which still displayed Unknown Island's Instagram account. She tapped the most recent pic, the group shot of them on the beach, to open and enlarge it. She stared at the faces, one in particular. Yeah, it was him all right, she was almost sure of it.

She pulled out her phone and opened her DMs, hoping they would still load even without Wi-Fi. She typed a few letters into the search bar. Sure enough, there he was. She felt her breath speed up a little. That was why she'd gotten a sketchy vibe from him. And it wasn't just a vibe. Emma Jane had seen him in action. Had he been lying about not knowing her? Or had he really just not remembered? She closed her phone again, quickly, as if she was worried someone might come up behind her. He was one thing. The rest of it was another, and someone really might come in any minute.

The caption of Unknown's post was what she really wanted to look at. They had all known it was weird, and most of them had laughed it off. Emma Jane read it again. "The guests are here, let's have some fun, counting backward ten to one. Their futures are bright, their pasts untold, three cheers for never growing old." One word was lodged in her brain. *Cheers.* That was what Chelsea had said, right before she raised her glass, drained it, and died. It had to be a coincidence, right? So then why did thinking about it give her goose bumps?

Emma Jane loved murder. She listened to podcasts about it, watched documentaries, read books, and dissected message boards. She had theories about Ted Bundy, Jodi Arias, and the Golden State Killer. She watched *The Staircase, Making a Murderer,* and *The Jinx* to fall asleep at night. Now that she was eighteen, she dreamed about being picked for the jury in a murder trial, though as one of her friends had pointed out, "You'll never get picked. You're too rich."

So maybe she was just seeing what she wanted to see. Maybe she was reading too much into it. But, still . . .

She looked at the table. Aside from everything that had been moved to take Chelsea to the freezer, nothing had been touched. Emma Jane played it back in her mind. There had been the *pop* of the champagne cork, and from that moment on, all eyes had been on Chelsea. In murder mysteries, there was always a distraction. A fire breaking out on the other side of the room, someone fainting, and then, when everyone's attention was elsewhere, the killer did what they needed to do.

Celia had fainted, but that was long before Chelsea died.

And the popping cork hadn't distracted everyone from the murder. Instead, it had brought their attention to it. If this even was a murder. Emma Jane walked over to the table, to where Chelsea had been sitting. There hadn't been anything in the champagne, because they had all watched her open the bottle and pour it. But what if there had been something in her glass? Chelsea's glass lay on its side on the table, and Emma Jane sucked in her breath as she looked at it. The glass was easily identifiable as Chelsea's by the bright coral lipstick ringed around the top. Now that Emma Jane thought about it, Chelsea had reapplied her lipstick several times during breakfast.

She looked at the rest of the glasses on the table. She hadn't been wearing lipstick, and she couldn't recall if Frankie, Celia, or Justice had been either. There was only one other glass with a smudge on it, a jammy pink stain that belonged to Margot, the only other person wearing makeup. Emma Jane remembered her nattering on at the helipad, as if she was the only one who knew about Glossier. Emma Jane used a napkin to pick up Chelsea's glass. She sniffed the glass but had no idea what she was sniffing for. It just smelled like champagne to her. She carefully set the glass back down where she'd found it and dropped the napkin on the table.

Chelsea's purse was still sitting there, so Emma Jane hooked a finger on one side and pulled the top open to peer in. Again, she wasn't totally sure what she was looking for. A pill bottle maybe or something that might hint at why Chelsea had died so suddenly.

"What are you doing?" Emma Jane jumped back, knocking the purse onto its side in the process. Robby was standing in the doorway.

"Looking for cigarettes," Emma Jane said. "I thought Chelsea might have some, and I wanted one after a morning like this." Robby was still staring at her, an intense look in his eyes.

"You don't smoke," he said. "And neither did she."

"How do you know that?" she asked, trying to sound defiant.

"She's a beauty blogger," he said. "Or she *was*. She would have known better than to smoke. And your teeth are too white. Plus, I went through all your pictures, and there wasn't a cigarette in any of them."

Emma Jane couldn't help it. "You went through all my pictures?" she said, feeling a bit like she was taking the bait.

"Yeah." Robby pulled a chair out from the table and sat down. Emma Jane did the same, not right next to him, but with a couple of chairs between them. When he sat back in the chair and crossed his arms, Emma Jane noticed the muscles in his arms. They weren't ripped like he worked out, just present, like he worked. "Hot asshole" was how Chelsea had pegged him. It seemed apt.

"At least you're honest about it," she said. He shrugged.

"I hate when people lie about that," he said. "Like, 'Oh, where are you from? Where do you go to school?' Like we don't look each other up and know everything about each other already."

"Did you go through everybody's photos?" she asked. "Or just mine?"

"Just yours," he said.

"Why?"

"They were good photos," he said. "Although I liked the ones without you in them the most. No offense. It's just that those seemed the most personal, like there was actually some feeling in them." Emma Jane felt her face starting to get hot. She ran a hand over the back of her neck. She wasn't sure what to say, but she wanted Robby to keep talking and thankfully he did. "There was one of a plate of prawn tails and a squeezed lemon," he said. "That was my favorite, of course, because it was food, but also it was one of those photos that make you want to be there. Like, you look at that photo and know how the sun felt, the way the air smelled."

"That was in Santorini," Emma Jane said. "The sun felt like a nap, and the air smelled like . . . lemon prawns." Robby smiled at her. He, too, had very white teeth.

"Can I ask you a personal question?" she said.

He scowled momentarily, then erased the look from his face. "Of course."

"What's up with the clogs?" Robby grinned.

"These clogs?" He held a leg out and flexed one of the aforementioned clogs back and forth.

"Yeah," Emma Jane said, the corners of her lips pulling up into a grin. "Those clogs."

"They're comfortable," Robby said, putting his foot back down on the floor. "I'm on my feet fourteen hours a day. If I didn't wear them, I'd be hobbling around like my grandma by close."

"Yeah, but what about sneakers?" she said. "Like a really cushy pair of Nikes or something?"

Robby shook his head. "Gotta consider the drips," he said. "I get barbecue sauce on my Nikes, they're done for. But these babies wipe right off at the end of the night. Mustard, honey, hot sauce . . . you name it, nothing fazes 'em."

"Ah, I see," Emma Jane said. She shifted in her chair and felt something in her loosen, relax just a little. "Comfy and practical. I can't really relate, but I understand."

"Yeah," Robby said, "and they're also sexy as fuck." She laughed. Robby seemed genuine. Unapologetic about who he was, not pretending to be anything else.

"So, for real, though," he said, "why were you looking in Chelsea's purse?" Emma Jane looked at him and then at the purse. She could have lied again, but in that second she decided she had to trust someone, and it might as well be Robby.

"I wanted to see if there was anything in there that might suggest why she just . . ." Emma Jane paused. "Died so suddenly. She seemed totally healthy and then . . . It's weird, right?" Robby didn't say anything, but he kept his eyes trained on her and nodded. "Do you really think she died of natural causes?"

Now Robby was the one who shifted in his chair, the hint of playfulness that had been in his eyes a moment before gone. "What if she didn't?" he asked, and it took Emma Jane a second to realize that he was actually asking her.

"I . . . I don't know," she said. She picked up a knife and used it to slide Chelsea's purse closer to her. "Don't you think we should at least look inside?"

Robby shook his head. "You do your thing," he said, "but I want no part of it. The Black guy can't get caught going through a white girl's purse, even if she *is* dead."

Emma Jane froze. She tried to keep her face neutral, but all of a sudden she could hear the blood rushing in her head, and her knees started shaking. Did Robby know? How would he know? No one knew, definitely no one on the island knew.

But that letter . . . The letter that had trumpeted Emma Jane's worst moment, her selfishness and ignorance. What if everyone knew? What if they were conspiring to make her confess? What if that was what this was all about? Maybe she couldn't trust Robby after all.

"You're right," she said, putting the knife down and standing up. "We should just leave it alone." Then she walked out of the dining room. When she glanced back, Robby was still sitting there, staring after her.

Margot was mad at herself. She hadn't handled things well, and she was worried she'd just made herself look incompetent. It wasn't her fault that she didn't know CPR, though she certainly would have made sure she did if she'd known it would come in handy on this trip. All these people were going to come back from the vacation and talk about how Justice had known just what to do and all Margot had done was scream. She figured she'd have to work extra hard from here on out to turn it around. She was a CEO, after all. These people would be looking to her to be a leader, so she needed to act like one.

She also wished that it had been her idea, not Frankie's, for everyone to post a joint statement. It was a good tactic and a pretty smart PR move, though Margot had no intention of posting anything that Frankie Russh had written. She'd post her own statement, and make sure she did it first. If the others wanted to use hers, and not Frankie's, she'd be okay with that. She should probably start working on her statement now. As soon as she had Wi-Fi, she would reach out to her PR team and have them start setting up interviews. People were going to be clamoring for the inside story of what had happened on Unknown Island, especially now that someone had died. It was a real bummer that someone was Chelsea. Margot had thought she could be really useful and had looked forward to getting to know her.

Margot looked around her room. God, it was a real shithole. Then she had a brainstorm. She whipped out her camera and started taking pictures. People who went to that fake music festival a few years back had had tweets go viral because of a sad cheese sandwich, so maybe she could leverage photos of her sad hotel room. She took a few more, then scowled at her phone. In pictures, it didn't really come across how thin the towel was or the low thread count of the sheets or that the light fixture in the bathroom made a weird buzzing sound.

Then she had an idea. The dining room. She could take pics of the spot where Chelsea had died. People would go crazy for those. Margot hurried out of her room, down the boardwalk, and back to the dining room. When she got there, she was relieved to find it empty, but also disappointed to see that, again, nothing really came across in the photos. She got some shots of Chelsea's purse and heels and lipstick-stained glass, but it only looked like a room where people had just eaten a meal. There was nothing spectacular or eerie about it. She swiped through everything on her phone—she didn't have a single photo that would make people stop scrolling. She cursed herself again. Emma Jane had taken all those photos of the dead body, and Margot should have done that too.

She paused and listened. The island was very quiet. She couldn't hear any footsteps or voices. If she was quick, she could get to the kitchen and find the freezer and no one would be any wiser. She wouldn't use any photos of Chelsea's dead body, but they would be good to have. They would at least put her on par with Emma Jane and ahead of the rest of them. Margot wanted to come out of this trip on top. She couldn't afford not to.

She turned, ready to take one last photo of the dining room, when she saw something that made her gasp. It would have made her scream, but she was smart enough to clamp a hand over her mouth, because the last thing she wanted to do was draw attention to herself. Moving as quietly as she could, she crossed the room, to the screen, which placidly displayed Unknown Island's account.

Margot felt herself flush with anger, and she stepped back and huffed in disgust. Unknown Island's social media coordinator should be fired. Everyone from Unknown Island should be fired, but when news broke of Chelsea's death, this caption was going to appear in very poor taste. Entire companies had been canceled for less.

Margot was beginning to get a really bad feeling about this. She didn't understand what was going on, but it was starting to seem like something had been flipped, like maybe the people who were behind Unknown Island weren't trying to celebrate their guests, but bring them down instead. Getting pictures of Chelsea's body seemed all the more urgent now. Something told Margot that when she got off this island, she was going to need all the leverage she could get to spin this story in her favor. She hurried out of the dining room and to the kitchen.

In the kitchen, dirty pots and pans were piled on the counters, and flies were starting to swarm. Opposite the door was a large walk-in refrigerator. Surely that was where they had put Chelsea's body. Margot made a beeline for it and had just grabbed the handle when a voice from behind her made her freeze.

"I don't think you want to go in there." Margot spun around to see Manny standing in the doorway. "It's not very pleasant."

Margot put on her most flirtatious smile. "Oh, yes," she said, "I was just looking for some ice."

Manny shook his head. "There isn't any," he said. He walked to the sink and turned on the faucet. He watched it run for a few seconds, then filled a large water bottle a little bit and held it up to examine it. He seemed to like what he saw and held the bottle back under the faucet. "The water in my room came out all brown and murky," he said, "but this seems to be okay." He took a sip. "Not very cold, though."

Margot waited for him to leave, but he just stood there, sipping that tap water like he had no place else to be. "No ice? That's too bad," she said, then hurried out of the kitchen before Manny tried to talk to her again. He'd killed nine people, and no matter what craziness was going down on this island, Margot didn't associate with murderers.

Manny felt like that moment when you realize you've had one drink too many. Only, aside from a few sips of champagne, he hadn't had anything to drink. He'd tried chugging water, but that hadn't made a difference, hadn't even cooled him down. He was used to the heat, but this was *hot*. His nerves were on fire, and he felt dizzy, like he couldn't walk a straight line. Even if this was an island off the coast of Antarctica, he'd still be sweating.

On his walk back to his room, Manny didn't see anyone else. It was comforting in a way, because he didn't particularly want to talk to anyone, but it also made him even more nervous. What if he was the only one here who didn't know what was going on? What if everyone else was together right now, conspiring against him? Fuck. He needed to calm down. He went into his bungalow, shut the door behind him, and took a few more gulps of water. The dizziness didn't go away.

Manny put his water bottle on the floor and walked over to his suitcase. He rummaged through it until he found the bottle. It was white plastic and said ANTIDIARRHEAL in big blue letters. It was some off-brand Imodium. If anyone opened the bottle, they likely wouldn't know what the pills were supposed to look like. And it was also kind of embarrassing. Manny could just grimace and shrug and say something like, "Traveling, man. It messes you up!" and then people would want to move on as quickly as they could.

There was no way he'd misinterpreted the woman on the phone. This was what she'd asked him to bring, but it wasn't for the reasons she'd hinted at. No one here wanted to party. It was a setup. The best thing to do now was flush everything and then just deny, deny, deny. He had started to unscrew the cap on the bottle when there was a knock on his door. Crap. "Just a sec," he called out.

He screwed the lid back on and shoved the bottle in a sock. Then he took it out and put it in his backpack, because no one keeps their diarrhea pills in a sock. He walked over and opened the door. Frankie was standing there. It hit him again how gorgeous she was, her dark hair pulled back from her face, revealing a smattering of freckles and hazel eyes.

"S-sorry," she stammered. "If you want to be alone, I can leave."

"No, no, come in," he said, moving out of the doorway. Frankie took a couple of steps inside but didn't come any farther. She seemed fidgety and upset. "You okay?" he asked, though it was a stupid question. Who would be okay after a morning like this?

"Yes," she said, "I mean no, not really. I'm pretty freaked out by all of this, and I think we should get off the island. It seems like you spend a lot of time on boats. Do you know how to drive one?"

Manny stared at her for a second, wondering why she thought he spent a lot of time on boats, and then it hit him: he never boarded a yacht without posting at least one picture of it. He felt like such a loser, and then a double loser for worrying about being a loser at a time like this. So what if Frankie had gone through his photos before they got here? It wasn't as though he hadn't gone through hers. Through everyone's, if he was being honest. Manny needed to pull himself together. "Yeah, well enough," he said. "Do you know where there's a boat?"

She shook her head. "No. But there has to be one somewhere on the island, for emergencies, and there's that boathouse off the dock down by the helipad. I don't think anyone's been anywhere near it since we landed." It took Manny a second to process that this was a proposition. That she was suggesting they go there now, together.

"Yeah," he said. "Let's go check it out." He opened the door, and they stepped outside. Dark clouds had gathered over the water again, but it was still sunny, and humid, on the island.

Frankie started walking down the boardwalk, and Manny followed. After a few steps, she fell back so that they were walking side by side.

"How long do you think until it starts raining again?" Frankie asked, and Manny scanned the sky.

"I don't know," he said. "A few hours maybe?" She nodded but didn't say anything. She was walking so fast that Manny had to make an effort to keep up.

"If there is a boat, I think we should just leave," she said, her voice low, as if the palm trees might overhear them.

"You and me?" he said, and she nodded.

"And Celia," she said. "She's so young. I knew her sister, so . . . I'd feel bad if we left her here."

"What about everyone else?"

"I don't know," she said. "I guess that depends on how big the boat is. But I have a really bad feeling about this place. Don't you?"

"Yeah, of course." Frankie jumped off the boardwalk and landed in the sand, then walked down to the water's edge. Manny followed. The waves lapped at his feet and ankles. Frankie slowed to a leisurely stroll.

"We shouldn't look like we're headed anywhere," she said, taking a step closer to Manny, their shoulders almost brushing. "If there is a boat, I just want to make sure we find it before anyone else." She took another lazy step and her arm knocked into his.

Her nervousness made Manny even more uneasy. "What do you think is going on?" he asked. "Or, what do you think is going to happen?"

Frankie shrugged and brushed against him again. "When

we first got the invites," she said, "I thought it seemed like the most random group of people. But now I don't think it's random at all. I think everyone was carefully chosen, and whoever is behind all of this is out to get us."

Manny swallowed, his mouth dry. Frankie's thoughts were so similar to his own. He'd hoped he was just being paranoid, but if she was thinking it too . . . "Get us how?" he croaked, barely able to get the words out.

"Ruin us," she said. "They want to destroy our careers and—" She waved her arm as though to finish her sentence, but Manny cut her off. Here, he disagreed.

"I don't have anything to ruin," he said.

She paused. "That's not true," she said. "You have your following and your music. . . ."

"I don't have the kind of following I can monetize," he said. "What I've got is a bunch of people who comment on my pics and ask me to intro them to Travis Scott, and they don't care about my music." It sounded harsh, but Frankie was the kind of person who probably got paid to put on lip balm. She opened her mouth, as if she was about to protest, but then shut it without saying anything.

"I'm not fishing for sympathy," Manny said. "I'm proud of the following I built, but I know exactly how I built it. It is what it is, but if Unknown Island is out to knock someone off their pedestal, I'm an odd choice, because I don't have far to fall." Frankie took a step closer. She had sunglasses on, and Manny wished he could see her eyes. Instead, he was staring at his own reflection, and the rest of her face was unreadable.

"These accusations, though . . . ," she said. Manny watched

himself shake his head in her lenses, and then something hit him.

"Nobody accused me of anything that isn't absolutely true," he said. "So, is it true for you?" Frankie stepped away from him like he had slapped her.

"No," she hissed. "Of course not! That's why I want to get out of here. Hannah was my best friend, she was like a sister to me, and for someone to . . . I just don't trust this place or any of these people."

"But you trust me?" he asked.

"Yes," she said as she turned and started walking again, her lazy stroll now a march through the surf. "I don't know you, but I know you're not a liar."

Manny started to say, "You'd be surprised," but Frankie had already picked up her pace.

"See," she said, pointing, "there could easily be a boat in there."

Unlike the other, open-to-the-air buildings on the island, the boathouse was completely enclosed. It sat facing the vast expanse of sea, with two long, skinny docks stretching into the water on either side of what looked like a garage door. Frankie was right. If there was a boat on the island, this was where it would be. When they got to the boathouse, Manny climbed up on a dock and tried the side door. No surprise, it was locked. There weren't any windows, just a few vents near the top of the peaked roof. He walked around to the front and inspected the rolling door, which looked like it extended a few feet below the surface of the water and then ended.

"I can swim under and see what's in there," he said.

"I can, too," Frankie said quickly, and then she pulled her shirt over her head. Manny did a double take when he registered that she wasn't wearing a swimsuit. Granted, her bra covered more than most swimsuits, but it felt more intimate than even the sparest bikini, and he wasn't sure if he should look away. He started to, but Frankie had already slipped into the water and was swimming over to the door. He jumped in after her.

"Should we go together?" he asked, and she nodded. "Okay, on three. One, two . . ."

Frankie dove before he got to three, so he gulped some air and followed. The water was warm and soft, and once he was under, Manny blinked his eyes open. It was something he was always proud of as a kid, that he could swim wide-eyed while the salt water made his cousins cry. He saw Frankie's legs disappear under the bottom of the door, and he swam after them.

Coming up on the other side was weird, as he was now swimming toward the dark and away from the light, and he blinked when he broke the surface. The boathouse was almost pitch-black. The only light came from under the door in the water, and the vent at the top of the roof, which sent down a few illuminating lines.

Manny could, however, see that there was a boat. A motorboat, bobbing in the water just a few feet from them. And in the little bit of light, he could also see that Frankie was grinning.

"You're a genius," he said, a smile stretched across his own face. She held out her hand for a high five, and when their palms touched, she laced her fingers through his and squeezed, still smiling. Then she let go and they both started swimming toward the dock.

"Now, we just have to find the keys and a way to open this door," Frankie said, pulling herself up out of the water. "You stay here and I'll go get Celia and come back."

Manny followed her out of the water. When he stood up, he tried to get his bearings. Out of the water it was even darker. He could make out shapes, but not necessarily what they were. He stepped on something soft and squishy, and he almost jumped back before he realized it was just a rubber flipper.

In front of him, Frankie was slowly feeling her way to the door. When they reached it, she felt for the doorknob. "Shit," she said, "it's one of those where you need a key from both sides."

"Just look for a switch on the wall—an opener," Manny said. "The one we came in under should be automatic." He held out his hands and started feeling along the wall, and Frankie did the same.

"I'm not even finding a light switch," she said. "Don't they use this place at night?" Suddenly, there was a thud, and Frankie yelped. She'd collided with a wooden beam, and from the way she was hobbling on one foot, Manny guessed she'd stubbed her toe. He was about to ask if she was okay, when a creak from above made him look up. Something cut across the shaft of light coming through the vent, and before he could even think, Manny grabbed Frankie and pulled her roughly toward him, wrapping his arms around her back as he pressed them both against the wall.

The tank fell so close to them that Manny could feel its breeze ruffle Frankie's hair. It made a deafening metal clang when it hit the ground in the exact spot where Frankie had been standing, and it hit hard enough that it didn't even roll. It splintered the wood and remained where it had landed. Manny didn't let go of Frankie, and she collapsed into him, her pounding heartbeat and ragged breath matching his own. When he finally dropped his arms, he realized he and Frankie were both shaking.

"What the fuck was that?" Frankie asked, barely able to catch her breath. She had pressed herself into the wall, as far away from the fallen tank as she could get.

Manny leaned forward and looked up at where it had come from. A few feet above them was a balcony, lined with heavy metal scuba tanks, all stored right up to the edge, which had no rail to keep them from doing what one had just done. "A scuba tank," he said. "Those things weigh like forty pounds. You must have shaken it loose when you bumped into the beam. It's a really stupid place to keep them. If it hit right, that thing could have killed somebody."

He held out his hand and Frankie took it, and they started to creep away, both pressing against the wall as though it could protect them.

Manny still couldn't hear anything but the sound of his own breath when, behind him, Frankie suddenly gripped his hand tight and froze. "What was that?" she said. "It sounded like a scream." Manny stopped to listen. This time, he heard it too. It was most definitely a scream.

Even though he was surrounded by water and heat, Xander decided to take a hot shower. He wanted to wash off the feeling of the dead girl in his arms, the way her head had lolled against his chest, and, even worse, the way it had fallen forward and bobbed with each step he took. Her hair had tickled his nose, and he could still smell her perfume, a mix of baby powder and the grocery store floral department, something that smelled like it came in a pink bottle.

He cranked the water as far as it would go, but the stream came out in nothing more than a weak arc. He stepped back to wait for it to at least warm up. Xander felt like he had been here forever and that he hadn't even arrived yet. This wasn't anything like he'd imagined, filming videos on the sand and among the palm trees. He'd planned to snorkel, surf, drink from coconuts. All that, and more. Instead . . . what even was this?

Seeing the name Damien Richards written on that piece of paper had been a shock. Xander never talked about Damien with anyone, so how could anyone know? It was just a freak coincidence. It had to be. Someone had thrown a Hail Mary and gotten lucky.

Xander stuck his hand out to feel the water. It wasn't cold, but it definitely wasn't hot either. There probably wasn't any hot water on the island, because why bother? He turned the water off, and that was when he heard it. A panicked shriek. Xander listened. One of the girls had found a lizard in her bed, probably something like that. But then he heard it again. A terrifying, guttural scream, and it was close. He ran out of the bathroom and threw open the door to his bungalow. Across the boardwalk, Justice had done the same and was stumbling out of her room with a look of confusion and terror on her face.

Their eyes met for a second, and then the scream ripped through the air again. It was coming from the bungalow two doors down, and this time, Xander and Justice started running toward it. Xander got there first. The door wasn't locked, and he flung it open. Margot was in the middle of the room, screaming and turning in circles, scratching wildly at her arms. Large, red welts were starting to swell on her pale skin, and when she wasn't tearing at her flesh with her nails, she was clawing at her throat. There were black things flying around her, and there were also several on her. They were what she was clawing at. Xander squinted, unable to make out what they were. Flies?

"What's happening? Are you okay?" Xander yelled, though it was clear Margot wasn't.

He could hear Justice behind him, breathing heavily. "I think she's having an allergic reaction?" Justice said.

"Yesshhh! Bessh! Bessh!" The sounds coming out of Margot were strained and hard to understand, and Xander realized that the black dots weren't flies or mosquitoes. They were bees. He took a few steps toward her and began swinging his hands through the air and slapping at Margot. He might as well have been doing nothing. The bees were swarming now, coming closer rather than moving away. Xander swatted one off his forearm and felt something crawling through his hair. There was a sharp jab of pain on his bicep, and then one on the side of his neck. They were stinging *him*! Justice was right beside him. A bee had landed on her cheek, and they both kept trying to brush the insects off Margot, whose face was growing more contorted by the second.

"Errrpipen! Errrrpipen!" Margot's words were slurred and hard to understand, and a few seconds passed that felt like years.

"EpiPen!" Justice shouted, as if she had suddenly deciphered a code. "She needs her EpiPen!"

Margot screamed again and doubled over. Xander picked her up and carried her outside, bees crawling over both of them. Margot was gasping. Without even thinking, Xander jumped into the water, slapping the surface with one arm as they hit so that their heads didn't go under. He could see the bees start to float off, spinning on the skin of the water. He kept one arm looped tight around Margot, holding her head above water, and kicked with his legs. With his free hand, he tried to pull the bees out of her hair. The water brought Margot no relief. She still sounded like she had a cheese grater in her windpipe.

Everyone else was starting to gather on the dock. Celia and Emma Jane came out of their rooms and stood there, shocked looks on their faces. "What's happening? What's happening?" Emma Jane asked.

"She got attacked by bees and I think she's allergic!" Xander yelled.

"I can't find her EpiPen!" Justice yelled from Margot's bungalow.

Manny and Frankie came running down the boardwalk, dripping wet like they'd been swimming, then Justice appeared in the doorway of Margot's bungalow. "Somebody help me!" she cried. "There are bees everywhere in here!"

Frankie immediately ran inside. Emma Jane, like she had finally been shocked into action, followed a second later.

Margot's gasps were growing shallower and shallower, her breathing a squeaking wheeze as her limbs stopped moving. It hit Xander that he was about to cradle his second dead girl of the day, and it wasn't even lunch.

"She can't breathe!" he yelled. "We need the fucking EpiPen!" Manny was kneeling on the dock, motioning to Xander.

"Swim over!" he yelled. "We can get her out." Kicking, Xander dragged Margot through the water to meet him. Manny looped his hands under her arms and lifted her out while Xander pushed from beneath. Then he pulled himself out of the water.

"We can't find it!" Emma Jane appeared in the doorway. Behind her, Xander could see Frankie tearing the sheets off the bed. Justice ran out with Margot's suitcase, dumped the contents on the boardwalk, and pawed through them.

"It's not here!" she said.

Seconds later, Frankie appeared and did the same with a smaller bag. Margot's makeup clacked and rolled across the boardwalk.

"There are hundreds of bees in there," Frankie said, as she frantically sorted through tubes and tubs. "Maybe even thousands! The bathroom is crawling with them!" There was a crash from inside the bungalow, and Xander turned his attention back to Margot, Manny kneeling next to her and holding her hand. Her dress clung to her, and mascara ran from her eyes, which were staring vacantly off into the distance. Her body still heaved, but it seemed like hardly any air was reaching her lungs. Her face, her arms, her neck, her legs, every visible bit of her was covered with large red welts that made her skin as bumpy as a gourd. Xander estimated that she'd been stung hundreds of times.

"There has to be something we can do," Manny said, turning to Justice, who'd given up on the suitcase and was now kneeling next to them. Justice shook her head.

"I don't know," she said. "Her throat is probably swollen, so I can't . . . I don't know, I don't know."

Graham and Robby had appeared at the end of the boardwalk and were taking in the grim scene. Emma Jane emerged from Margot's room. She had a bee crawling on one thigh, but she either didn't notice or had chosen to ignore it.

"It's not here," she said. "The EpiPen. We looked everywhere."

Xander glanced at Manny, and then at Justice, and then at Frankie, who was sitting on the ground, surrounded by Margot's makeup. Celia stood off to the side, frozen, her arms wrapped around herself. Suddenly, she darted forward to rearrange Margot's dress, which had twisted up around her waist. Then she ran into Margot's bungalow and emerged with a pillow. "We should at least make her comfortable," Celia said. She passed the pillow to Justice, who placed it under Margot's head after Manny lifted it. Then Justice reached for Margot's wrist to feel her pulse.

"It's there," she said, softly. "But it's very weak." She leaned over Margot so that she was looking into her eyes. "You're going to be okay. Help is on the way."

"No it's not! We are stranded here!" All heads swiveled toward Graham, who was wringing his hands and breathing heavily.

"Shut the fuck up," Manny hissed. Robby grabbed Graham's arm and pulled him away from the rest of them. Xander kept his eyes on Justice, who still had her fingers on Margot's wrist, and he knew what had happened as soon as she started shaking her head. Justice choked back a sob.

"She's dead," Frankie said, and Justice nodded. Xander stood up and looked down at his arm. Three stingers dotted his skin, but he wasn't allergic. He'd grown up with a cherry tree in his backyard, and bee stings were often the price paid for cherries as sweet as sugar. He walked into Margot's bungalow and looked around. The sheets and pillows were thrown on the floor, and bees still buzzed through the air. The bathroom door was closed, and he walked over and opened it.

The bathroom was a beehive. When Xander looked up, he saw that the light fixture was clogged with them, a crawling, dark mass. He flipped the switch, turning the light off. He shut the bathroom door behind him and then shut the bungalow door too. Back on the boardwalk, he looked out at the ocean. The sun had gone behind the dark clouds, which massed right above them. Manny looked at him, and then they nodded at each other. It was time, once again, to put a body in the freezer.

Robby felt like he should do something more to help, but truth be told, he was happy to let Xander and Manny shoulder the body again. When they'd put Chelsea in the freezer earlier that morning, Robby had gone with them to make room. Standing in there, he'd remembered how bare it was. He hadn't needed to move anything because there wasn't anything to move. He'd never seen a hospitality kitchen so empty. It was almost totally devoid of staples, as though they had planned to send someone to the store every day for even the basics.

The only thing that had been stocked in the kitchen was junk food. Tons and tons of junk food. There had also been an inordinate amount of hummus and several jars of tahini, as if whoever had done the ordering had decided that was a great dip for Doritos. Robby had tossed all of the hummus and tahini in the trash.

Now, he threaded his way back through the kitchen to once again open the heavy metal door to the walk-in freezer. He wrenched the handle and pulled the door open, and then stifled a gasp. Not at Chelsea's body, which was still lying on the floor, covered with a tablecloth, just like they had left it an hour before, but at the jars on the shelf. The same hummus and tahini that Robby had thrown in the garbage.

"Sorry, can we get by?" Manny's voice snapped Robby out of it, and he jumped aside, out of the doorway. He mumbled something about how he didn't think they needed him. He looked back before he left the kitchen, to see Justice and Frankie looking in the walk-in door as Xander and Manny settled the new body on the floor next to the old one. The clock on the wall showed that it wasn't even eleven.

Graham was nowhere to be found, but Emma Jane and Celia were in the dining room. Robby paused for a second, as neither of them were looking in his direction. Celia was sitting on a chair, her knees up under her chin, and her arms wrapped around them; Emma Jane was standing and staring at the screen that displayed Unknown Island's account. She was just inches away from it, and rocking back and forth slightly, totally absorbed in what she saw. She had on pale green drawstring pants and a matching bikini top, and there was no doubt she was gorgeous. That wasn't what Robby liked about her. What he liked was that she was unpredictable. She was smarter than she looked, and maybe a little mean, and probably the kind of girl who even once you got to know her well, you still had no idea what was going on in her head. That was the kind of girl he liked.

Tiffany was like that, though in the end, Robby had started to suspect that the whole reason he never knew what Tiffany was going to do next was that she didn't take her medication consistently. Robby's mother had hated her ever since the time Tiffany had broken up with him and then parked her car in their driveway and sobbed for three hours when he wasn't even home. "You need to tell that girl to move," his mom had said when she called him at work. "I need to go to the store."

He had met Tiffany where she was, though. Between the YouTube channel and the restaurant, Robby had felt overwhelmed, like if he made one mistake he'd find himself a has-been before he was even old enough to vote. His relationship with Tiffany was how he blew off steam. He hadn't even known he took it that seriously until they got back together after the driveway incident, and she went and cheated on him with Braxton Ross. The very next day, Braxton Ross came into Hock & Jowl with his family. Robby felt nauseated just thinking about it.

Emma Jane turned around and looked at him, and he crossed the room to stand next to her. "What?" he asked. They'd been flirting before, Robby was sure of it, but then it was like a door had come crashing down and she'd shut off, and now it seemed like she was weighing something, judging him. Then she faced the screen again and spoke.

"They posted a new photo," she said, pointing at a picture Robby hadn't seen before. It was a solo shot of Chelsea, and it must have been taken some time during breakfast, before they had received the awful letters, because Chelsea was smiling. It was a good photo, her lipstick bright, her skin flawless, a flower tucked behind her ear.

"When?" Robby asked.

"I don't know," Emma Jane said. "It was here when I walked in."

Robby felt anger shoot through his veins. Graham was clearly holding out on them about the Wi-Fi, since he apparently had no problem texting Unknown Island photos to post. Emma Jane read the caption, which was just as obtuse and nonsensical as the first one. "Chelsea Quinn is far from the worst, and that's why she was chosen first. There's lots of buzz about number two, so we'll make sure she gets her due."

Celia must have heard them, because she walked over. Robby and Emma Jane turned when Celia gasped a little. "The caption," she said. Robby nodded and saw that Justice, Frankie, Manny, and Xander had joined them. Frankie rushed forward and practically pushed Robby out of the way to get to the screen. She tapped the post, making it fill the screen. "I don't understand," she said, her face red and her eyes filled with tears. "What are these trying to say?"

Robby was about to say he had no idea, but then Emma Jane spoke. "The rhymes are clearly referencing the deaths," she said. "And how Chelsea and Margot died." Silence enveloped the room. Emma Jane turned back to the screen and opened the first photo, the group shot of all of them on the beach. "'Three cheers for never growing old,'" she read. "And then Chelsea dies after toasting with her champagne. 'Buzz about number two,' and then Margot gets attacked by bees."

Justice gripped the back of a chair like she was holding on to it so that she wouldn't fall over. "Can't it be a coincidence?" she said. It didn't seem like a real question, but Emma Jane answered.

"Maybe," she said. "But it's not."

Celia yelped. "Look!" she said, and they all looked to see what she was pointing at. Another photo had just gone up. Deep in the pit of his stomach, Robby wasn't surprised to see that it was a picture of Margot, a faraway shot, taken while she was walking down the beach. When no one spoke, Justice read the caption: "'Margot Bryant is our number two, for lots of reasons, old and new. Number three must watch where they tread, when seeking a way to get ahead.'" Her voice cracked on the last word, and no one said anything. Robby wasn't focused on the caption, though. He was thinking about something else.

"That motherfucker still has internet," he said, and looked around. Graham was nowhere to be seen.

When it was clear that Margot was dead, Graham had hurried back to the office as quickly as he could. His plan was to lock himself in there, but the door had no lock. Still, he had shut it and sat down at the desk, and he was still sitting there when the door burst open, hard enough that it hit the wall and bounced back.

Before Graham could think or say or do anything, Robby

marched forward and grabbed Graham's phone off the desk. Frankie was right behind him, and then Manny and Xander and Justice . . . all of them crowded into the small office. Graham felt like he couldn't breathe. Robby shoved the phone in Graham's face, inches from his nose. "Enter your passcode," he said. Graham looked up at him. Robby's eyes were dark and his nostrils flared.

"What?" Graham asked.

"Enter your passcode," Robby said again, and shook the phone. Graham reached out with one finger and tapped in the code: 1108, the day in November when he'd won the election. As soon as Graham was done entering the code, Robby snatched the phone back and started tapping through it. "What'd you do, erase everything as soon as you sent it?" he asked. "Or do you have a laptop around here somewhere and you emailed the photos?"

Graham stood up, the chair scraping across the floor. "I don't know what you're talking about," he said, trying to keep his voice steady as he looked Robby in the eye.

"The photos that were just posted," Frankie said, stepping up so that she stood behind Robby. Graham looked at her, and with a start, he realized that what he'd assumed was a bikini was actually underwear. "You need to come clean, right now, and tell us what the fuck is going on."

Graham stuttered, "I—I . . ." He looked at Robby, then back at Frankie, then over her shoulder at Manny, and at Justice in the doorway. All of them looked pissed, murderously pissed, and he felt their rage directed right at him. "I really don't know what you're talking about," he finally managed to say. Graham felt like he was going to cry, which was the reason he had locked himself in the office in the first place. He didn't want any of them to see him cry.

"Unknown Island posted two new photos, one of Chelsea and one of Margot," Emma Jane said. Graham swiveled to look at her. He hadn't even known she was in the room. "Both of the captions reference how they died, and the only way any of this is possible is if you took the photos and wrote the captions and then sent them to be posted or posted them yourself."

Graham felt dumbfounded, like a sweating snowman. "I swear to god," he said, when he finally found his voice, "I didn't do any of that. I didn't know that any new photos had been posted."

"Come look," Frankie said. Graham thought her voice might have softened the smallest bit.

"You believe me, right?" he asked as he followed her into the dining room. "I don't have anything to do with any of this." He thought maybe he should let go and cry in front of all of them so that they could see just how innocent and upset he was. Graham felt like he was dying, this heat and this awful island and now this, a game of seven-on-one that he was destined to lose.

But everything they were saying was true. There were two new photos that Graham hadn't taken or sent. "I've never seen those before," he said. "I haven't been able to connect to anything since I sent that first group photo to Sharon." As soon as Graham said her name, he felt stupid. "Or the person I thought was Sharon. I keep checking to see if the Wi-Fi has come back on, but it hasn't." He looked over at Robby, who was still holding his phone. "That thing's a brick," Graham said. "You can look through it all you want. I haven't taken any pictures since those first ones."

Graham turned back to the screen. The picture of Margot had been up for a few minutes, and the comments were already rolling in. It seemed, though, that the tide was shifting, and the earlier enthusiasm was waning. "I'm unfollowing," someone wrote. "This is too weird for me." "You lost me, Unknown," wrote another. "I wanted to see pics of hot girls on the beach, not solve riddles."

Frankie was scrolling through the comments and as she hovered above one, Graham stepped forward to read over her shoulder. "I don't care about the captions or the photos," someone had written. "I'm unfollowing because Chelsea Quinn and Margot Bryant are both awful people. I don't want to see them celebrated like this." That comment already had 268 likes.

"Same," said another. "Chelsea Quinn ran someone over with a car and everyone knows Margot Bryant doesn't give her employees health insurance. A girl in her company literally died."

Graham felt like he might throw up when he saw his name in another caption. "That's nothing," a user had written. "Graham Hoffman straight up murdered someone. He pushed a photographer down the stairs at a party and the dude died. My friend knows someone who saw it happen." The likes and replies were already starting to pile on, and Graham felt like he was seeing his worst nightmare, his biggest secret, written out on the internet for the entire world to dissect. He scrambled to close the window, to get in front of Frankie, but she had already read it.

"You pushed a photographer down the stairs?" she said, her voice rising as she said it again, louder so that everyone in the room could hear. "Someone on here is saying Graham pushed someone down the stairs."

"I did not, I did not!" He stepped in front of Frankie, blocking the screen with his body, and Frankie did nothing to stop him.

Emma Jane had picked up one of the letters, which were still scattered across the table. "Is that who Tommy Bledsoe is?" she said, holding the letter up. Graham felt like he might explode. The tears were coming, and he didn't even try to stop them. Why was someone doing this to him? Why were they all ganging up on him like this?

"I did not push anyone down the stairs," he sputtered. "He deserved it. It was an accident, I didn't do anything wrong."

"Which one was it?" Manny said, his voice level and cold. "You didn't do it, it was an accident, or he deserved it? Can't be all three."

"You are a murderer." Justice was getting in on it now, too. They were all stabbing him, twisting the knife, helping someone ruin everything that Graham had worked for. Graham remembered the smile on Tommy Bledsoe's face as he stated matter-of-factly, that he had evidence to prove Graham had been stealing from the campaign. Graham also remembered the way that smile had disappeared when his hands connected with Tommy's chest, and Tommy realized he was falling backward. Graham hadn't meant to kill him, but he had definitely meant to give him a shove.

Now, frantic, he looked at all the faces staring back at him. It felt like they were closing in, the circle getting smaller, even though none of them had moved. He hated all of them, and if the seven of them had been standing at the top of a staircase, Graham would have pushed with all his might. He ran from the room, back into the office, and slammed the door.

Graham felt like he was choking; he couldn't breathe, and he was gagging. This couldn't really be happening; he couldn't be stuck here with these people, with no escape from any of it. He always kept control; he always knew just what to do. When Tommy hit the floor at the bottom of the stairs, Graham had known instantly that he had broken his neck. People who were still alive didn't lie like that.

The first thing he had done was scan around, insanely grateful that he and Tommy had been alone and that there were no cameras in the stairwell. It took him only a split second to decide what to do. "Someone call 911!" he yelled. "Tommy just fell!" For weeks afterward, the only thing that comforted Graham was that no one had seen what happened. He had told himself that over and over, and he had believed it. Until today.

A knock on the door made him jump. He spun around and saw the knob turning and the door opening. He braced himself for all of them, but just Frankie stepped into the room and then closed the door behind her, so softly that it barely made a *click*.

Graham looked at her, panicking, but the look on her face was soft, and she was smiling. "Hey," she said, "I just wanted to make sure you were okay." Graham bit his lip and nodded. "That was rough, back there," she said, "and I wanted to apologize. Everyone is tense and looking for someone to blame, and all of us should know that commenters are full of shit."

Graham felt his breathing slow and his muscles start to relax. Frankie Russh had come to check on him, maybe she was even on his side. She took another step and laid a hand on his arm. She was still in her underwear, her wet hair still glistening. "We all know you didn't kill that person," she said. "We were all accused of things we didn't do."

"Yeah, I know," Graham said, wishing he wasn't so sweaty.

"Listen," Frankie said, "we have to get out of here." Graham started nodding furiously. That was what he wanted more than anything. Out of here, off this island. "I think I know how," Frankie said. "I found a boat in the boathouse, but it's locked up behind a big door. We just need to figure out how to get that door open and then we can get the boat out. You don't know where the keys are, do you?" Her hand was still resting on his arm, and it was the first welcome bit of warmth that Graham had felt all day.

"I don't," he said. "I'm not lying. I really just got here an hour before everyone else. I have no idea what is going on or where anything is."

Frankie nodded and smiled, her face full of understanding. "Of course," she said. "I know that. But can you keep an eye out? Not just for the keys, but for anything that could help us?" Graham nodded again, and she dropped her hand from his arm. She took a few steps to the door, then turned back.

"Thanks, Graham," she said. "It's great to know there's at least someone here I can trust."

When she left, Graham watched her go, and he then walked back behind the desk and sat down with a thud. His breathing was slowing down, and he felt better. Frankie Russh was a silver lining, a glimmer of hope. She trusted him, which meant that she and her one hundred and thirty million followers were on his side. But what now? He didn't feel better enough to not be miserable. He put his elbows on the desk and his face in his hands.

He had to slow down, take it one step at a time. The first thing he needed to do was get off this island and away from these people. He *and Frankie* needed to get away from these people, and everything else, dealing with the rumors and accusations, could come later. Graham looked around the office and his eyes fell on something he couldn't believe he'd forgotten. The set of keys he'd found earlier, still dangling from the closet door from when he'd opened it to find the champagne.

He was across the room in two steps, his hands trembling so bad that, for a few seconds, it seemed like he wouldn't be able to get the keys out—that he might pull the doorknob off. With a final jerk, he yanked them free and then ran out of the office to find Frankie.

She was nowhere in sight, though. In fact, no one was. They must have all scattered, which was fine with Graham. He would go to the boathouse, see if he could figure out how to get the door open, and then lock everything back up and find Frankie. That was better, anyway, he thought. He didn't want to get her hopes up if the keys turned out to be useless. He began jogging down the beach. The sky was starting to spit, and when he looked toward the horizon, he could see that the rain was already coming down hard over the ocean. There were even some waves. They didn't have much time. Drops hit Graham on the forehead and clouded his glasses. He broke into a full run.

He was out of breath by the time he got to the boathouse.

In spite of the rain, the air was still hot, and breathing felt like sucking in shaving cream. He fumbled with the keys as he tried each one. He hit the jackpot with the third. It slid into the lock and turned, and Graham pulled the door open. He walked in and paused, looking around. Light from the open door poured into the boathouse, and he saw the boat that Frankie had been talking about bobbing in the middle, not tied to anything, just caged inside. He could also see the door she'd mentioned, the one that would need to be raised to get the boat out of its dock.

Before checking out the door, Graham took a few steps toward the boat and peered down into it. He almost pumped his fist in the air. The reason the boat was locked up was that the keys were right there, in the ignition. He walked back to the door and pulled the key out of the lock. If one of them opened the big, roll-up door, then he and Frankie were in business.

He started to snake along the wall, searching for a switch, a keypad, anything that looked like it might control the big door. There was nothing on the left side of the boathouse, so he started to make his way back, stepping over a big steel scuba tank that had rolled into the middle of the dock. Then he saw it, by the door, right where he'd come in. A nondescript button, small enough that it was easily overlooked. Graham pressed it, and the whole boathouse started to rumble as the door opened. Then a metallic clang from above made him look up.

CHAPTER SIX

Justice raced back to her bungalow. She felt like she might throw up or cry, or both, and she wanted to be alone. She opened the door, slammed it behind her, and then slid down the wall. She couldn't wrap her brain around what was happening. She was trapped on an island halfway around the world with a bunch of strangers. Two people had died, and a third had just admitted to killing someone.

She started to add it up: Chelsea and Manny hadn't even denied that what was said about them in the letter was true. Everyone seemed to know it was true about Margot, and then Graham . . . If the letter had been true for the four of them, then was it true for everyone else? She thought back to the very first post, the group shot with the strange caption. "Counting backward ten to one . . ." Was this a sinister game, some twisted joke that had gone wrong, and that was why there were only eight people now? Justice didn't want to consider that maybe the opposite was true. Maybe the game was going right. Who would do this to all of them, and why? Justice pressed the heels of her hands into her eyes, trying to make her thoughts make sense, make herself get a grip, but still, she could barely breathe.

The air inside her bungalow was thick and unmoving, and she could feel sweat dripping down the back of her neck. Just a few hours ago, the idea that she was so far from home was thrilling. It had made her heart flutter like a butterfly, but that butterfly had turned into a nest of hornets, and her chest hurt with panic. Now home was the only place she wanted to be.

For as long as she could remember, Justice had known the truth: that she was the only average person in a family of exceptional people. Her father the judge, her mother the neurosurgeon, her brother the child prodigy, a Stanford grad at eighteen, and her little sister, only nine but eerily intelligent. "I swear to god," her mother would joke about Janelle, "that child can already beat Jerome at chess!"

Her mother had never said anything like that about Justice. Her grades were average, her test scores unimpressive. She tried to study, but she could never concentrate long enough to really absorb anything. Extracurriculars were her ticket to Harvard, that was what she could never make her parents understand. Her environmental work, her online following—it was all to give Justice something that would make her stand out, that would make people take notice. And it was about the environment, that too, of course. That was very important. When Justice had been invited here, she thought it was a sign that she was about to make it. Someone had noticed her, all right. But it was clearly the wrong someone.

Last Thanksgiving, her brother had gotten drunk. Even though he worked in the tech industry (making more money than God, as their dad liked to joke), Jerome had sworn off technology. He didn't text or send emails, just an occasional FedExed letter. Justice made the mistake of telling him that she'd reached two hundred thousand followers that week. She'd expected him to be proud or to congratulate her, but instead he ripped into her for posting so much about her life online. "You're not even selling your privacy," he'd said, "you're just giving it away, and you have no idea what anyone is going to use it for." It soon devolved into a shouting match, and the spray of his vitriol expanded to include their parents.

"She's underage!" he'd yelled at their mom. "And anyone out there can find out anything about her that they want." Justice was used to her brother the know-it-all, but what had really pissed her off was how seriously their parents had taken what he said. They started discussing making her account private and approving her posts, dismantling her hard work and her dreams right in front of her, as if it was their right. Then Jerome suggested that she delete her profile entirely, and Justice had lost her mind.

"You're such a hypocrite!" she'd screamed. "Google pays your bills. You're talking about the industry you work for!"

At that, Jerome had just smiled and drained his glass of cabernet sauvignon. "Of course," he said. "That's why I know what I'm talking about."

Just remembering it made her shake. Justice and her brother had never gotten along. There were times in her life when she had hated him, but she would give anything to talk to him right now. First, she would admit that he was right, and then she would ask him to help her get out of this hell.

She pushed herself up off the floor and walked over to the

bed, where she'd dropped her phone when she heard Margot scream. She crawled onto the bed and sat at the top, leaning back against the wall. She tucked her knees under her chin and then she grabbed her phone. She opened the camera, flipping the phone around so that she was staring at her own face, hit Record and started talking. "I'm seventeen, and this morning I watched two people die on Unknown Island . . ." She kept talking until she felt her mind drain, at least somewhat, and only after did she stop recording. Then she stood up too fast, making the world spin.

Not only was she going off no sleep but also no food. She'd hardly been able to eat anything at breakfast, and she was feeling it. She had to eat something, even if it meant seeing other people. She tucked her phone into her back pocket and headed out of her bungalow and back to the kitchen. She must not have been the only one who wanted to be alone, because the only other person she saw was Xander, sitting by the pool, seemingly oblivious to the fact that it was starting to rain again.

Justice felt hot and dirty, but the rain brought no comfort. It just felt like bugs tickling her skin. As she approached the kitchen, she tried to think about what sounded good. Maybe she could find a piece of fruit or a handful of almonds, something that would tide her over until they were able to get out of here. Because they were getting out of here. They had to.

The kitchen appeared to be empty, but when she rounded the corner of the counter, Justice yelped and jumped back. Robby was on his hands and knees, picking something invisible off the floor. He jerked upright at Justice's scream, whatever he'd been painstakingly collecting flying out of his hand and scattering back across the floor. The fright made Justice's stomach twist and her heart was pounding again, and she did the only thing that seemed to appeal to her anymore. She sank down and sat on the floor.

A few feet away from her, Robby turned and leaned against the counter. He tilted his head back and looked up at the ceiling. His own chest was heaving. "What are you doing in here?" he asked between breaths.

"I came to find a snack," Justice said. "I didn't know you owned the kitchen."

When she had calmed down, she could see that the palm of Robby's hand was dotted with small white things. She leaned forward to get a closer look. Sesame seeds. In fact, they were everywhere, scattered across the floor.

"What are *you* doing in here?" she asked, motioning at the seeds.

"There's no broom," Robby said, by way of explanation. "And I want them out of here. I said no sesame in the kitchen, it was a condition of my coming here to cook, but they didn't listen. It's everywhere. There's so much hummus, gallons of it . . ." Justice thought he sounded like a mad person, but her eyes flicked to the counter above Robby's head. He wasn't lying. There were several tubs of hummus, sesame bagels, bottles of tahini dressing, sesame crackers, and that was just what she could see from her spot on the floor.

She was about to tell him that she liked hummus and ask what he had against it, when she heard a dog bark. For the past several months, Justice had seized up every time she heard a dog bark, and now the sound sent her scrambling to her feet.

"Where is it?" she said, spinning in a circle to scan the kitchen. The sound was so close, the dog had to be in the room.

It sounded like a little yapper, and it could be hiding anywhere. Under the counter or even in a cabinet. "Get it out of here," she said, running around the counter to the other side. "Help me find it!" She turned around to see that Robby had stood up. But rather than help her find the dog, he just stared at her, a puzzled look on his face.

"Are you afraid of dogs?" he asked.

Yap yap! Yap yap! Yap yap!

"No," Justice said, furiously. "I just don't like them."

The dog kept barking. *Yapyapyapyapyapyapyap,* like it planned to go on forever. Justice clamped her hands over her ears. She felt like pulling her hair out. Robby walked up to her, brusquely grabbed her by one shoulder, and spun her around so that she was facing away from him. Then he pulled her phone out of her back pocket. At that moment, the barking blissfully stopped. Justice stood there, not moving, and then she slowly took her hands away from her ears. Beautiful silence. She turned to see Robby standing there, her phone in his hand. He reached out to hand it back to her and she took it from him.

"If you don't like dogs, then why do you have your alarm set to one barking?" he asked.

"What are you talking about?" He didn't say anything, just motioned for Justice to look. Hands shaking, Justice tapped open the clock to see that he was right. She dropped her phone, and the screen cracked as it hit the floor.

Justice had dropped her phone like it had burned her, and she made no motion to pick it up. After they both stared at it for a bit, Robby bent down and retrieved it, but instead of handing it to Justice, he put it on the counter. He got the sense that she didn't want to touch it.

"I didn't . . . ," she started. "I don't know. . . ." She faltered, then took a deep breath. "I didn't set that," she said. "I didn't even know that that sound was on there. This is the first time it has ever gone off." She looked at Robby. Her eyes were the size of cucumber slices, her irises dilated with fear. She stumbled a little and gripped the countertop to keep from falling. "I need to sit down," she said, and sank back to the floor. Robby followed her, landing right on top of several sesame seeds.

They sat in silence for a few minutes, or maybe it was a few hours.

"We're being tortured," Justice said, finally. "This is some sick game, and whoever is playing it doesn't even care if people die."

"Who do you think is playing it?" Robby asked. Justice shook her head, and a single tear ran down her cheek.

"It's someone who knows us really well," he said. "They know all our weaknesses." That was what he had thought when he walked into the kitchen to retrieve the chef's knives that he had brought with him from home, and then saw the sesame seeds everywhere, the tubs of hummus that he kept throwing in the trash stacked back on the counter, taunting him.

"Why do you hate sesame?" Justice asked, and Robby took a deep breath.

"I'll tell you if you tell me why the sound of a dog barking freaks you out so much," he said. To his surprise, Justice nodded.

"Okay," she said. "But you first." Robby nodded back and looked down at the floor, wondering where to start. He pressed his finger into a sesame seed on the floor and cut it in half with his nail. "Start at the beginning," Justice added, and Robby nodded.

"The past couple of years have been a blur," he said. "My YouTube channel took off and then I had my own restaurant. Even though those were things that I wanted, it felt out of my control. I guess because people thought they knew me from YouTube, they assumed they had a say in everything I did. It was as if they felt like they owned me." Justice nodded, and Robby went on. "And I let them. People in the comments would say they hated a shirt, and I'd never wear it again. Then, when the restaurant opened, I became a fucking zoo animal. People would walk into the kitchen all on their own and demand to take a photo with me, even though I'd be right in the middle of cooking. If I said yes, I'd burn the food, and if I said no, they'd leave a bad Yelp review." Justice grimaced.

"I hear you on the comments," she said. "And don't envy you on the reviews. That must have been brutal."

"Yeah," Robby said, "and I had investors to think about. I was still filming the show, and I had to drop out of school, and never saw my friends, and it just felt like so much pressure. My girlfriend was my last link to my old life, but then she cheated on me."

"Oof," Justice said. "I'm sorry." Robby looked up at her and knew that she meant it.

"You want to know what's really crazy?" Robby said, and she nodded. "I got obsessed with the guy she hooked up with, and it wasn't even about her. It was just that I was so jealous of him and his normal life. I couldn't stop looking stuff up about him online." Robby paused and thought of how much he had been able to learn about Braxton Ross with Google and an hour and half when he was supposed to be planning the menu for a private party.

Braxton Ross's birthday was September 27. He played midfield on the lacrosse team, attended First United Methodist Church, was student council vice president, and was probably flunking calculus (not that flunking calculus would matter to a guy like Braxton Ross). He was the youngest of three siblings. His oldest sister had pledged Chi Omega at the University of Georgia; his older brother had gone to Northwestern, where he was studying journalism. His father had a law degree from Emory and was a prominent real estate attorney. As an undergrad, he had been a Sigma Chi. Braxton's grandfather had also been a Sigma Chi, and an attorney, and so everyone knew what Braxton was going to do after graduation. Braxton Ross's life was an open book, and it was as normal as fuck. He was also allergic to sesame.

Robby took a deep breath, and looked at Justice again, weighing what he was about to do in his mind. He hadn't told anyone. He had kept a straight face and a straight story the whole time, and now he was about to spill his guts, give someone all the ammunition they would ever need to bring him down. He reconsidered for a split second, and the reality hit. Telling Justice didn't matter, because Robby had been kidding himself when he thought no one knew.

"I found out the guy was allergic to sesame," he said, "because he'd once gone as hummus for Halloween, and in the video he posted of his costume, he made a joke about it being a killer. The same day I found that out, I got to the restaurant and saw that his family had a reservation." Robby stopped, put his head in his hands, and then continued. "I don't know what I thought I was doing," he said, "but I made a trip to the store to buy sesame seeds, and when his order came through, I put a few in his shrimp and grits."

He looked up at Justice, who sat watching him. She was so motionless that it seemed like she was holding her breath. "I swear to god, it was only a few," Robby said. "I thought it would just give him an upset stomach or something like that. It wasn't until the next day that I found out he'd died." He gulped. "His family blamed the ice cream shop down the street. They had a black sesame ice cream, and they thought someone didn't wash the scoop." Robby's heart was racing and he could hear the blood rushing in his ears. "Nobody even questioned the restaurant," he said, "and we had an all-staff the next night to talk about the importance of food safety. The ice cream shop went out of business because the guy's family sued them into the ground." Robby exhaled.

Now that he had finished, he felt himself deflating and it felt strangely nice, like his coiled insides were finally unwinding. But now Justice knew the truth about him. He was a murderer, and he couldn't look at her. He kept his eyes on the ground and pressed another sesame seed with the tip of his finger so that it stuck to his skin. Then, without really knowing why, Robby put the sesame seed on his tongue.

"Gross," Justice said. "Don't eat that. It was on the floor." He looked up and saw that she was smiling. It wasn't a happy smile or an amused smile, but one of sympathy. He spit the sesame seed out.

"I'm a monster," Robby said, and she shook her head.

"I'm the monster," she said. "I killed a kid."

"What?" She said it so bluntly that Robby didn't believe her. Then tears started running down her cheeks, and he knew it was true.

"I didn't mean to," Justice said. "I was trying to poison a dog."

"A dog that barked all the time?" She nodded, looking every bit as miserable as Robby felt.

"It was the week I was supposed to retake the SAT," she explained. "I took them once, but I don't test well, so I had to take them again, but that dog kept me up all night. I had a white noise machine and earplugs, but I could still hear it. It would start at around eleven and go until four in the morning, late enough that as soon as it stopped, the birds started. I swear, for like a week, I only slept like two hours a night, max, and the closer I got to the test, the more I started to freak out." Justice didn't look at him as she spoke, and Robby could see that her hands were shaking as she fiddled with the brightly colored string bracelets that encircled her wrists.

"I should have just asked them to keep the dog inside," she said, tears dripping off her face and landing on her chest. "I don't know why I didn't, but one night it was like three in the morning and I got up and went down to the garage. I was looking for tape, so I could tape something over my windows. I didn't find any, but I did find some rat poison, and the next thing I knew, I was sneaking over there to put it in her bowl."

"Her?" Robby asked, keeping his voice soft and gentle, and Justice nodded.

"Princess Petunia, the dog," she said, and Robby's eyebrows involuntarily shot up at the name. "I didn't want to kill her; I just thought that maybe it would make her sick and they'd keep her inside for a few days, long enough for me to get some sleep and take the test."

"But the little boy ate it?" Robby asked. Justice nodded.

"He was only two," she said between sniffs, her voice quavering. "And you want to know what's really fucked up?" She didn't wait for Robby to respond. "They kept the dog inside after that!" A cry ripped through her like she was being torn in two, and she leaned forward, burying her head between her knees and wrapping her arms around them. Her sobs shook her whole body.

Robby wasn't a hugger, but Justice clearly needed some sort of comfort right now, so he shifted on the floor until he was sitting right next to her, close enough so that she could feel him even with her eyes closed.

"You didn't mean to do it," he whispered.

"I know," she choked between sobs, "but I did." Even though she couldn't see him, Robby nodded. He knew how she felt so precisely it sliced him in half, a clean cut. He hadn't meant to do it either. But he had.

Frankie felt gross. She couldn't believe she'd flirted with Graham, and it wasn't until she was walking back to her bungalow that she realized she had done so in her underwear. The entire time she'd spent on the island felt like a fugue state, and when she'd stripped down to dive under the boathouse door with Manny, she'd forgotten that she was the only one who hadn't changed into a swimsuit. She had assumed she wouldn't be on the island long enough to swim. How wrong she had been. She already felt she had been here forever. It hadn't even been a day.

She was desperate to leave, and that was why she had flirted with Graham. Off the island, he was nobody, but here, he was the only one who'd had contact with anyone from Unknown Island since they arrived. Sure, he was nothing more than an errand boy, but right now, it was all she had to go off. Graham might know something that he didn't even know he knew. Or, more likely, he was going to be called on to deliver some other message, and whatever tiny, infinitesimal bit of leverage Graham had, Frankie wanted in on it.

Frankie walked into her bungalow and locked the door behind her. She stripped out of her damp bra and underwear—both of which were solid black cotton, thank god—and put on the most modest swimsuit she could find. Once she got it on, she realized it wasn't very modest: a pale pink one-piece with a deep dip down the front and an improbable belt that tied in a giant bow. Ugh. That would not do.

She pawed through the rest of her luggage until she found a plain old bikini that seemed to at least be sturdy. If she had to swim far, she wanted to make sure she was prepared. She changed again, and then looked at her stuff, strewn on the floor. It all seemed ridiculous. Everything she had brought with her still had the tags on it, and if she had been able to connect to the internet, she could also have pulled up a detailed spreadsheet of when she was supposed to wear what and what kind of post went with each.

Frankie didn't have set rates, as Roger painstakingly negotiated her fee for every sponsorship. A pic in the feed was about the price of a luxury car. A story where she waxed on about the virtues of a particular moisturizer—and helpfully told her followers they could swipe up to find where to buy it—was about two luxury cars. Some brands wanted her to tag and talk about them, others preferred to keep it on the DL, knowing that a commenter would inevitably ask where her dress was from and then Frankie could reply and tell them (and everyone who wasn't asking).

For the clothes she didn't post about, Frankie had a stylist who chose her outfits. She made sure to keep Frankie in the right mix of luxury brands so she seemed successful, underground labels so she seemed cool, and a few Target or Brandy Melville pieces thrown in so she still seemed accessible. Frankie couldn't remember the last time she'd picked out her own clothes. Looking at all the stuff that wasn't even really hers, Frankie felt a lump rising in her throat. What she really wanted right now was Hannah's vintage Hard Rock Cafe T-shirt, the one she'd bought thrifting when they were thirteen, and which they'd fought about for days after, as Frankie insisted she had seen it first.

Hannah was the rightful owner, though. Frankie would have lost it within a week, but Hannah had managed to hold on to and wear it right up until the very end. It was so soft and sheer that moonlight showed through. She was pretty sure that Hannah had had the shirt at the hotel, but after that, she had no idea. Frankie sniffed and shoved the thought down. She had so many regrets about Hannah, and now was not the time to start cataloging them.

She reached into the pile and pulled out the most practical thing she could find—a frilly floral sundress that at least wasn't micromini or über-maxi—yanked off the tags, and pulled it on over her head. Then she sat down on the bed and tried to think.

A few things were obvious. Everything about Unknown Island was fake. Frankie tried to remember the first time she'd heard about it, when people online started to talk about the luxury island that didn't charge its guests a cent—it was months ago, certainly. Someone, some sociopath, had put so much planning and money into this. The online campaign, the invites, the contracts, the logistics of the transportation alone were a complicated spiderweb.

Frankie herself hadn't thought anything was suspicious until the guest list was revealed. That was another stroke of genius on Unknown's part. By revealing the guests so publicly, and so last minute, Unknown was pretty much guaranteeing that no one would back out. Frankie felt regret pierce through her.

As soon as she'd seen the names and the accounts of the people she was going to be spending the week with—Graham Hoffman, 121K; Margot Bryant, 643K; Manny de La Cruz, 1.3M—she'd known something was up. But she'd been too worried about her image to listen to her gut. She could have saved herself all this trouble. Saved her life. Because Frankie was pretty sure of that now. The guest list wasn't random. Every person on it, herself included, had been carefully selected. Not for their following, not for their accomplishments, but because Unknown Island wanted to kill them.

Frankie got up and started to pace the room. There was no way Chelsea's and Margot's deaths were accidents. Twenty percent of the population doesn't just happen to die within a couple of hours. Their deaths had been planned. Their deaths were murders. Someone was going to be next, and Frankie was going to make sure it wasn't her. Her first option, and what she wanted more than anything, was to escape, to get off this island. If that didn't happen, then she was going to do whatever it took to survive. She left the bungalow to go look for Graham.

She was halfway down the beach when she noticed the side door of the boathouse was open. Frankie glanced around, making sure that no one was around, and then she broke into a run. She wasn't getting left behind.

Frankie clambered up on the dock and swung herself through the door, then gasped in shock. The automatic door was wide open. Sunlight poured in and there was nothing between the boat and the freedom of the turquoise sea. Then she looked around and what she saw made her scream.

Frankie clamped her hands over her mouth, wishing she could shove the sound back in. Graham, or what was left of him, lay on the dock just a few feet from her, blood and brains splattered as if they had been sprayed by a sprinkler, a steel scuba tank resting on what used to be his head. Flies were swarming and Frankie gagged, vomit rising in her throat, but she forced herself to swallow it. She shouldn't have screamed, people were going to come running, and now she only had seconds.

She jumped from the dock into the boat. She turned the keys that were dangling in the ignition, but nothing happened. Shit, shit, shit. She knew nothing about boats, but she could do it. There was a steering wheel, and out on the open water, there'd be nothing to crash into. She just had to get far enough out and then she'd flag down the first people she saw. She turned the keys again, pressed buttons, flipped switches, and spun dials. But still nothing.

She heard people shouting and running, and they weren't very far away. She turned the keys again, as hard as she could, then slammed her fists against the steering wheel in frustration before clambering back out onto the dock before anyone got there and found her in the boat. She stepped in something squishy and looked down to see that her toes were in a puddle of blood and gray gelatinous globs. She retched again, and this time she didn't stop herself, bending over to vomit into the water. She stood up to see Xander and Justice in the doorway panting, their eyes wide.

"I saw the door was open," Frankie gasped, "so I came in . . . and . . . and . . ." Manny appeared in the doorway, then Robby. As she gestured, she looked back at the boat and saw the keys still in the ignition. She should have grabbed them before anyone else saw them, and the realization of her mistake made her throw up again.

The next thing she knew, Xander had his arms around her and was trying to lead her toward the door. "Don't look," he said. "Just close your eyes. You can wash your feet off in the water. Do you want me to carry you?"

Frankie shook her head and resisted. Every step toward the door was a step away from the boat.

"I think she's in shock," Xander said, pulling her as she stumbled. At the door to the boathouse, Frankie stopped and turned around just in time to see Manny jump into the boat and inspect the console. Her knees felt weak and she started to fall. Xander bent down, swooped one arm under her knees and scooped her up, then carried her out of the boathouse and to the beach. He set her down in the sand, close to the water's edge so that the sea could wash the bits of Graham off her feet.

Justice kneeled beside her. "Take deep breaths," she said.

"Don't go in there," Xander said turning to Celia and Emma Jane, who were now standing at the edge of the boat-house dock. "It's Graham, and it's bad." Celia nodded.

"What happened to him?" Emma Jane asked.

Justice gulped. "Head smashed in," she said. "There's blood, and um, bits . . ."

A look of disgust washed over Celia's face, and then she and Emma Jane sat down in the sand, not far from Frankie. Robby followed, and Manny came out of the boathouse. He sat down with the rest of them and shook his head.

"Frankie and I were in there earlier, and one of those fell and missed us by an inch," he said.

Frankie's head shot up and she looked at Manny. She wanted him to stop talking, but he was gazing out at the water.

"Why were you in the boathouse?" Emma Jane asked, and Frankie swore she sounded suspicious.

"We wanted to see what we could find," Manny said. "And then we heard Margot's screams. . . ."

Frankie rubbed her face and nodded, like she was helping tell the story too.

"What did you find?" Emma Jane pressed, apparently deciding she wasn't going to let it go.

"Same thing that Graham found," Manny said. "A boat that's not going anywhere."

Frankie swallowed. "What do you mean it's not going anywhere?" she asked.

"He was clearly trying to escape," Manny said. "It looks like he was fiddling with a bunch of dials, but the batteries are dead and it's out of gas."

Frankie's heart started to pound. "There are other ways to make a boat go, right?" she asked.

"Sure," Manny said. "You can always row it, but that's not going to happen either."

"Why not?"

Manny finally turned to face her. "There are no paddles. I looked."

Frankie bit her lip to choke back a sob. Her ticket out was dead in the water.

Emma Jane stood up and brushed the sand off her butt and started to walk toward the boathouse. "Where are you going?" Justice called after her.

"I just want to see something," she said.

"I wouldn't go in there if I were you," Manny said. "He's not in good shape."

Emma Jane kept walking.

"Wait! I'll come with you."

Emma Jane turned to see Celia scrambling up and running toward her.

"What do you want to see?" Celia asked when she caught up.

"I don't know," Emma Jane said. "I guess I'll know it when I see it." She was slightly annoyed, as she had wanted to look around alone, but out of everyone, Celia seemed the least likely to get in her way. "Why do you want to come with me?"

"I don't, really," Celia said flatly. "But there's a smashed-up body in there, and I don't want you to have to see it alone."

Emma Jane stopped midstride and turned to stare at the

small, mousy girl next to her. Celia couldn't have been more than five feet tall, and her skin looked like it had gotten more sun in the past few hours than it had in the past few years, but she was clearly tough. Emma Jane thought that this was the nicest thing anyone had said to her since Sergio died.

"Thanks," she said. "But don't tell anybody what I do in there, okay?"

Celia nodded and they started walking again. Emma Jane's brain had been in a nonstop whirl since Chelsea had collapsed. It reminded her of the few times she had done mushrooms—there was a thought, an idea, just outside the perimeter of her mind. She didn't know what it was, but she knew it was there, and she couldn't grab it. At least not yet. So she was trying to collect as much information as she could to lure it closer.

Earlier, she had waited for Robby to leave the dining room, then snuck back in and took pictures of everything she could—the tables, the chairs, the dirty dishes. She'd noticed that not only was Chelsea's glass ringed with coral lipstick but that there was also a coral smudge on the tablecloth where her face had hit. No one else was wearing this kind of lipstick, and this meant that the glass was obviously Chelsea's glass. They had all watched her *pop* a new bottle of champagne and pour it herself, which meant that if she had been poisoned, the poison had been in her glass, not the champagne.

Chelsea had been drinking from the same glass all morning, and they had all been in the dining room the entire time. If there was poison in her glass, then someone had put it there right before she drank from it.

One of them had put it there right before she drank from it.

Then, when everyone left to move Margot's body to the freezer, Emma Jane had snuck into Margot's bungalow and taken pictures of everything in it. She'd climbed up on the counter in the bathroom to peer into the light fixture full of bees. She'd gotten stung a couple of times, but what she had seen hurt more. The bees hadn't been nesting in the light fixture; their hive had been *placed* there. It wasn't attached to anything.

Emma Jane had spent less than three hours total with Margot, and she had not enjoyed it, but she still knew that Margot was not the type to forget or misplace something as important as an EpiPen. Someone had known Margot was allergic to bees. Someone had put the bees in Margot's bathroom. Someone had taken her EpiPen so she wouldn't have it when they attacked.

Now, at the entrance to the boathouse, Emma Jane paused. "You really don't have to come in," she said to Celia. "I'll be fine."

Celia nodded, looking a little paler than before, but she seemed determined. "I'll just stand here at the door," she said, "and that way, you can yell if you need me."

Emma Jane smiled, and resisted the urge to pat the girl on the head. Then she went in.

Manny had been right. Graham was not in good shape. The scuba tank had caved his head in like a cantaloupe. She stood there and looked at it and noticed the strange feeling she'd had twice already that morning: dead bodies didn't freak her out. Sure, she felt bad that someone had died, but if she blocked out the fact that these were people she knew, she found the whole thing very interesting. A crime scene was like a puzzle, and you had to take inventory of everything, because you didn't know which pieces were going to be useful.

Emma Jane turned to see Celia watching her and raised a finger to her lips in a gesture of secretive solidarity. Then she took out her phone and started snapping away. She took pictures of Graham, of the boat, and of the scuba tanks, staying close to the wall as she did so. The scuba tanks were stored on a narrow balcony that was about twenty feet high. It had no railing, and the tanks were lined up right to the edge. Over it, actually. She could see the space left by the two that had fallen, the one that Manny had mentioned and the one that had hit Graham. They could easily be dislodged by anything that shook the balcony. Or by the teeniest, tiniest push.

Emma Jane looked back at Graham's body and at everything around him, and she noticed a small white button. Flattening herself against the wall, she pressed it, and the big door at the front of the boathouse started to roll down. Sure enough, she could hear the scuba tanks shaking above her. She quickly pressed the button again and the door stopped. Pressing this button was likely the last thing Graham did, but that didn't make sense. Manny said it looked like he'd tried to start the boat. Why would he try to start the boat if he hadn't even gotten the door open yet?

She looked from his splayed body to the boat, and then beyond that, out the door to the flat horizon, and then it hit her. Frankie. *She* was the one who had been trying to start the boat, because the door was already open when she got there. Emma Jane snorted a quick breath in through her nose. That bitch had been trying to leave them.

Emma Jane pocketed her phone and stepped back out of the boathouse. Celia had a strange look on her face. "You like stuff like this, don't you?" she said. It was an odd question, but somehow Emma Jane knew exactly what she meant.

"I guess I do," she said. "I've always liked murder, though I cannot say I like it this close to me."

Celia swallowed. "Murder?"

Emma Jane inched backward so that she was leaning against the boathouse, and lowered her voice. The others were still sitting on the beach, quite a ways away, but she didn't want to take any chances.

"I think Chelsea was poisoned, someone put the bees in Margot's room and stole her EpiPen, and someone pushed that tank onto Graham."

"I don't get it, though," Celia said, eyes wide. "We're the only ones here. . . ."

Emma Jane leaned in. "Exactly," she said, and jerked her head toward the others.

Celia sucked in a quick breath and put a hand to her chest, slumping back against the boathouse wall. "Oh god" was all she said.

Emma Jane knew she should be terrified, absolutely panicking right now, but instead she felt a calm excitement. Whenever anyone asked her, or teased her—"Emma Jane just *loooooves* murder"—she'd always told them that it made her feel safer. "That way, if someone is trying to kill me, I'll know what to do." She meant it as a joke, of course, but now she couldn't help but think it was somewhat true.

Whoever had murdered Graham, Margot, and Chelsea was all about careful planning, and it would take careful planning to stay one step ahead of them. She had to remain calm and keep things close. She couldn't do it alone, and so she would trust Celia, and only Celia.

"You and I should stick together," Emma Jane said. "Be each other's eyes and ears. Look for anything unusual or weird, anyone acting strange. Someone is pretending to be someone they're not, and they might mess up. And we shouldn't go off alone."

"Chelsea didn't go off alone," Celia pointed out. "She died right in front of everyone."

"I know," Emma Jane said, "but that was when we weren't expecting anything. It will be harder for the murderer to do that now. Everyone's on edge."

"I thought of something," Celia said.

"What?" Emma Jane asked, looking at the younger girl.

"Well, if Graham was the one sending pictures to be posted, that should stop now," Celia said. "And if he wasn't, then . . ."

Emma Jane nodded. She knew exactly what Celia was getting at. She turned to leave but Celia caught her arm.

"I want to tell you something," Celia said, "because . . . I want to tell someone."

"Okay," Emma Jane said, suddenly very curious.

"I lied," Celia said.

Emma Jane raised her eyebrows and waited for Celia to go on.

"That name in the letter," she continued, "Stacia Lindstrom?" Emma Jane nodded. "I said I didn't recognize it. But I do." Emma Jane stayed silent. Celia shifted uncomfortably, and her eyes were growing red.

"I first saw it on the cover of a magazine at a CVS," Celia said. "I took a bet. Online. For a pizza. People use the word 'hacking' when they talk about getting into someone's email, but that's a misnomer. There's no hacking involved. It's just making educated guesses, that's all."

Emma Jane had wanted to give Celia space to tell her story, but she had no idea what the girl was talking about. "I'm not following," she said.

Celia took a breath and started over.

"I made a bet with someone I met online about how fast I could get into someone's email account. He said he'd buy me a pizza if I could do it in less than twenty-four hours, and I told him I could do it in less than twelve. I didn't know who he was, and he didn't know who I was. He picked the person, and it was Stacia Lindstrom. I didn't ask why he'd picked her." Celia stopped. She pulled off her glasses and wiped her eyes.

"It was so easy. I just went through her social media profiles and got all the answers to her security questions. Most people pick obvious stuff, like their best friend's name or where they went to high school, so they won't forget. Then I reset her password." Celia sniffed. "The guy I made the bet with tried not to send me the pizza because he said it was only temporary, but he finally relented. And I guess even though it was only temporary, it was enough for him to get what he needed."

Tears were streaming down Celia's face now, and mucus bubbled from her nose. "I never would have done it if I'd known why he wanted it. It was just a stupid bet, and I was trying to show off. I'm usually one of the only girls in these places, and I sometimes feel like I need to prove myself, show that I'm better than the rest of them." She wiped her nose, stretching a snail trail of snot across her cheek. "It was just ego," she went on. "It was so dumb. Some woman died because I was trying to make a bunch of strangers in an online forum who don't even know my real name think I was smart."

Emma Jane reached out and squeezed Celia's hand. "He was a stalker," she said. "He would have found a way to kill her even if you hadn't helped."

"Maybe," Celia said. "Or maybe not."

"Did you ever tell anyone?" Emma Jane asked, and Celia shook her head.

"After I saw the magazine, I put it together," Celia said. "I left the store and went straight home and deleted the account I'd used to make the bet and everything that was linked to it." Celia swallowed. "But there was plenty of time for someone to find out."

Emma Jane nodded. "And someone did." She looked at the group on the beach. Everyone was standing now. "Come on," she said. "We need to go back before they start wondering what we're talking about."

If Celia had confessed in hopes of getting a confession in return, she had hoped wrong. It wasn't that Emma Jane didn't want to confess. She did, desperately. It was that she didn't know if she could. She couldn't even type the words. There was no way she could say them out loud.

Sergio had been Emma Jane's first friend. At her father's insistence, their housekeeper, Silvia, had started bringing her son to work with her once a week. "EJ needs a playmate," he'd said. Emma Jane was four. Emma Jane had made Sergio sit in her frilly pink bedroom and have tea parties, pink pretend cakes and pink pretend tea.

All through elementary, he came after school, and then he kept coming. In junior high, they'd study together, Sergio doing most of Emma Jane's homework after she grew frustrated with his nineteenth attempt to explain it so that she could do it herself. They were maybe fourteen when she suddenly realized that Sergio was old enough to stay home by himself, and probably had been for years.

As they got older, her friends started to tease her about him, asking for hookups. "Yo, your housekeeper's son is so freaking hot. EJ, bring him out!"

"He has a girlfriend," Emma Jane would insist, even though she had no idea, really. She always had guys in her life, so she assumed Sergio had girls in his. She never asked. She never asked why a seventeen-year-old was still coming to her house every day after school. She never asked herself why she was always there to meet him. It was a perfect bubble, iridescent rainbows in the sun, and to acknowledge what was happening would have burst it right there.

It had been a Wednesday. Emma Jane pulled up in her Tesla right as Sergio was about to walk up the driveway, having just taken a bus for an hour and a half to get to her house so that he could make a futile attempt to keep her from failing geometry. It was winter, that time of year when the golden hour came early and could easily slip through your fingers if you didn't reach out and grab it the moment it arrived. The light was too beautiful to waste on anything like homework. "Get in," Emma Jane said to him. His answer was a smile, and he obeyed.

"Where are we going?" he asked.

"I have no idea," she said, flipping a U-turn.

"Awesome," he said.

He was too pure for her. Too good. She'd known that since

she was four. Emma Jane dreamed about him every night, her conscience tormented. She was worried that if she confessed, the dreams would stop, and then he'd really be gone.

Manny remembered the days after the fire like they were just last week. He had stayed in his room, the curtains drawn, and barely got out of bed. He couldn't eat. His mom kept making his favorite foods, but he could barely keep down water. After a couple of days, a pattern started to form.

They would find a body in the ashes. Then, after a few hours, the body would be given a name. A few hours after that, the name would be given a story. Manny refreshed his phone constantly, learning the identities, the families, the personalities of the people he had helped incinerate.

His dad barely spoke. His mother cried, and his little brother suddenly had no one to play with and didn't understand why. Manny was sixteen and had just ruined his family. This was even before the legal fees, and the trial, and his sentencing. Before his mother's diagnosis and her dying two months after that. Manny hadn't spoken to his dad in a long time, and he knew this was because his father blamed him for his mother's death. Manny understood, because he blamed himself too. That year was a scar. He lost forty pounds. He only slept a couple of hours a night. He barely saw anyone. He hated himself when he looked in the mirror, and he thought about suicide daily. He'd been close. So close.

That had been the darkest time in his life. Until now.

The sky was clouded in patches, and the sun peeked through directly overhead. It must be almost noon, they'd been here for less than a morning. Manny pushed himself up off the sand. "We can't just sit here," he said.

"What else can we do?" Frankie said. "Should we put Graham in . . . with the others?"

Manny shook his head. "I don't think we can move him," he said. "He's too . . ." He couldn't think of the right word, a word that described the condition of Graham's body without sounding insensitive. But Frankie nodded, knowing what he meant. Manny could tell, even though she was trying to hide it, how upset she had been about the boat. It had been a good idea, albeit a suspiciously easy one if it had worked out. In their short time on Unknown Island, Manny already knew that it was not the kind of place where you could find a boat ready and waiting to zoom away to freedom and safety. Finally, he thought of something they could do.

"We need to eat lunch," he said, and Frankie laughed, caustic *ha ha*s.

"No, I'm serious," he said. "We're not doing ourselves any favors if we start passing out from hunger."

Emma Jane and Celia came back from the boathouse and joined them.

"What were you doing in there?" Frankie asked, a note of accusation in her voice.

"I just like to look at dead bodies," Emma Jane said, causing everyone but Celia to shrink from her a little.

"Manny's right," Xander said, standing up, "we should go eat." He started trudging toward the dining room, and everyone followed. Manny couldn't help but notice that people were pairing off. Celia and Emma Jane walked together, Justice and Robby were side by side, and Frankie fell back to walk with him. She took very slow steps, and the distance between them and the others started to grow.

"I'm sorry," he whispered. "About the boat." She shook her head.

"It was a long shot," she said. "Someone wants us stuck here. They're not going to let us get away that easy." Manny agreed but didn't say anything. "Who is it?" Frankie asked. The question, barely a whisper, was almost carried away by the wind.

"I don't know," he whispered back, which was a half-truth. Manny felt like he knew, even if he didn't know. It was someone out for revenge. Unknown Island was a place of retribution, conceived and orchestrated by a mysterious vigilante. That sentence felt stupid in his brain, like a theory someone would come up with after reading too many comic books, but no matter how far-fetched it was, nothing else made sense. Someone, or some*ones*, had carefully selected these ten to make them pay. Manny knew what he was paying for, and he suspected that everyone else knew what they were paying for too, though some of them wouldn't admit it. Including the beautiful girl beside him.

"Were you the one who tried to start the boat?" he asked Frankie. He kept looking straight ahead, but out of the corner of his eye, he saw her give a little nod.

"I was going to come back for you," she said.

"It's okay," Manny said, because he knew she was lying.

"I just want out of here so bad," Frankie said.

"We all do," he replied.

"I'm worried about Celia," Frankie said, and Manny looked at her. Ahead of them, everyone else had started up the path from the beach to the dining room. "She's so young," she added.

"How old is she?"

"Sixteen."

"How old are you?"

"Eighteen."

"That's not much of a difference."

"I know," she said, pulling out her bun so that her dark hair fell down her back. "But she's been through so much already. I've known her for years, since she was a little kid. I used to be friends with her sister, Caroline. Caroline was an influencer too, though she never really got that big. She had this horrible video go viral, and that kind of ended her career. She killed herself, probably because of it."

Manny inhaled through his teeth. "That's rough."

Frankie nodded. "They were close too," she said. "So, to go through that, and then come here, and have all of this . . . I just feel like I should watch out for her. Try to make sure nothing happens to her." Manny nodded. It was a noble sentiment, but he didn't ask Frankie how the hell she was going to do that. Or how watching out for Celia figured into her plans when she was trying to get the boat to start all by herself.

They entered the dining room to find Emma Jane and Xander standing in front of the screen. The likes and comments and follows were rolling in, even though no new photos had been posted. Manny came to stand right behind Emma Jane, who was scrolling through the comments.

"People love it," she said. "They're trying to figure out the riddles and wondering who's going to be posted next."

"No one's going to be posted next," Xander said. "Graham

was sending the photos and that's . . ." He turned around, looking at Manny for confirmation, but Manny didn't have any to give him.

"People think it's a game," Emma Jane said.

Manny read the comment she had stopped on.

"This is kind of dope," someone had written. "Unknown has taken all these wack influencers and I feel like they're setting them up to be humiliated or something."

"I thought it was weird at first, but now I'm super into it," read a reply. Emma Jane was reaching out to tap on another when Manny grabbed her hand.

"Don't," he said. "We should be ignoring this thing."

"It's okay," she said, "I'm used to the haters. They don't bother me." She resumed scrolling. Everyone always said the haters didn't bother them, and everyone always lied. Manny turned away.

Justice came into the room carrying her water bottle. She sat down at the table, folded her arms, and dropped her head onto them, like someone who was intending to sleep through English class. Frankie was nowhere to be seen.

"Where did Frankie go?" Manny asked.

"I don't know," Justice said without lifting her head, her voice muffled by her arms. Seconds later, Celia walked into the room.

"Where'd you go?" Manny asked her. She looked at him like he'd just accused her of something.

"I had to get something from my room," she said.

"What?" he asked. Without saying anything, Celia pulled something from her pocket and held it up for him. Manny leaned in to get a better look. It was small, and white, and . . . Shit. It was a tampon.

"Sorry," he mumbled, and Celia gave him a little smile before shoving it back in her pocket. Manny looked over his shoulder to see that now Xander had disappeared. Frankie was still nowhere to be seen, and he hadn't seen Robby since the beach.

"I think we need to stop going off on our own," he said, raising his voice so that everyone in the room could hear him. "We don't understand what's—"

Emma Jane's scream cut him off. A new picture had been posted.

Justice jolted upright, and she and Celia raced across the room. Seconds later, Frankie appeared. "What's going on?" she said, then, without waiting for an answer, she joined the crowd around the screen. Xander arrived, breathing quickly like he'd run. Manny moved slower, sure that whatever had been posted was something he didn't want to see.

It was a picture of Graham, taken on the beach when the helicopter had just landed and the boat carrying Justice and Xander had arrived. Graham had his arms outstretched in a gesture of welcome and a pained smile on his face. There were dark circles of sweat visible underneath his arms, sand under his feet, and palm trees behind him. The photo was clear and in focus, nothing pixelated or grainy about it. No one spoke.

Manny thought back to his arrival on Unknown Island. It was a moment of excitement, when he still thought, when they all still thought, that they were in for the week of their lives. But that feeling had lasted only a split second. He remembered the pilot throwing their bags down as if someone was timing him, the helicopter taking off when its passengers were barely out of range of the propellers. He remembered Graham coming through the palm trees, almost crashing onto the beach, and he remembered the boat rocking as Xander and Justice climbed out of it onto the dock.

What he didn't remember was anyone else on the beach.

"'Graham Hoffman got off scot-free, and that's why he is number three,'" Emma Jane said, reading the caption. "'Stabbing backs, clawing to the top, lies and dishonesty that never stop.'"

Xander was the first to speak. "Someone here took that photo," he said. "Justice and I had just gotten out of the boat and were walking across the beach. I remember seeing Graham like that, because I thought, 'Who's this nerd?'"

"Ha!" Frankie laughed, and then kept laughing hysterically. She doubled over, unable to catch her breath.

"Shut up!" Emma Jane hissed at her, but Frankie kept laughing. Manny took her by the shoulders and led her to a chair. She melted into the chair, and then she hiccupped.

"I'm sorry," she said. "I feel like I'm losing my mind. This is all so surreal. I don't know what to do but laugh."

"Just sit," Manny said. "You want me to get you some water?" She started to nod, but then stopped and shook her head.

"It's okay," she said, standing up, "I'll get it myself." She got up and started walking toward a pitcher at the end of the table, and Manny went back to the screen.

Emma Jane cleared her throat and turned around. "We

were all there when this picture was taken," she said. "Does anyone remember anyone else on the beach?"

"The helicopter was taking off as we were pulling in," Justice said. "And there was the guy in the boat, and the two employees who got in when Xander and I got out. But they were too far away to take this picture. Someone had to have been standing on the beach."

"The helicopter had already taken off when Graham and Robby got there . . . ," Celia said. "So the pilot—"

"Wait!" Manny said, cutting her off. "Where *is* Robby?"

"He went to get . . ." Justice started to speak, but then fell silent. For a split second, the six of them stood there, looking at one another, and then Manny sprinted toward the kitchen.

His heart was hammering in his chest when he burst through the door. There were snacks stacked on the countertop, and a trash can full of hummus, but the kitchen was quiet. Too quiet. For the briefest of instants, Manny thought that maybe Robby had spilled beet juice on the floor, and then his stomach seized. He held out his hand and gripped the countertop, because he felt like he'd fall over if he wasn't holding on to something. Then he put one foot in front of the other and walked to the end of the counter to look around the corner, at the source of the puddle of beet juice.

It was Robby, facedown on the floor, a chef's knife buried deep into his back.

Everyone agreed with Manny. From now on, they were sticking together. But they still needed food. Xander's stomach growled like a guard dog, even though eating was the last thing that sounded appealing right now.

"I don't really want to go in the kitchen," Celia said.

"You don't have to go," Manny said.

"Yes, she does," Justice said. "We all have to stick together."

"Well, we can all go there, and some of us can go in the kitchen and some of us can stay in the hall," Manny said.

"I'll go in the kitchen," Emma Jane said.

"I'll go with you," Manny said. "We'll grab whatever we can and come right back out." Frankie volunteered to go too. The six of them walked back to the kitchen, and Manny turned around at the door. "You three stay right here," he said, addressing Justice, Celia, and Xander. "And sing."

"What?" Justice asked.

"Sing," Manny said. "That way we know you're still standing here. We'll sing too."

"What song?" Emma Jane asked.

"Something we all know," Manny said.

"What song could all six of us possibly know?" Justice asked.

"'Who Let the Dogs Out'?" Xander suggested. Lip-synching to that had been one of his first videos to go viral.

"No," Justice said, shutting it down with one word. If Xander hadn't been so hungry, he might have been offended.

"Fleetwood Mac?" Frankie offered.

"I don't know who he is," Emma Jane said.

"'Wheels on the Bus'?" Celia said, and they all looked at her. "Everyone knows 'Wheels on the Bus.'"

"Anyone here not know the words to 'Wheels on the Bus'?" Manny asked. Emma Jane nodded.

"You don't know 'Wheels on the Bus'?" Frankie asked.

"No, I do," Emma Jane said.

"Then why were you nodding?"

"Because I know the words."

"Okay," Celia said, "so, on the count of three. One, two, three . . ."

"The wheels on the bus go round and round, round and round, the wheels on the bus go round and round, all the way to town . . ."

Xander was glad they were going to eat, and also that no one had expected him to go into the kitchen. He wasn't sure he could handle it. He wasn't sure he could handle what he was doing right now, standing in a hallway, staring at the wall and singing a children's song that he wasn't sure he knew the words to.

"You're getting the words wrong," Justice said, and Xander glared at her. Like it mattered. He started to sing louder.

"The wheels under the bus go around, go around, go around . . ." Justice glared back, and he resisted telling her that even if he wasn't sure what a tune was, he was pretty sure she couldn't carry one.

"I need to pee," Celia said.

"What?" Xander said. "The muffler on the bus goes . . ." Crap. What did a muffler sound like?

"I've been holding it forever," Celia said.

"Fine, let's go," Justice said. Xander rolled his eyes and nodded in assent. He could see the bathroom door from where he was standing. He felt like a hall monitor, but if he was being honest, the few seconds alone were blissful after the last couple of hours. He felt like he was made of dust and his entire body would crumble if someone so much as flicked him.

He'd been with these people for less than six hours. He barely knew them, and yet . . . he couldn't really believe that one of them was a murderer. It didn't make sense. Robby was not a small dude. He was probably five eleven, six feet, and not that Xander had been looking or anything, but he was well-muscled. Strong. None of the girls could have taken him down like that. That left Manny, and from what everyone had said, he and Emma Jane were the only two whose whereabouts were accounted for the entire time. Everyone else had gone off alone. Celia said she'd gone to the bathroom, Justice had gone to get her water bottle, Frankie said she'd stepped outside for some air, and Xander himself had gone to try to take care of his mutinous bowels. Since breakfast, his guts had been bubbling like they were being boiled, and he didn't know whether it was the biscuits and gravy or the stress. Probably both. There had to be someone else on the island. That was the only thing that made sense.

He could hear Justice and Celia singing in the bathroom, and now he just belted out words—"Wheels and bus and wah-wah-wah"—and soon they were back. Frankie and Emma Jane and Manny were in the kitchen a few minutes, and when they returned, each had armloads of food. Xander felt an inordinate amount of relief to see the packets of beef jerky that Frankie had wedged under her arm.

Emma Jane was carrying hummus. "This was all in the trash," she said, "but it's unopened and not expired."

"Um"—Justice cleared her throat—"I think Robby just really hated hummus."

Manny had a bunch of chips and crackers and a case of Perrier, and they carried everything outside. It was the kind of lunch you bought on a road trip to hold you over when you didn't want to stop, but it was food.

Xander ripped open a packet of beef jerky and started eating. The jerky turned to dry crumbs in his mouth, and he could feel his stomach start to roil again, so he grabbed a can of Perrier, cracked it open, and chugged.

"We need to search everyone's phones," Emma Jane announced. Xander choked. Bubbles tickled his nose.

"What?" he said when he had finally recovered, wiping his face with the back of his arm.

"We need to know if anyone here has been taking those pictures and posting them," Emma Jane continued. "So everyone put your phones in the middle of the table, now. No prepping." Manny tossed his phone onto the table, its fall cushioned by a bag of pretzel chips. Justice, Emma Jane, and Celia followed suit. Only Frankie seemed to hesitate, but just for a second.

"I have a lot of confidential information on there," she said.

"Someone is trying to murder us," Emma Jane chided her, "so don't worry, we're all too busy to leak your nudes."

Xander thought he saw Frankie blush, just a little. Xander was still hesitant. He hadn't taken those photos, but he still didn't want anyone going through his phone. Since everything had happened with Damien, Xander had treated his phone like it was public property. Every night before bed, he scrubbed it. Deleting photos, texts messages, browser history, anything and everything that could harbor any incriminating evidence. He'd learned the hard way that apps are the window to the soul.

He sensed that everyone was looking at him, intrigue

mounting the longer he delayed. He pulled his phone from his pocket and dropped it on the table with the others.

Emma Jane picked up the six phones, stacked them like a deck of cards, and then shuffled them. "Okay," she said, "this is how this is going to work. Everyone is going to close their eyes and pick a phone at random. Whoever's phone you pick will give you their passcode, then you go through their phone. Look for anything that seems shady and that could be related to Unknown Island. Pictures, messages, et cetera." She paused. "And to Frankie's point, we all have stuff on our phones that we don't want other people to see. So be discreet."

She held out the stack of phones to Celia first and then went around the table, everyone taking one. Celia got Justice's, Justice got Frankie's, Emma Jane got Celia's, Manny got Emma Jane's, Xander got Manny's, and Frankie got Xander's. He gave her his passcode, and she gave him a weak smile before she started typing away.

Xander looked around the table. Everyone's heads were bent, their faces furrowed in concentration as they sifted through each other's digital garbage. Xander looked down at the phone in his hands, a nearly new iPhone with a lock screen photo of a pretty, dark-haired woman standing on a beach holding a baby with one arm and trying to keep the wind from blowing her hair into her eyes with the other. The woman's clothes were old, out of style, and the picture looked like it was a snapshot of a print. Xander figured it was a picture of Manny and his mom. He glanced up at Manny, at the tattoos that covered his skin, a spider's web of fine-line ink from his collarbone to his wrist. Xander would not have pegged him

174

as the kind of guy to keep a pic of his mom on his phone, but then, everyone was full of surprises.

He typed in Manny's passcode and the photo disappeared. Xander had to admit that it was kind of thrilling. Going through someone's phone was about the closest you could get to being in someone else's head, and the first thing that stood out to him about Manny's was just how popular he was. He had hundreds of unread texts, most from numbers he didn't have saved in his contacts. Xander clicked through a few of them, but they revealed little: the majority seemed to be just saying "hey" or some other greeting that Manny had never responded to. Xander wondered if someone had written the guy's number on a bathroom wall or something, because it certainly seemed like his number was out there.

Manny had saved a lot of contacts as just initials, and when those people texted him, he seemed to text back. The texts were pretty simple, lots of thank-yous and plans to meet up, and a lot of them were sent postmidnight. Xander read a few and started to get a good idea of what Manny did that made everyone so grateful.

He clicked out of the texts and into the photos. Here, Xander recognized the pattern immediately. Dozens of shots that were virtually identical, the amount of photos needed to get one that was worthy of posting. He tried not to linger on Manny's shirtless bathroom selfies and went into Instagram. Here, the DMs were as crowded as the texts, and Xander's eyebrows raised at seeing a few names that he recognized. He clicked on a conversation between Manny and a very famous rapper. It was more of the same, the brief lines of text, and then a larger one from Manny, asking the rapper when he could play him some of the new tracks he had been working on. The guy had left Manny on read. Xander felt embarrassed for him, and quickly closed the app.

He went through everything else he could think of, and found nothing out of the ordinary, except for the fact that Manny's Wordle score was *very* high. Xander leaned across the table and handed Manny his phone.

"He's clean," he said.

"So are you," Frankie said, handing Xander his. He felt himself relax a little as his fingers closed around it. "Though suspiciously so, if you ask me."

Xander swallowed. "I like to stay organized," he said, meekly. He looked around the table, and everyone seemed to display at least some degree of relief to have their phones back in their possession. The searches had turned up nothing, and Xander had to admit that made him feel kind of relieved too.

"So, what do we do now?" Celia asked.

"Now we search the island," Xander said. "There has to be someone else here." Everyone nodded in agreement.

Much of Frankie's phone was exactly as expected. The girl had a lot of pictures of herself. The only thing that really surprised Justice was Frankie's texts. She didn't get a lot of them. No group chats, and not a ton of friends. Frankie was almost all business. She texted a lot with someone that was saved in her phone as just "R." At first, Justice had thought maybe R was a boyfriend, but going through the conversations, it seemed like R was actually her manager. It looked like right up until Frankie had gotten on the helicopter to the island they were still debating whether or not she should come. R kept reminding her that she didn't have to do anything she didn't want to do, but also that her fee for this trip would recoup a lot of what they'd paid out last year. Justice found his wording odd. Paid out? It made it sound like Frankie was a bookie. But it wasn't suspicious enough to raise a flag, so Justice had handed the phone back without a word.

When Celia handed Justice's phone back to her, Justice felt relieved but also like she wanted to throw it into the ocean and never see it again. Watching Celia go through her phone had been brutal, and she had noticed that she wasn't the only one around the table who looked painfully uncomfortable. She had nothing to hide on her phone except her true self, rawly on display in the late-night, crying confessional videos she recorded when she felt desperate for someone to talk to. The whole time she'd been going through Frankie's phone, she'd kept an ear out for her own voice, but mercifully, Celia hadn't played the videos. At least not out loud. It felt like another horrible way in which her brother had been right: a smartphone was too much information concentrated in one place.

Justice's stomach growled. All she'd managed to eat was fruit leather and some nuts. Robby's confession had put her off hummus permanently, and for a brief moment she found herself jealous of the carnivores, who had miserably scarfed down beef jerky. She looked around the table at the five faces that surrounded her. Everyone looked wretched. Puffy eyes, pale faces, nails bitten down to the quick, more and more twitches emerging by the minute. Justice watched as Frankie put her sunglasses on, then took them off and put them back on top of her head, then repeated everything two seconds later.

Everyone's phone had been clean, which was the smallest balm to Justice's unraveling psyche. She still didn't want to believe that one of these people was a murderer. When Xander suggested they search the island, that there had to be someone else, hiding out among the palm trees and sand, Justice had nodded vigorously with everyone else. Celia was the only one who seemed hesitant.

"If there is someone out there," she said, "what do we do when we find them?"

Justice could see Xander's nostrils flare, and he sat up a little straighter.

"We'll make that decision when we come to it," he answered. "We'll go together, and we won't go empty-handed."

Celia didn't seem totally convinced, but it was clear that she also didn't want to be left behind. They all stood up to prepare for their expedition, filling water bottles, putting on sunscreen, stuffing what was left of the snacks into backpacks. It wasn't that easy for Xander to fulfill his promise of not going empty-handed. Not surprisingly, Unknown Island was fairly devoid of things that could be used as weapons.

He and Manny settled for destroying a chair and breaking it into pieces of wood that were somewhat sharp on the ends. Emma Jane and Celia went into the kitchen and returned with butcher knives. Justice shivered when she saw that they were engraved with Robby's initials, but she didn't think about it for too long. At this point, she was getting good at putting things out of her head. She and Frankie each grabbed one of the pieces of the broken chair, and then the search party set out.

They had barely stepped on the beach before Justice was chugging water. The sun had gone behind a cloud, and it looked like it might start to rain again soon, but that only made the air on the island oppressively humid. Justice could feel the sweat seeping uniformly out of her pores, from head to toe. When it got humid like this back home, everyone longed for thunder and lightning, and the inevitable downpour brought a collective sigh of relief. Here, even when the rain came, there would be no relief.

On the boat over, when Unknown Island had first come into sight, a thrill had run through Justice. It was so breathtaking, like a little slice of heaven that had been dropped into the middle of the ocean. The pristine white-sand beaches on one side, and the dark mountain and lush jungle on the other. As soon as she had seen the mountain, Justice had wanted to explore it. She had figured maybe she'd wake up early one morning and hike to the top to watch the sunrise and experience a perfect moment of peaceful beauty.

Now that the jungle was their destination, Justice found it ominous. "Has anyone been out here yet?" she called, and was answered by a string of nos.

They walked in a line, Xander in the front and Manny in the back. It was hardly stealthy and they certainly weren't going to sneak up on anyone, but they had agreed to stick together. A small trail snaked through the trees, and as they trudged along it, Justice saw a flame-colored bird flit through the leaves overhead, alighting for a moment on a branch of gorgeous egg-yolk-colored flowers. The air smelled like perfume, and a chorus of birds and insects rose and fell like a symphony. Sunlight drifted down through the trees, camouflaging all of them in dappled shade. Justice dug an almond out of her pocket and forced herself to chew and swallow it, hoping that it would keep her from throwing up, passing out, or both.

A new sound was audible, like a low roar in the distance. Xander had ripped apart one of his T-shirts and tied a strip of it around his head to keep the sweat from his eyes. He hiked quickly, whacking bushes out of his way with a broken chair leg. Celia and Emma Jane were both out of breath. Manny occasionally trailed behind too, but Frankie kept up. Justice climbed easily, and she had a momentary sensation of being thankful for her strong body, for the hours of swim practice that had conditioned her muscles. She knew that if all else failed, she could run and swim a long ways.

"Holy shit!" Xander yelled, coming to a stop so quickly that Justice almost crashed into him, and the others piled up behind them. The low roar had gotten louder and its source had come into view. A rushing waterfall, no bigger than an arm's width across, cascaded down the rocks into a pristine azure pool. A sharp sound from above made them all jump, and they looked up to see a flock of the flaming-red birds loop and soar above their heads.

Justice was soaked with sweat. "I wish we could go for a swim," she thought. She wondered why everyone turned to look at her, and then she realized that she had said the words out loud.

"Why can't we?" Frankie asked, and Xander nodded.

"If we all stick together, I think it should be fine," he said.

The next thing Justice knew, everyone was shedding shoes and backpacks and T-shirts, and she almost smiled for what felt like the first time in as long as she could remember.

Xander was first in the water, but she was a close second. She dove in and felt the coolness rush over her, the familiar feeling of the rest of the world disappearing, sounds and feelings muffled as she became weightless. She kicked a few strokes, gliding through the water. She should have been a mermaid, someone who never even set foot on land. When she finally broke the surface, she'd swum almost all the way across and emerged only a few yards from the waterfall. Droplets flew up and hit her face and Justice couldn't help it. She laughed with glee.

She wished she could stay here forever, but when she turned around, some of the others were already climbing out. She dove under again and swam back slowly, trying to make the moment last as long as she possibly could. When Justice got to the other side, the only person still swimming was Xander, and she realized that he'd stayed in the water to make sure she didn't need help getting out.

"I've got it," she said to him before pulling herself onto the rocks. She didn't bother to put her wet clothes back on, just slipped into her shoes. She took her scarf from her backpack and dipped it into the water, then tied it around her head.

It was clear from their slightly quicker speed that the dip had buoyed everyone's spirits, but still, no one spoke. The entire time they walked, Justice scanned the jungle around her, looking for caves where someone could hide or shelters made from branches and trees that could be used as a makeshift camp. She saw nothing.

The waterfall had been close to the highest point on the island, and in less than ten minutes, they had reached a clearing. Justice turned and took it all in. It was spectacular: dramatic views of the ocean and sky from every direction. From this high up, the water was dozens of shades of blue—she could even make out some reefs below the rippling surface.

"Oh my god," Frankie yelped, pointing. "A boat!"

Justice spun to look, and sure enough, there was a boat. It was far enough away to be just the size of a fly, but in an instant, they were all jumping and screaming and waving their arms. But the boat cruised along. Gradually, they grew still. Frankie was the last to give up as the boat disappeared on the horizon.

"I wonder if any of those other islands are inhabited," Celia said, pointing at dark smudges in the distance. Justice found herself wondering how far away they were and if she could swim it.

"We should come back up here when it gets dark and build a fire," Manny said. "Somebody might see it and come check it out."

Even though it was a good idea, no one could gather the energy to be excited. "If we're still here when it gets dark," he added.

"I really hope we're not," Justice said, and an echo of "me toos" followed.

Without a word, they all seemed to know it was time to go back. They turned and started down the mountain. Going down was easier than coming up, and it took less time to reach the beach. Justice stopped next to the pool and looked up at where they had just been. Sure, they hadn't looked behind every rock and peeked under every leaf, but still, it was pretty obvious. There was no one else on the island.

The dip in the pool under the waterfall seemed to have reminded everyone of the power of water, and it didn't take long for the group to end up in the swimming pool. Emma Jane took in everyone—all of them in the pool except for Celia, who sat on the edge and dangled her feet in the water. With every passing moment, Emma Jane was more and more convinced that the murderer was one of the five people she now shared the shallow end with. But who? And, more important, how?

The phone search they all agreed to earlier had been fruitless, and she had expected it to be. Whoever was secretly taking pictures and posting them wasn't going to do it with the phone they carried with them. This had taken months of planning, and probably millions of dollars, and no one here had the motive, or the funds. Frankie probably cleared five to six million a year, but that wasn't enough for something like this. Celia probably didn't do too bad either. Emma Jane had met a gamer at a party once who made a big deal of telling her he made seventeen million dollars the year before. He'd backed off when she'd replied, "Seventeen? Oh, what a coincidence, that's how old I am." She doubted Celia was in that echelon, but maybe two to three million. If Emma Jane was being honest with herself, she was the only one here who had access to the kind of money needed to pull off a stunt like this, and even then, she didn't really have access to it. It was her father's. "Hey, Daddy, can I borrow twenty million for a deadly game of cat and mouse?" Yeah, no.

Justice seemed like a stress case, almost a goody-two-shoes, though those types of people could really spin out when things stopped going their way. But put together something like this? No, Justice was way more likely to dump a bunch of oil in the ocean or start a forest fire when she finally broke.

That left Manny. Yeah, he was sketchy, but he was also bona fide small time, if even that, and he wasn't a liar. He had been the first one to admit that what he was accused of was true. Chelsea had admitted it also, and then Celia had confessed to Emma Jane, even if she hadn't shared her secret with everyone else. Hmm. Now she started thinking about Celia again. That was pretty smart, how she had hacked into that woman's email account. Although, as Celia had pointed out, there wasn't really any hacking involved. It was just information gathering, putting the pieces together from a puzzle scattered across the internet.

What had landed Emma Jane on the island was a selfish act of stupidity, and she was willing to bet the same held true for the rest of them. But in this case, what Celia had admitted to was different. She'd messed up not by being stupid, but by being smart. What if by letting Celia in on her suspicions earlier, Emma Jane had made a huge mistake? She couldn't do anything about that now, but Emma Jane decided she was going to be more careful. From here on out, the only person she would trust was herself.

She thought carefully about what to say. She didn't want to say the word "clues" out loud, because it was too grandiose, and also because she didn't want to let anyone know what she was thinking. If the murderer really was one of them, then they had to have left a trace somewhere, and that somewhere was highly unlikely to be out in the trees or under a waterfall. No, any clues left would be at the scenes of the crimes, or in someone's room. There was no way she was going to get to search all those places by herself, but with the peanut gallery in tow, at least there would be safety in numbers. If that was really a thing.

"I think we should keep searching," Emma Jane said. "Go through all the buildings, everyone's rooms."

"There aren't that many buildings," Manny said. "It'd be hard for someone to hide so close to all of us."

Emma Jane shook her head. "No, not for someone," she clarified. "For some*thing*. Or some *things*. We've hardly looked, and there could be something to help us get off the island or send a message. Like a two-way radio or flares."

Soon, everyone was nodding and climbing out of the pool, with only Justice hesitating, like she wanted to stay. Ultimately, though, she climbed out as well and followed the group back to the bungalows.

Searching the rooms went faster than Emma Jane had imagined it would. No one had spent much time in theirs, so aside from Margot's, which had been turned upside down and was still crawling with bees, each bungalow was pretty tidy and clean.

Luggage was searched, too. Manny and Celia both had a lot of computer equipment, his for recording music, hers for gaming. Xander had workout stuff, including a pair of dumbbells that he had put in his backpack and lugged halfway around the world, suggesting that he was a bit of a dumbbell himself. Like Emma Jane's, Frankie's was full of clothes, but hers mostly still had tags on them, and she had an inordinate number of vitamins. Justice had brought a couple of books, some blank notebooks, and several bottles of nail polish. "I thought I'd paint my toes," she said with a shrug. Promises of heaven unpacked in hell.

From there, they moved on to the kitchen, which was also sparsely furnished and had clearly been stocked just for Robby to cook his one meal. There were no closets or cabinets in the dining room, but they checked in on the screen. There were no new posts. By now, though, they knew whose photo would be shared next.

They moved on to the lounge, even though there was nothing to search there. Just the same barren room furnished with crappy furniture.

Emma Jane sighed. "Zero stars," she said. "One out of ten. Would not visit again."

She wondered briefly if she should be making jokes, then she caught Justice smiling. "What's left?" she asked. "I think we've looked everywhere."

"There's the office," Manny said. "Though it's small."

Emma Jane brightened at the suggestion. She'd forgotten about the office. Manny led the way down the hall and entered the room first. It was barely bigger than a closet, though it had a closet—its door open wide, revealing a mini fridge. Manny opened it, the cold air wafting out in clouds. It was half full of bottles of Veuve.

"I'm not even going to ask if anyone wants any champagne," he said, and slammed it closed.

Emma Jane sat down at the small desk, in the lone, uncomfortable chair. She jiggled the mouse, and the computer woke up, asking her for a password.

"Hey, Celia," she said, motioning for her to come over. "Can you do anything about this?" Emma Jane saw the girl blush and wondered if she had come too close to revealing her secret, but Celia said nothing as she and Emma Jane switched places.

"Passwords are generally pretty protected if you don't know whose password it is," she said, running her hands under the desktop and behind the monitor. Then she picked up the keyboard and looked underneath it.

"What are you doing?" Justice asked. Celia had picked up a pencil cup and was dumping all the writing utensils onto the desk.

"There's always a chance that someone wrote it down somewhere close," Celia said. "You'd be amazed at how many security breaches are due to Post-its." She pulled open the desk's only drawer, and her face lit up. "See!" She held up a tiny piece of yellow paper with a series of numbers written on it in black pen.

She closed the drawer and quickly typed the numbers in and pressed enter—and was denied. Celia scrutinized the Post-it and tried again, and then again. Emma Jane watched as the girl's fingers moved across the keyboard, referencing the numbers but typing out letters this time.

Finally, Celia shook her head. "It's not a phone number," she said, "but it's not the password, either."

"Can I see?" Emma Jane asked, and Celia held the Post-it out to her. She examined it, still stuck to the tip of Celia's middle finger. It was six digits, almost like a . . . *Oh my god.* Emma Jane looked up and across the room at the weirdest thing in the office: a large metal safe. Xander and Frankie were spinning the dial back and forth. The safe was unyielding, its contents still locked tight. Just looking at it made Emma Jane's stomach clench. She'd cracked a safe once, and it had been the second worst thing she'd ever done.

The first time she and Sergio had hooked up, he had surprised her. He had always been so sweet, so gentle, that she hadn't expected him to take control, hands in her hair, pulling her head back so that he could kiss her neck. Emma Jane liked it, and it was the first time, ever, that she'd been with someone and not faked it, not one bit. From that moment on, it felt like she was addicted to him. If she went more than a day without seeing him, she couldn't sleep, felt dizzy. And then when they were together, even an inch of air between them felt like too much. She wanted him all the time, and he wanted her just as bad.

It was like a game. They'd pass a tree and he'd pull her behind it. They'd walk down a hall and she'd shove him into whichever room happened to be open, kissing furiously surrounded by mops and brooms or up next to a water heater. That was how they'd ended up in the bedroom closet at that party. They'd been quick and quiet and were fixing themselves up, catching their breath and exchanging suddenly shy glances, when Emma Jane spotted the safe. It was just on a lark that she walked over to it. It was a combination lock, and she wanted to see if she could open it. She and Melanie were forever cracking into each other's lockers in junior high. It was easy. So she'd spun the dial, not actually expecting it to open. Now, Emma Jane swallowed. Irony, cruel, cruel irony: opening that safe was what had ultimately brought her to this one. She pulled the Post-it off Celia's finger and walked toward it, Xander and Frankie making way for her.

"No way. Do you think . . . ?" Justice said.

"I don't know," Emma Jane said, "but I'm going to try."

"Wait!" Suddenly, Manny was at her side. "Don't open it," he said.

Emma Jane looked at him, surprised. "We don't even know if I can," she said.

"Of course you can," he said. "No one puts a giant safe in the middle of a room and then leaves the combination to that safe in the very same room unless they want someone to open it."

Someone laughed uneasily.

"Whoever is behind all of this isn't stupid," Manny continued. "They want us to open it."

"What do you think could be in there?" Xander asked. "You think it might blow up?"

"I have no idea," Manny said. "The only thing I'm sure of is that it's a trap."

"But what if it's not?" Emma Jane asked.

"Do you really believe that?" he said.

"Of course I don't," she said. "But I know that I can't be on this island, where someone is trying to kill us all, and find the combination to a safe and then not open it!"

"Don't you see? We keep playing into their hands," Manny said. "We're doing everything they want us to do, and we don't even know who they are."

"I don't think we have any other options," Emma Jane said. "I'm going to open it."

She faced the safe again and before she knew it, Manny had snatched the piece of paper out of her hand.

"Okay," he said. "Then I'll do it. Everyone else go wait in the hall."

"What the hell?" Emma Jane shot back. "So that you can get first dibs on whatever is in there?"

He scowled at her. "No," he said, his voice flat. "So that if it blows up, it won't take us all with it."

"Nice try, Mr. Chivalry," she said, "but you're not getting me out of here until I see what's in that safe."

"Um, I will happily wait in the hall," Frankie offered.

"Me too," Justice added, and Celia and Xander both nodded.

"I'd go farther than the hall," Manny said, his gaze still fixed on Emma Jane. "Like maybe out by the pool."

Emma Jane heard the other four shuffle out into the hall and then it was just her and Manny and the safe. She thought for a second about asking him if he remembered her, but then, they'd never really met. Just exchanged a few messages on a night that never really came together, and who hadn't had a million of those?

She snatched the paper back from him and turned to the task at hand. She spun the dial to the right and stopped on ten. Then she spun it back and stopped on twenty-seven, and then right again, stopping finally on eighteen. Then she gestured at the handle. "Since you are such a gentleman," she said, "I'll let you do the honors."

"No way," Manny said. "Ladies fir—"

The words weren't even out of his mouth before Emma Jane grabbed the handle, twisted it, and yanked the door open. There were no explosions, but what they saw made them both suck in a quick breath of air. The safe was empty except for a handgun.

"You were right," Emma Jane said. "It was a trap."

CHAPTER SEVEN

Thunder crashed, and they all jumped. The rain had started again. In the hall, Frankie felt like she was going to crawl out of her skin. They must have opened the safe by now, and there hadn't been an explosion. In fact, there were no sounds coming from the office at all. Panic seized her. What if the safe held something that could help them get off the island, and Emma Jane and Manny were keeping it to themselves? She turned and ran.

She careered into the office to find Emma Jane and Manny standing there, staring at the open safe.

"What is it?" she asked breathlessly, and Manny stepped aside so that she could see. The safe was empty except for a gun. "Oh," Frankie said, her heart still pounding. "Is it loaded?"

"Who knows?" Manny said. "I'm not touching it."

Emma Jane nodded in agreement. "I don't think anyone should touch it," she said.

"What's going on? What was in the safe?" Xander asked from the doorway. He, Celia, and Justice had followed Frankie, and now everyone was back in the office.

"A gun," Frankie said. "We don't know if it's loaded." She looked down at it. She had never held a gun before, hadn't even seen one in years, not since her mom had stopped dating that guy who was into the NRA. She'd always thought of herself as anti-gun, but now she wanted it. A gun was protection. If used correctly, it could protect her, protect all of them, from . . . someone.

"What should we do with it?" she asked.

"Nothing." Manny stepped forward and slammed the safe door closed. "If Unknown Island is giving us anything, it's not for our benefit. How do we lock this so that it stays locked?"

"We can reset the combination," Emma Jane said. "Three people can pick one number each, and then no one person can open it."

Frankie felt the panic rise in her again, but she wasn't sure how she could stop this without looking suspicious, at least not right now. Maybe she could make it so that she picked one of the numbers and then she could convince the other two people to tell her what number they had picked.

"How do we pick who gets to choose a number?" Celia asked, and they all looked at each other.

"Rock-paper-scissors," Emma Jane said, taking charge. "Line up, three and three, facing each other. The winner from each game picks a number."

Frankie bit her tongue to keep from protesting aloud. Rock-paper-scissors was too random. There was no way for her to make sure she was chosen to pick a number. They should vote, she thought, vote on the three picked. It would all be in how she suggested it. . . .

But before she could say anything, everyone was lining up

and she had no choice but to join them. Justice versus Manny, Celia versus Emma Jane, and Xander across from her. She just had to beat him, which should be easy. He certainly wasn't that smart, so what was he likely to throw? Rock! Xander was brute strength, so of course he would throw rock! And she would throw paper! No one ever expected paper!

Justice threw rock and was covered by Manny's paper. Emma Jane threw scissors and was crushed by Celia's rock. Frankie triumphantly threw paper, but then Xander messed it up. He threw scissors and cut Frankie's paper to shreds!

The gun, her hope, her protection, was receding further and further from her grasp, and Frankie felt like she might cry. She forced herself to be quiet. If she couldn't have the gun, the next best thing she could do was make sure that everyone liked her. She just had to be the nice girl, everybody's favorite, the person no one would ever suspect. She could do that. She'd been doing that for years, she'd made a career out of it. Frankie made herself smile.

"I hate guns," she said. "I'm so glad we're locking it back up."

"No shit," Justice said.

Emma Jane stepped up to the safe, opened the door, and turned the dial several times to the right. "This will make it so that we can reset the combination," she said.

Frankie wanted to ask how she knew so much about safes but figured that pointed questions were not how she would make Emma Jane like her.

Xander went first. "Nobody look," he said, and everyone turned around. He entered his number, then Manny, and Celia went last. When they were done, someone shut the door and they all turned back around. No one knew what they should do next.

Celia wanted to go back to her room to be alone, but they had agreed that no one was going off by themselves. The bungalows were too small for everyone to be in one, and it was raining, so they sat in the lounge. Celia on one end of the couch, Justice on the other, Emma Jane in the lone chair, and Xander, Frankie, and Manny sprawled on the floor.

There was a bit more airflow in this room, so it wasn't as stifling. It was also a room that no one had died in. At least, not yet. Every fifteen minutes, they'd make a group trek to the dining room to check the screen, but so far Unknown Island was staying silent. No new posts.

Celia thought of her parents. Were they checking her feed, waiting for pics of glamorous dinners and smiling selfies with Frankie Russh? Maybe they were wondering why she hadn't posted anything yet, but then she reminded herself that she hadn't been on the island for half a day. Her parents had to at least be checking Unknown Island's feed and wondering what the heck was going on. Perhaps they had texted her about it and were concerned that she hadn't replied.

Surely people all over the world were looking at what Unknown Island was posting and wondering why they'd gone so off-brand. Maybe people were starting to get concerned. But then, maybe not. Maybe they thought Unknown was trying to start some new trend. Maybe it already had, and rhyming couplets were popping up in the captions of all sorts of accounts. Still, it likely didn't matter either way. There was a vast canyon between commenting about your concern and actually doing something about it.

It was hard to predict what was going to happen on the internet. Her family had learned that the hard way with Caroline. After she'd killed herself, she got almost a million new followers overnight, and the comments on her posts became real-time battlegrounds. It was shocking what horrible things people would say about the dead, even when the dead had just died. After a few days, Celia had deleted Caroline's accounts. She was tired of everyone feeling like they were entitled to a piece of her sister.

Across the room, Xander stood up, and the movement rippled through all of them. "I'm going to go get in the pool," he announced.

"There's lightning," Frankie said. "It's dangerous."

Xander laughed. "It's dangerous in here," he said.

"I'll go with you," Justice said, standing up. "I'm tired of sitting here."

"Well, we're sticking together," Manny said, "so if you guys go, we all go."

That was how Celia found herself sitting in the rain, wondering how the black-and-white snake had gotten itself out of the pool.

Manny sat by the side of the pool and then lay down. He barely felt the rain, but the warm cement under his back reminded him of being a little kid lying on the ground to soak up the heat after swimming. His mom had called him a lizard.

The gun made him nervous, even more nervous than before.

Their plan had been solid, locking it back up and changing the combination so that no one could open it, but still. Unknown Island had wanted them to find the gun, so he doubted it was just going to go away so easily. Shutting monsters in the closet doesn't make them disappear. The thing about monsters is that they're patient. They can sit forever, just waiting for someone to open the door.

Manny's eyes shifted to Frankie. She was sitting with her knees tucked up under her chin. Manny still wanted to talk to her, but he had no idea what to say. How do you make small talk when you've just witnessed four murders and one of you might be next? He knew that her trying to escape in the boat without him was a red flag, but instead of making him like her less, it had made him like her more. She, too, was only human.

Back home, he imagined that she was the kind of girl he'd make a dinner reservation for. There would be no late-night "wyd" texts. It would be calls on Tuesday to make plans for Saturday, that kind of thing. He shut his brain off from going there. It hurt too much to think about home, to think about all the things he wanted to do differently. Over the past couple of years, he had perfected the art of living in the moment. It was a survival technique, because it had been too painful to think about the past. Now it was too painful to think about the future.

Swimming laps gave Justice's body something to do while her mind raced. Instead of doing flip turns at the wall like she normally would, though, she stood up briefly each time. Listening, hoping to hear something. A helicopter, a boat, her parents yelling at her on the phone, telling her to stay right where she was, that they were on their way and she was grounded for life. Justice would happily take grounding for life, because it would mean that she was still alive.

She'd lost count of how many laps she'd swum, and she didn't want to tire herself out too much, so she stopped and flipped over on her back to float. The day had become elastic, moments compressed or stretched beyond her comprehension. Four dead bodies in one morning, death coming faster than they could blink, but now each minute felt like a lifetime. "How long have we been out here?" she asked.

"An hour and fifteen minutes," Celia called back. "Seventeen if we're being precise."

Justice looked over. Celia had taken on a gnome-like shape, huddled under a beach towel, her glasses speckled with rain.

Emma Jane pushed herself up from where she'd been lying. "I think we should go see if anything has been posted," she said.

Justice stood up in the water. "I don't want to," she said. "I don't want to know, I don't want to look, I don't want to give it the satisfaction of an audience."

Emma Jane nodded. "I know," she said. "I don't either, but even if we ignore it, it's not going to go away."

Justice nodded. She knew this. She knew that whatever happened online kept happening even when you closed the computer, but she wanted to pretend, just for a moment, that it didn't.

But this wasn't that moment. She swam over and pulled herself up and out of the pool. She took a few steps, meaning to grab her headscarf from where she'd dropped it before diving in, but it was gone. Justice spun in a circle, scanning the pavement around the pool, but the bright red piece of fabric was gone.

"Where's my scarf?" she asked. "I dropped it right here before I got in the pool."

Celia stood up, her wet towel pooling into a puddle on the ground. "Are you sure you had it?" she asked.

"Yeah, I was definitely wearing it," Justice said. "I've been wearing it the whole time I've been here." Frankie joined the search too, but Justice could tell that the two girls were just being nice. After sitting out in the rain, by now her scarf would be as wet as if she'd worn it in the pool. There was no way it had blown away. Maybe she hadn't had it. Maybe she was losing her mind. Justice really, really wanted to go home.

She followed the rest of the group inside to check the screen, but there were no new posts.

The rain had stopped and the sun was setting. Xander looked out over the ocean, at the flat line of the horizon and the orange and pink reflected in the rippling water. The sunset made him feel cold. It marked a full day on Unknown Island, a day that had lasted years.

All afternoon they had checked the screen. All afternoon they had waited. Nothing had happened. They switched positions around the pool. Sitting, lying, swimming, feet in, feet out. Now Frankie paced up and down the side, her arms wrapped tightly around her stomach.

Xander wondered if they were thinking what he was thinking. It seemed like such an absurd thought, yet at the same time, an obvious one. They'd been together all afternoon, and nothing had happened. No one had died, and no new posts had gone up.

Staying together kept them safe. Because one of them was a murderer.

Xander kept telling himself he had nothing to fear. He just had to keep his wits about him. He was larger than everyone here. He could wrap Celia around his neck and wear her like a scarf. Manny was his only real competition, and while Xander figured that Manny had been around enough to know how to throw a punch, Xander still had several inches and about thirty-five pounds on him. He just had to make sure no one snuck up on him. Robby clearly hadn't been paying attention.

But there was a gun, and Xander figured that whoever had put that gun in the safe also knew how to get it out, even with a new combination. There was no way to outweigh, or outlast, a gun. His mind went in circles, like one of those snakes that won't stop eating its tail. Also, Xander was hungry, and he could never think straight when he was hungry. Finally, he stood up.

"We should gather firewood," he said. "When the sun goes down completely, we should do what Manny suggested earlier and climb back up that cliff and build a fire."

"Everything is soaked," Emma Jane said. "I don't know how we're going to find any dry wood."

"We have to find something," Xander said. "A fire is the only way we're going to get someone out here, and if the rain holds off, we don't want to waste time."

"The furniture in the lobby is wood," Celia pointed out. "And in the dining room, too."

They all stood there for a second, just looking at each other, and then Xander broke into a run. He leaped down onto the sand and then up onto the boardwalk and was in the lobby in two steps. He picked up the first piece of furniture he could find, a side table, raised it over his head, and then brought it crashing down onto the floor. Two of the legs broke off and the top splintered in half. He felt a surge of joy, like when he'd just completed a nearly impossible pass.

He heard a loud crack and turned around to see that Frankie had picked up a chair and was hitting it as hard as she could against the wall. Xander walked over and helped Justice upend the lightweight couch, flipping it over quickly so that one of the arms broke off when it landed on the floor. Justice started kicking the remaining arm and had soon dislodged it enough that Xander could wrench it off. He smiled. This was the most fun he'd had all day. And then Emma Jane yelled.

Emma Jane and Celia had gone into the dining room to gather the chairs and anything else they could find that might burn. Celia was the first to take a chair and smash it on the floor, and then Emma Jane joined in and it felt great. Destructive. A small way of getting back at Unknown Island. A small, insignificant, inconsequential way, but a way nonetheless.

Emma Jane had smashed one chair pretty thoroughly and was raising a second over her head to bring it down hard on the ground when she noticed that while they were busy smashing furniture, Unknown Island had posted a new photo. It was, of course, of Robby, hard at work in the kitchen, his apron on and a towel thrown over his shoulder. He was concentrating on the task at hand, sprinkling herbs onto the plates of biscuits and gravy on the counter. Someone could have stood quietly in the doorway and snapped away, and Robby wouldn't have even noticed them. Emma Jane tried to remember breakfast, or right before it, who was sitting at the table and who was up and about, but it was futile. At that time all she'd been paying attention to was how crappy the hotel was, and how crappy she felt.

Her scream caused everyone to stop smashing and come running. She could hear their breathing as they gathered behind her.

"I don't . . . ," Celia started. "I mean, it's three rhymes, instead of two, and this caption doesn't even make sense!" And then she read aloud, "'Robby Wade's goose is cooked, funny how little it took. For the five to stay alive, the sixth must leave, no time to grieve.'"

Celia was right only about the rhymes, though, because the caption made perfect sense to Emma Jane. "It wants us to kill someone," she said. Frankie laughed.

"You've got to be kidding," she said. "That's insane."

"Exactly," Emma Jane said.

"Fuck that," Frankie said. "Nobody is killing anybody. We're sticking together." Celia reached her hand out, then paused before she touched the screen.

"Do we even want to read the comments?" she asked.

"No!" the five of them answered in unison, and she withdrew her hand.

Emma Jane was trying to think. She read the caption again, and again. "If we do what it says and kill someone, then it succeeds in turning us all into the murderers it has already accused us of being," she said.

"It doesn't say 'kill,'" Frankie said. "It says 'leave.'"

"Poetic license," Emma Jane said. "But what if the message is straightforward? What if it's telling us how to save our own lives?"

"Okay, Sylvia Plath, how is it doing that?" Frankie asked.

In spite of herself, Emma Jane cracked a smile. She had to give credit where credit was due—that was a good one.

"One of us is the murderer," she said. "We figure out who that is and get rid of them, and then the other five stay alive. Just like it says."

"*If*," Frankie added. "*If* one of us is the murderer."

"Of course," Emma Jane said, even though she didn't really believe it. "*If*."

"Come on, it's getting dark," Manny said, changing the subject. "We want to climb up while there's still some light. It won't be easy, carrying all this wood. We need matches, lighter fluid, and flashlights, if we can find them."

"Ha!" Emma Jane barked a laugh. "There won't be any flashlights on this island. Not deadly enough."

"I don't know about that," Xander said. "I think you could definitely kill someone with a Maglite."

He had a point, Emma Jane thought, so maybe they could find a flashlight after all.

Just as Emma Jane had predicted, there were no flashlights. In the kitchen, they found one book of matches that Robby must have brought from home—they were embossed with a gold Hock & Jowl logo—and a half-empty bottle of lighter fluid. It wasn't much, but it would have to do. After that, everyone went back to their rooms to grab backpacks and shoulder bags and anything else that would be useful for hauling broken furniture up a cliff.

Celia couldn't be certain, but she was pretty sure that today was the first time she'd ever been hiking, and now she was doing it twice. Her family wasn't outdoorsy, and Celia herself would have been the first to admit that she was an indoor kid. One doesn't get really good at video games by playing outside.

The hike up the cliff in the afternoon had been hot, but now that they were carrying packs filled with broken furniture, each step felt like the last mile of a marathon. Celia's heart pounded, and she couldn't catch her breath—the humidity felt like being underwater. Manny led, and he moved quickly. When Celia paused, about a quarter of the way up, Xander offered to carry her bag for her, and she agreed with a "thanks" as she handed it to him. The truth was, though, that a bunch of broken chair legs didn't actually weigh all that much and handing her backpack off barely made a difference. She was still struggling.

They were almost at the top of the mountain when Celia lost her footing and careered forward. She yelped and managed to catch herself, sharp rocks digging into her palms, but that was nothing compared to the pain that ripped through her shin. Justice and Xander were instantly by her side, Xander not even asking before he lifted Celia up. Celia glanced down and saw a rivulet of red running down her leg.

"Are you okay?" Justice asked breathlessly. "Nothing's broken, right?" Fear was visible on both her and Xander's faces, not just because of Celia's injury, she realized, but for anything out of the ordinary that might snap the already thin filament of their plan.

"I'm fine," Celia said, glancing down at her leg again before quickly looking away. She pointed and flexed her toes, then rolled her ankle. "Nothing's broken. I just don't like looking at blood."

Emma Jane, Frankie, and Manny had turned back, and everyone gathered around Celia while Justice opened her Hydro Flask and dumped some water over Celia's leg. Celia winced.

"It's not deep," Justice said. "More like a scrape." Celia nodded.

"I hate to say it," Manny said, "but we have to keep going. The sun's almost down and we don't want to have to try to get this fire going in the dark."

Celia nodded and started to push herself to her feet.

"You all go ahead," Frankie said, shrugging off her backpack full of furniture and then holding it out to Manny. "I'll stay with her and we'll catch up later." Manny hesitated before he took Frankie's bag.

"Are you sure?" he asked, looking first at Frankie and then at Celia. "I don't like splitting up."

"We're sure," Celia said, getting to her feet. "I don't want to hold anyone up."

Manny nodded as he hooked Frankie's bag over his shoulder and then turned back to the others, the four of them resuming their hike. Celia watched them go and then took a few steps. Even without the pain blossoming across her shin, she doubted she would have been able to keep up. Frankie reached out and touched her elbow.

"You okay?" she asked, and Celia nodded.

"Thanks for staying with me," she said.

"No problem," Frankie told her. "I do think we should get going, though. We don't have to keep up with them, but we don't want to fall too far behind, because—"

Celia didn't let her finish. "Yeah, I know," she said, and started limping up the trail. "I'm already dreading coming back down in the dark."

"I know," Frankie said, and screwed up her face like she was thinking hard. "It's tough out here, too, because all you can hear is the wind and the waterfall."

"I know," Celia said. "It sounds just like my white noise machine."

Frankie gave a little smile. "Under other circumstances, I would have enjoyed laughing at that."

Celia nodded and they climbed in silence for a few moments.

"Do you think what Emma Jane said is true?" Frankie asked.

"What do you mean?"

"That the killer is one of the six of us, and that if we figure out who, and kill them, then we'll save our lives," she said.

Celia paused for a moment before answering. "I don't know," she said, finally. "Maybe, but maybe not. It seems very open to interpretation, and to jump to that conclusion . . . that would make everyone a murderer."

"I think you're right, in that killing isn't the only interpretation," Frankie said. "But I do think she was right in one way."

"How so?" Celia asked. They were close to the top now, and the splash of the waterfall was even louder, so she had to raise her voice to make sure Frankie heard her.

"I think the island is telling us that we have to get rid of someone," Frankie said, taking a big step up over a large rock and then turning to Celia and holding out her hand. "I think that's what it's saying. We have to vote someone off, or else it will do it for us."

Celia grabbed Frankie's hand and let her help pull her up. "But how do we vote someone off?" she asked. "There's no place for them to go."

"There's the boat," Frankie said.

"Yeah, but Manny said it doesn't have gas," Celia said, wondering what Frankie was trying to say. "It's not going to go far."

"I know," Frankie said. "But it can drift. It might actually be a good idea. Maybe they'll run into another boat or something. If we put someone in the boat and send them out to sea, they might even get rescued faster than the rest of us."

"And then it fulfills the island's request," Celia said. It came out almost like a question.

"Yeah, it does," Frankie said.

"And you think that if we do this, then no one else will die?"

Frankie sighed. "I don't know," she said. "But if this fire doesn't work, we have to try something."

Celia nodded. "It's actually not a bad idea," she said, truthfully.

Frankie let out a breath. "I'm glad you're on my side," she said, just as they crested the top of the mountain.

The sky was awash in pinks and oranges and otherworldly light, and Frankie headed over to help the others build a fire. For a second, Celia stood there, watching her. She'd said it wasn't a bad idea. She hadn't said anything about being on Frankie's side.

• • •

Xander had never been a Boy Scout, but even he knew that these were not the ideal conditions for building a fire. They had hiked up the mountain to the tallest point, just beyond the waterfall, and stopped at a patch of flat, exposed ground. Under almost any other conceivable circumstances, the spot would have been breathtaking. A steep plunge down to the sea on one side, lush jungle on the other, and a storm-cloud-tainted sky playing host to the last glimmer of a spectacular sunset as the darkness rolled in.

But the open expanse meant wind, and the ground was wet, so their task wouldn't be easy. They gathered a few rocks to make a platform so that their meager pile of wood didn't have to sit in the mud. The pieces of wood had been a pain in the ass to drag up, and now, as they tried to stack them into a bonfire, they looked pathetic. Xander glanced around. He itched from head to toe, his skin dotted with large red welts. Bug bites that were probably poisonous. Celia sat off to the side, the blood on her skin drying to a rust color. Emma Jane had a streak of mud across her face, and Justice's hands were caked with it. Only Frankie, sitting next to Celia, still looked somewhat like herself. The rest of them looked feral and suddenly, Emma Jane's suggestion didn't seem so ridiculous. They were all here because they had been accused of murder, so maybe they were capable of it as well.

Xander joined Emma Jane, who was staring at their lame excuse for firewood. "You really think the murderer is one of us?" he asked.

"I'm not talking to anyone privately," she said.

Surprised, Xander fell back a step. "What?" he pressed.

"If the murderer is one of us, that means it could be you," she said. "Or me."

"You can't be serious," Xander said. "I haven't killed anyone here."

"I am serious," she said, spinning around. "Listen up! All of you! We can't pretend this isn't happening. We are kidding ourselves if we think that someone's going to see our burning pile of chairs and come rescue us!" Xander turned back to the pile of wood and tried to block Emma Jane out. "No one is coming! We have to take matters into our own hands!" Emma Jane was still shouting as Xander took out the bottle of lighter fluid and doused the wood with the accelerant.

"You're insane!" Manny shouted at Emma Jane. "We're not murderers."

"Five of us aren't," Emma Jane shot back. "And one of us is! And one of us is going to be next. Or all of us, unless we do something about it!"

Now Frankie was yelling too. "You need to shut up!" she screamed at Emma Jane. "You are not helping anything! We need to stick together and we need to stay calm!"

"I'm perfectly calm!" Emma Jane wasn't backing down. "I'm the only one here who is. Go on, burn your chairs. Burn everything you can, and when the fire dies down, we're still going to be here! No one is going to save us, that's why we have to save ourselves!"

Justice started yelling then, about how they were all sitting ducks. Xander heard one of the girls—maybe Frankie—yell something about the gun. Xander lit one of the seven matches and tossed it onto the pile. With a *whoosh*, the lighter fluid caught and the pieces of furniture went up in flames. The smoke was acrid and black, but they had their bonfire and the yelling stopped.

Celia hobbled up to join the rest of them. "Wait," she said, her voice at a normal volume. "Frankie had a good idea."

Fire was supposed to be regal, powerful red and orange flames that licked the sky and sent out showers of sparks. But this fire was sad, more a scurrying mouse than a roaring lion. The furniture must have been treated with something that made it fire-resistant. The flames were small and blue, and the smoke smelled like chemicals. Frankie's eyes watered and her throat itched, and she could tell by all the coughing that she wasn't the only one.

Xander tried to stoke the fire with an arm of the couch, but it was a hopeless endeavor. This fire wasn't going to save them. Everyone moved as a group, trying to avoid the smoke, but the wind wasn't going to let them off so easy. Wherever they moved, it followed, and it was picking up more and more, sending out little gusts that would have felt refreshing any other time.

"Let's hear this good idea," Justice said, holding her T-shirt up over her nose and mouth, trying to make it easier to breathe. Their circle had widened, everyone trying to stay away from the heat and the fumes from the fire, and they all sat at the edge of the firelight, more than half into the shadows.

"We don't have to kill anyone," Frankie said. "We just have to vote them off."

"Ha," Emma Jane said. "And how are we going to do that? Put them in time-out and make them go sit on the stairs?"

Frankie swallowed and told herself to remain calm. Nightfall and the dying fire were making them all desperate, that was clear. Frankie could see it in their faces and their bodies, the way Manny looked at everyone, the way Justice stood away from the group, the way Xander didn't speak and just kept trying to stoke the fire. But desperation didn't have to make them murderers, and Frankie didn't see why Emma Jane couldn't understand that.

"We put them in the boat," Frankie said, simply, "and send them out to sea."

"So they die a slow death," Emma Jane said, and Frankie shook her head.

"Not necessarily," she said. "They could be found, they could be rescued before the rest of us." Frankie dug into her backpack and pulled out a notebook and pen. "We don't have to vote out loud," she said. "We can each write down the name of who we think should leave the island, and then count the votes."

"Wait a minute," Emma Jane said. "So is getting voted off a punishment or a privilege? Are we voting for who we think is the murderer or who we think deserves the best chance to get rescued?"

Frankie sighed. "I don't know," she said. "Everyone has to decide that for themselves." Frankie did know, though. Deep down, she knew that her idea wasn't all that different from Emma Jane's. Maybe there was a slim chance that sending someone out to sea to drift around, during a storm, in a part of the world that was known for its big-wave surfing, would get them rescued. The most appealing thing about Frankie's plan, though, was that it let them pretend it was a possibility.

"And who's going to count the votes?" Emma Jane asked.

"I don't know," Frankie said, trying to keep her voice calm. "It doesn't matter. I can read them first. . . ."

"Of course you can," Emma Jane sneered. Frankie stifled a sigh, frustrated that Emma Jane was making it so difficult.

"And then everyone else can read them, too, okay?" she said. "Unless you want us all to read together on the count of three, someone has to read them first, and it was my idea, so I'm volunteering."

"Fine," Emma Jane said, so Frankie went on. She took a piece of paper and folded it in half and licked the crease. Then she folded that half into thirds and licked the crease again. When she tore the paper, it tore easily and cleanly, and she had six identical squares of paper. She passed them around the circle and everyone took one. Then she held her pen up. "Keep your eyes closed until the pen comes to you," she said. "And write in block letters if you're worried about your hand-writing giving you away."

It was like the sun had started its descent slowly, and then all of a sudden plummeted past the horizon. It was dark now, and she could barely see everyone's faces in the orange glow of the fire. They all nodded and then closed their eyes. Frankie bent her head and wrote. From the moment she'd had the idea, Frankie knew who she was going to vote for. She had known who everyone was going to vote for, because after she'd suggested that they needed to unite and kill someone, it was obvious that Emma Jane had to go. The girl was trying to bring them all down to her level, that was her sick game. With each letter Frankie wrote, she became more and more convinced— Emma Jane was the murderer. She had to be.

Frankie folded her paper in half and passed the pen to Justice, who was on her right. Then Frankie closed her eyes and waited. In the darkness, she listened to the crackle of the fire. The wind that was picking up, ruffling her hair and clothes. Someone coughed, no doubt from the smoke, and then the wind shifted and Frankie coughed too. Then someone was putting the pen back in her hand. Frankie opened her eyes and held out her hands, and one by one, everyone deposited their slips of paper into her outstretched palms. As each vote was delivered, Frankie felt herself getting calmer and calmer. They were about to get Emma Jane off the island. That might not make them safe, but Frankie was sure it would make them safer.

Everyone sat back down and Frankie stood up. The moon was behind the clouds and the sky was totally dark now. Frankie took a few steps and then kneeled by the fire, close enough so that she could read the votes by its weak light. The smoke instantly overwhelmed her nostrils and made them sting. The wind changed direction again, pushing everyone else back farther.

She unfolded the first piece of paper and kept herself from smiling as she read EMMA JANE spelled out in block letters. She smoothed the piece of paper and put it on the ground in front of her. Then she unfolded the second one and kept her face blank as she read her own name. She was surprised to see that someone had voted for her, but then, it was probably Emma Jane herself, since she must suspect by now that Frankie was on to her. She smoothed out that vote and lay it on top of the other.

She unfolded the third, and a shock went through her. Who

would vote for Celia? She placed that awful vote with the other two. Then a vote for Manny, and another vote for Celia. Seeing Celia's name shocked Frankie even more than seeing her own. It felt so cruel, and in that moment, Frankie knew her earlier instincts, to protect Celia, had been right.

Frankie felt her breathing quicken. This wasn't what she had expected. She had thought that everyone else could see what she saw, but instead, they were blind and cruel. There was only one vote left, and she was glad for the cover of darkness as she opened it, because otherwise she was sure that the rest of them would see her hands shaking. The final piece of paper was blank. Someone hadn't voted. Frankie swallowed and looked up. There was no way she could let anyone else see these votes. She knew what she had to do. "Emma Jane," she said, "it's time for you to go."

Manny hated this. He hated where they had ended up and he hated where they seemed to be going. When the pen had come to him, he had held it over the paper and found that his hand wouldn't move. So he had passed the pen on and left his piece of paper blank. Let it play out, he thought. He knew that everyone was desperate and that they all felt like they needed to do something, and if this was what they felt like they needed to do, then so be it. When they were putting someone in the boat, wading out to waist-deep waters to push it on its way into oblivion, they'd realize the magnitude of what they were about to do, they'd stop then. And if they didn't, he'd stop them.

"Emma Jane," Frankie said, "it's time for you to go."

Emma Jane scrambled to her feet.

"You're lying," she hissed at Frankie.

Frankie stood up, too. In the darkness, both girls' features were smudges as the firelight flitted across their faces.

"I'm not lying," Frankie yelled. "We all agreed! This was your idea in the first place!"

"The only person here that would have voted for me is you!" Emma Jane shouted back. "Because you're threatened by me! You don't really think I'm the killer, you think I'm competition!"

"You got the most votes!" Frankie screamed. Now everyone was standing, their gazes volleying back and forth between the two girls like they were watching a tennis match.

"I want to see the votes!" Emma Jane shrieked.

"Fine!" Frankie hissed back. "There they are!" She gestured at the pile of paper on the ground, but when they all looked, there was just one piece of paper remaining. While they had been watching Emma Jane and Frankie fight, the wind had blown the votes into the fire.

Someone gasped as the wind picked up the last square of paper and sent it dancing across the mud into the darkness.

"You sneaky bitch!" Emma Jane yelled as she darted after it. "You did that on purpose!"

"I did not!" Frankie yelled back. "It was an accident!"

Emma Jane ran away from the fire chasing the lone remaining vote.

"Ha!" she called out. "I can barely read it, but I can tell this one's blank! You—" And then she screamed. And kept screaming, only it sounded like the scream was getting farther and farther away.

Manny jumped to his feet, wondering why that was, and then it hit him—Emma Jane had fallen over the side.

Feeling around carefully with each step, Manny made his way to the cliff's edge. Behind him, everyone was talking and someone was crying, but he kept his attention focused in front of him.

"Emma Jane!" he called out. "Can you hear me? Are you okay?" He was met with only the sound of crashing waves, and his blood went cold. "Emma Jane?" he called again.

Earlier, Manny had taken his T-shirt and ripped it into shreds, and then tied those shreds around the top of a stick. He planned to use it as a torch to light their way back down the trail, but now he felt his way back toward the dying fire, and squirted the last of the lighter fluid on the T-shirt shreds, then touched it to the flames. With the torch lighting his way, he hurried back to the edge and got down on his hands and knees to peer over the side.

In the dark, it was hard to tell what shape was what, but in the small light cast from his torch, he could just make out something about twenty feet down. It wasn't moving. "Emma Jane?" he called again, softer this time.

Justice and Xander had joined him, one on each side. "Can you see her?" Justice asked.

"I don't know," Manny said. He turned and held the flaming stick out to Xander. "Hold it out so I can climb down."

Xander nodded and took it, then dropped to his stomach and held the torch as far as he could over the edge.

"Be careful, dude," he said, but Manny didn't answer, all of his attention focused as he lowered himself over the side. It wasn't a straight drop, but it was steep, and there were large rocks every few feet. Manny kept a tight grip on a branch above him as he felt around with his feet for a hold. When he found one, he gripped another branch and lowered himself a little farther down. The light from the torch wasn't much, and Manny thought it actually made things worse, because the shadows didn't stay still and he constantly thought he was seeing things moving on the side of the cliff. Shadows, animals, ghosts . . .

From above, Xander and Justice were trying to be helpful, telling him where to reach, where to put his feet, but Manny tuned them out and went by what he felt. He was about ten feet from the top, still only halfway to the dark shape that he thought might be Emma Jane. He called out to it. No answer. Manny knew he couldn't go any farther, so he started to climb back up the way he had come. When he was close to the top, he held up a hand, and Xander grabbed on, pulling him up and over the top. The three of them sat there in silence.

Manny looked at the fire. It had almost totally died out, and Frankie and Celia sat huddled together, their arms around one another, one or both of them crying softly.

"So?" Justice asked, and Manny shook his head.

"I don't know," he said. "I couldn't see anything, and I didn't hear anything." As he spoke, the clouds parted, revealing the moon. It was full, and it cast enough light that they could suddenly see clearly. It was eerie, as if the clouds were trying to help them out. Justice flattened herself on her stomach to look over the edge and Manny followed suit.

"What do you see?" Xander asked.

"Nothing," Justice answered. Manny nodded as he pushed

himself back. Emma Jane was nowhere to be seen. They had done what she wanted them to do. Even if they hadn't meant to, they'd killed someone. Manny felt dizzy and rolled over, the wet ground beneath his back, and stared at the moon. A few hours before, when he'd searched Emma Jane's phone, he'd opened up her DMs and been shocked to see a conversation with himself. She'd been in Miami and someone had given her his name. She'd reached out, asking if he could hook her up. They'd gone back and forth a bit, and then he'd stopped responding. He tried to remember the particulars of that night, where he was and who he was with and why he never came through for her, but the truth was, he couldn't remember. His whole life was littered with those conversations. He'd thought he was keeping things low-key, but he was kidding himself. Everyone knew. That was what he was known for, that was why he was here, with yet another loop he would never close.

Xander stood over him and held out a hand. Manny took it and let himself be pulled up. No one spoke as they gathered their stuff, then started back down the way they had come. Xander led, carrying the torch, but it turned out they didn't need it. With the full moon out now, there was plenty of light, and all the way back down to the beach, no one even stumbled.

CHAPTER EIGHT

Celia sang as they hiked. Not out loud, just in her head, the song she and her sister had sung on long car rides, an anthem guaranteed to annoy their parents. *The ants go marching one by one, hurrah, hurrah; the ants go marching one by one, hurrah, hurrah; the ants go marching one by one, the little one stops to shoot a gun and they all go marching down, to the ground, to get out of the rain.* Celia identified with the ants.

No one said anything until they were standing in front of the dining room. "What do we do now?" Justice asked.

When no one else spoke, Celia answered. "I know we agreed to stay together," she said, "but I would really like to go back to my room and try to get some sleep. Alone."

Justice and Xander both nodded.

"Me too," Justice said.

"Let's get whatever we need from the dining room," Xander said. "And then we'll go into our rooms, lock our doors, and not come out until morning."

To Celia, this was the best idea anyone had had all day.

Xander went into the dining room, and she followed him. After the darkness of the mountain, the bright lights of the hotel seemed harsh and glaring. Celia felt like a cockroach that wanted to scurry away to a dark corner.

In the dining room, Xander grabbed more snacks, and Justice refilled her water bottle in the nearest bathroom. Frankie and Manny didn't take anything, and Celia felt like her stomach couldn't handle food right now. In the pile of snacks on the floor, she spotted a few bags of peppermint tea, and she picked those up and tucked them into her pocket. Hot water was probably too much to ask for in her bungalow, but if she soaked the tea bags long enough in cold water, that would maybe do, and would be enough to wash the taste of bile and blood from her mouth. The bile taste had been there since right after breakfast, and the blood since they were on the mountain. When Emma Jane had gone over the side, Celia had been so shocked that she'd bitten her tongue in surprise, and the taste of metal had flooded her mouth instantly. It reminded her of going to the dentist.

They all looked at Xander, who shrugged and nodded, and then they began the walk back to the bungalows. The clouds were starting to float over the moon again, and the bungalows were dark silhouettes that looked like nothing more than shacks. Now, half of them were empty. They reached Xander's bungalow first, and he disappeared inside. Justice's was next, and she did the same. Celia's was right beside Frankie's; Manny's was on the other side of the boardwalk.

Celia turned and waved to them before she went in, and Frankie waved back. "Have a good night," Celia said, and then regretted it as soon as she closed the door. It was such a rote, preprogrammed thing to say. There was no way any of them were going to have a good night. Celia walked into the bathroom to make her tea.

When Justice had first seen the bungalows, tiny houses perched on stilts above cyan waters, as if they were cottages at the end of the earth, her heart leaped. This, she had thought, was truly getting away from it all. Now she shivered at how isolated and flimsy and out in the open they were. She would have been more protected sleeping in a tent.

She shut the door behind her and locked the dead bolt. The sparsely furnished room seemed like another liability—there was nothing she could shove in front of the door. She walked over to the bed, kicked off her shoes, and climbed under the sheets, pulling them up to her chin even though it was still hot. She shut her eyes, and then felt something brush her cheek. Her eyes flew open and she jerked upright, swiping at her face. It was a thread, a thread from the pillowcase.

She lay back down. Her pounding heart was the only thing she could hear. Finally, it slowed, and then there was a creak that set it hammering again. "It's just the wind," she said aloud, startling herself. Even the sound of her own voice set her on edge.

The curtain moved even though the window was closed. Justice got out of bed to double-check that it was locked. That was when she noticed the lock was on the outside. Of course! Why even pretend she could make herself safe? She crawled back into bed. There was a rustle in one corner of the room and then a rustle in another corner. Maybe a lizard? Justice closed her eye, this time squeezing them so tight that her whole face scrunched up. Go to sleep, she had to go to sleep.

Then there was another sound, one that caused her to bolt upright in bed again. Frantically, she strained to see in the dark, hoping the sound wasn't what she thought it was. But what else could it be but the sound of a doorknob turning? The sound of someone trying to get into her room?

"Go away," she whispered. "Please just go away." The turning stopped, if that had even been what it was.

Justice fumbled for her phone and pressed it to check the time. The blue light was comforting, but the time it displayed was not. She still had hours before the sun came up. She had to try to get some sleep. She closed her eyes, and then opened them.

The curtain moved again.

Justice started to cry silently. She didn't know if she'd ever wanted anything as bad as she wanted off this island, right now. Her whole body shook with her tears. She had killed someone, and now someone was trying to kill her. The curtain moved yet again.

"I'm sorry," she whispered to the curtain, her voice thick and choked. "I'm so, so sorry." She turned onto her side, curling into a fetal position as she hugged a pillow. Underneath the cool side of the pillow, her fingers hit something hard and round, and Justice felt her whole body go cold. She grabbed the object and sat up, clicking on the light on her phone so that she could see what it was.

It was an EpiPen, Margot's name clearly visible on the prescription label. The same EpiPen Justice had searched so hard for this morning, her bee stings still smarting as proof. She opened her mouth to scream, but nothing came out. Fear had been flooding her body for so long that she had nothing left, she was simply as scared as she had ever been, as scared as she ever could be. She lay back down, holding the EpiPen tightly, and tried in vain to go to sleep.

Frankie hadn't spoken the whole way down the mountain, and she hadn't spoken in the dining room either. A steady river of tears streamed down her face, and every minute or so she would sniff. She hadn't wanted this. She had wanted Emma Jane gone, certainly, but off the island. Not dead. Frankie tried to tell herself that it was a good thing, that they were safer now, but she didn't believe it. Standing in front of her bungalow, she finally found her voice again.

"Will you come in?" she asked Manny, looking not at his face but at a spot on his shoulder. "You don't have to, obviously. Especially if you think . . . but I'm not. I promise. I swear, up there, I was just trying to save everyone. . . ." She couldn't look at Manny until he responded.

"Yeah," he said, "I'll come in."

"I just really don't want to be alone right now," Frankie said, and he nodded.

"Me neither."

Frankie turned the knob and they entered her room, which was even darker than it was outside. The darkness made her shiver as she thought of Celia and Justice going into their rooms alone. They were braver than she was. Everyone was braver than she was. For as long as she could remember, Frankie had been scared. Of everything. Of failure, of being a nobody. She'd always thought of herself as a survivor, but now she wasn't so sure. Maybe she survived because she was too scared to let go, too scared to surrender.

The only thing that was calming Frankie right now was the sound of Manny's breathing.

"I don't think we should turn on any lights," he said. "Just in case someone's watching us. I don't want the others to know we're together."

Frankie nodded, and they both shuffled toward her bed. She crawled over to the far side and sat with her back against the wall. Manny sat down next to her, their shoulders touching. Frankie reached up and felt her own face with her fingertips to see if she was still crying. Her cheeks were wet, but it didn't seem like the tears were still flowing, so she decided she wasn't.

"Want to play a game?" she asked. "To try not to think about . . . it."

"Sure," Manny said. "What game?"

"Twenty questions," she said.

"Okay," he said. "You go first."

"How many tattoos do you have?"

"One," he said. "It's just really big." Frankie gave a small laugh, and Manny continued. "Forty-three last time I counted," he said, "and there have been more since then. I regret them."

"Why do you regret them?" she asked, surprised.

"Nope," he said, "that's another question, and now it's my turn."

"Okay, go."

"What's the significance of sixteen?" The roman numeral sixteen was Frankie's only tattoo, the size of a dime, inked on her left ribs. It wasn't visible in the bikini she had on now, so

Manny must have seen it earlier, when she'd been in her under-wear. Frankie felt her body flush, knowing that he'd been look-ing at her closely enough to spot the tattoo. Frankie was used to people looking at her, but for some reason, with Manny it felt different.

"Sixteen stands for the age I was when my life really started," she said. "Now, my turn. Why do you regret your tattoos?" Manny shifted slightly, and Frankie couldn't be sure, but it felt like he was closer now, his arm touching hers from the shoulder to just below the elbow.

"It'd be nice to be a blank slate," he said. "When I look at these tattoos and how many of them there are, I realize I haven't left myself any room for new stories. When I started getting them, I didn't think it mattered. I didn't think I'd live past twenty-five, but now . . . I want to be old someday. And I don't want my life to be defined by everything I did before I was twenty." Frankie nodded in the dark. "Now me," Manny continued. "Why did your life start when you were sixteen?"

"That was when I emancipated myself," she said, and added, "Who's Carolina?" She'd been wondering about the name inked across Manny's chest from the moment she saw it.

"My mom," he said. "She died of cancer a couple of years ago."

"I'm sorry," Frankie whispered.

"It's not your fault," he whispered back. "Why'd you eman-cipate yourself?"

She took a deep breath and let the air escape out of her as a sigh. "Oh, it's a long story," she said. "But basically my mom had no idea what I was doing until I had almost fifty million followers, and as soon as she found out, she decided she was my manager, even though she knew nothing about social media." Frankie couldn't remember the last time she had talked about her mother, and now that she had started, she couldn't stop. The words keep coming.

"I have to give her credit, it was her idea to start monetizing my following. I hadn't even thought of it at that point; I was just stoked to be posting videos that people liked, and when people sent me product, I would post about it because I genuinely liked it. But my mom started charging, and then whatever money I made, she spent. The more money I made, the more money she spent. We moved into a fancy new apartment, and she bought herself a car, bought her boyfriend a car. My whole life, she'd treated me like a roommate and barely paid any attention to me, and now she was in everything I did.

"She quit her job, and started her own social media accounts, and she'd make me be in her videos, because she knew that would get her followers. She was forty, you know? She should have just stuck to Facebook." Frankie's anger surprised her. She knew she hadn't forgiven her mom, but she thought that maybe time had made her less bitter. It hadn't.

"She'd promise people that I'd do posts on my account for stupid stuff, like a cheesy, expensive steak house in New Jersey so that she and her boyfriend could get a free date night. But the worst was when she'd threaten posts. Like, we'd be somewhere and she'd think that someone was rude to her, and so she'd start yelling, 'Do you know who my daughter is? She has sixty-five million TikTok followers, and we can make it so that no one ever comes to your store again!'"

"Jeez," Manny said. Frankie swallowed.

"Yeah," she said. "I never liked my mom, if I'm being

honest. Even as a little kid, I could tell that she was selfish, but then I started to hate her. She was drinking all the time too. She'd do this thing where she'd cut the tag off a tea bag, tape it inside a to-go mug, and then fill it with vodka. She thought she was so clever, but no one was fooled. You could smell it, and she'd just sit there all day, sipping from this mug, never asking anyone for a refill of hot water. The first big campaign I booked was for Aéropostale, and she got shit-faced and the makeup artist offended her somehow. The next thing I know, she's yelling and screaming and literally dragging me off set— like, the photographer was shooting. And I didn't protest, because I knew that'd be even more embarrassing than just going with her, but I was humiliated." Frankie paused. "I went home that night and started researching lawyers, and a few months later I was on my own."

"Do you miss her?" Manny asked.

Frankie had to think. No one had ever asked her that before. From the time she'd contacted the lawyer to when that lawyer had set her up with Roger, a real manager, and the entire time it took to get the court order, no one had asked her that.

"No," Frankie said, "I don't. It took a while to get used to living on my own, but once I figured out I could order toilet paper and soap on Autoship, it was easy. Or easier, I guess." She moved her left foot a little so that the side of it brushed against Manny's right foot. He didn't pull away.

"You and your mom were close?" she asked him.

"Yeah, very," he said. "She was my biggest supporter. She believed in me, even after all the shit that went down with the warehouse fire. She didn't miss a minute of my trial, just sat behind me the whole time and came in every day looking so nice and respectable. When I saw her, I thought she looked tired, you know? I figured it was because of everything I put her through. Then I found out that she'd been sick but had been putting off going to the doctor until after my sentencing. By then, it was too late."

"Oh, Manny," Frankie said, and without thinking, she reached out and found his hand in the dark and wove her fingers through his.

"She loved music like I love music," he said. "She was always dancing around our house and singing, and she had great taste. Old-school R&B, jazz, folk . . . And she would always tell people, 'My son is going to be a famous musician someday. He is so talented.'" Manny sniffed. "I still want to make her proud of me, and I told myself she was the reason I was doing all of this."

"All of what?" Frankie could feel him shrug.

"The brand building, the following, all that shit," he said. "But I got it backward. I put too much emphasis on the famous and not enough on the music. I thought that if I got enough people to care about me, then they'd care when I put out an album. But that's . . . I got it all wrong. Just because they follow doesn't mean people care."

"That's the truth," Frankie said. "So, you're working on an album?"

"Yeah. I work on it every day."

"What kind of music?"

Manny groaned. "That's the ten-million-dollar question," he said. "I know this sounds pretentious, but it's hard to put into words. I guess it's comedown music?"

"Huh? I have no idea what that means." Frankie's voice was gentle, and he took a breath.

"Okay," he said, "so you go out and you have a lot of fun, and it's like a really great night, but then you come home late and alone and you put on something that makes you feel sad. But it's a good sad, because you feel something, and as long as you feel something, you know you're alive. And you imagine that someday you'll meet someone who feels sad in the same way that you do, and . . ."

"You'll be happy?"

Manny squeezed her hand. "No, of course not," he said. "You'll just be sad together."

Frankie laughed. "Ah, the dream," she said. "I had no idea you were such a romantic."

"I am," he said. "I've seen *The Notebook* at least thirteen times."

"Stop," she whispered, laughing.

"I can't help who I am."

"I'd love to hear it sometime," she said. "The album." Frankie could hear him swallow.

"I'd love to play it for you."

"When we get out of here," she said.

"When we get out of here," Manny echoed. They sat in silence for a second, Frankie waiting for him to say something else, and when he didn't, she filled in the gap.

"I kind of envy you," she said.

"Why's that?"

"You have a thing," she explained. "Something you love. Music."

Manny cleared his throat. "I heard you were working on an album," he said, and she laughed quietly.

"Auto-Tune and I recorded a couple of songs," Frankie said. "They're okay, but I hate performing. I can't even do karaoke."

"What about dancing?" he asked, his thumb moving back and forth lightly on hers, making that inch of skin pop and fizz.

"Yeah," she said, "I like it, but I never took classes or anything. My mom couldn't afford it. I taught myself dances from watching YouTube videos."

"You've got so much going on, though," Manny said. "Like all your collabs. Fashion and beauty and all that stuff. You're not passionate about any of it?" His fingers had moved and instead of tracing the back of her thumb, he ran them lightly over her palm.

"If I had to pick a collab I was most passionate about," Frankie said, "it would probably be my signature Baskin-Robbins ice cream flavor."

Manny was silent. "No shit?" he asked. "You got to make your own ice cream? What was it called?"

"Frankie's Sugar Russh," she said, smiling to herself. "Pink bubble gum ice cream with mini gummy bears, sprinkles, and a ribbon of vanilla frosting."

Manny gave a low whistle. "Wow," he said, "that sounds . . . intense."

"It sold out," she said. They were still holding hands, and Frankie turned to face Manny, who was already facing her. In the dark, they were so close that her nose bumped his, and for the first time that day, Frankie's pulse quickened in a good way.

A beat of silence passed and then another, and Frankie found herself wishing that it wasn't so dark in here so that she could see his eyes, his tattoos, his lips. Finally, Manny broke the silence.

"Do you mind . . . ," he said.

"Yes?" Frankie leaned forward so that her forehead rested on his.

"If I use your bathroom?"

Manny didn't need to pee. He just needed a minute. He closed the door behind him and sat down on the edge of the tub. His heart was going a mile a minute and he felt dizzy. He took a few deep breaths, trying to slow his body down.

He'd almost kissed Frankie, and she'd wanted him to. It was too dark to see the expression on her face, but he could feel it in the energy radiating off her. He was sure his was the same, their essences tangled up in the space between them even though their lips hadn't touched. And really, what the fuck?

Five people had died today. Frankie had yelled at a girl, and she fell off a cliff. Someone was a murderer. Someone was trying to murder them. And yet here they were, sitting on a bed in the pitch-black darkness making incremental movements to bring them closer together, to make a cascade of touches seem accidental.

Manny put his elbows on his knees and his head in his hands, pulling his hair back so hard that it almost hurt, stretching the skin on his forehead and straining his roots. He had no idea what was real anymore. All day, he'd been waiting to wake up, waiting for this nightmare to end, yet that end seemed to get further away with each passing minute. So maybe it didn't matter? Maybe he should just do what he wanted to do and go back out there and kiss Frankie. But not a hesitant kiss, not a smiling kiss, not a soft little kiss where they broke apart to stare in each other's eyes, giggle, and say hi. Not a kiss like that. It would be an urgent kiss. A hard kiss, a kiss like he was trying to suck her soul out of her body, a kiss like their lives depended on it.

This morning, when he had first seen her, next to the helicopter, Manny would have said she was perfect. But Frankie had fallen off her pedestal since then, and that only made him like her more. Because he wasn't perfect, and what would he have done with a perfect girl?

If they got off this island—*when* they got off this island— they were going to fall in love. They'd make out on the beach, eat tacos at two a.m., cook elaborate meals that turned out totally mediocre, fall asleep over FaceTime when they couldn't be together, steal each other's chargers. They'd fight. She'd annoy him, he'd annoy her, but they'd be real together. Cracks and flaws and mistakes all on the table. They'd be happy, but more important, they'd be sad together. They'd be alive.

Manny took a deep breath and stood up. He felt around for the faucet and turned it on, a trickle of water coming out. He cupped his hands underneath it, and then when they were half full, he splashed the water on his face and ran his hands through his hair. He turned the faucet off and heard something. A crash, and then a thud, like something falling over. Instantly, all of the hair on his arms stood on end.

His first thought had been Frankie, but no. The sound

wasn't coming from inside the bungalow. His heart was pounding again, and it felt like it was in his throat. He pushed the bathroom door open.

"Manny?" He could tell by Frankie's voice that she had heard it too. "I think that was coming from Celia's bungalow. . . ." The bed squeaked as Frankie scrambled across it, and Manny felt across the room to the door of the bungalow. He opened it, and then Frankie burst past him, running the few feet down the boardwalk to Celia's bungalow. She started to pound on the door.

"Celia! It's Frankie! Are you okay?" she shouted. "Open the door."

There was no sound from inside. Manny ran up and grabbed the doorknob. It was locked, and he gave the knob a shake. Frankie pounded on the door and called, "Celia? Are you in there? Open up!"

The sound of footsteps pounding down the boardwalk made them both spin around. It was Xander, his hair a mess and his eyes wild, clutching the table lamp from his room like it was a weapon. "What's going on?" he asked.

"We heard a crash," Frankie said. "Now she won't open the door. Celia!" She pounded harder on the door, and then she stopped, her arms falling limply to her sides. "Oh god," she said, "what do we do?"

"I guess we break it down?" Manny offered, and Frankie nodded, weakly.

"These doors are crap," Xander said. "It won't be hard." Justice had appeared behind him.

"What's going on?" she asked. "What happened?"

"We don't know," Frankie said. "We heard crashing and

Celia won't . . . she can't open the door." Justice took a few steps back. Xander motioned for Frankie to move aside, and when she did, he stepped up to the door. He took the lamp, raised it over his head, and then brought the base down, as hard as he could, on the doorknob. The sound of metal on metal rang out like a broken bell and erased any hope Manny had that maybe Celia was just a heavy sleeper.

Xander smashed the doorknob again and again, and finally it broke off. He reached into the hole and felt around. The door opened a few inches, and the four of them just stood there. Frankie took a deep breath.

"I should—" she started, but Manny shook his head, cutting her off. Before anyone could say anything else, he pushed Celia's door farther open and stepped inside the room.

The smell hit first, rank and rotten, and it made Manny gag. He covered his nose to try to block it out.

"Celia?" he called softly, even though he knew she wouldn't answer. He stepped to the side, felt around for a light switch, and flipped it on. The sight made him throw up in his mouth, and he swallowed, forcing it back down.

Celia lay facedown on the floor, by the bed, one of her hands still gripping a sheet that was half on the bed, the rest puddled next to her. She looked like she had exploded. The stench came from the shit and vomit that covered the room, even the walls. There were puddles and trails of it everywhere, as if Celia had stumbled from one side of the room to the other before collapsing. Manny backed out of the room, gasping for breath as soon as he could, trying to keep the contents of his stomach in place.

Justice had a hand over her nose and mouth, and a wild

look in her eyes. "I should check and see if she's still alive," she said, and before anyone could stop her or warn her or assure her she didn't have to, she darted into the room, stepping over puddles and trails of bodily fluids to squat down by Celia and check her pulse. It was clear from how quickly Justice was back up and out of the room that Celia didn't have one.

"What happened to her?" Xander asked. His voice was small, and he was still clutching the lamp, now dented and cracked. They moved away from Celia's bungalow.

Manny looked at Frankie, who hadn't said a word yet. She had her arms wrapped around herself and was rubbing her hands up and down them.

"Poisoned, I would guess," Justice offered, and Frankie let out a sob.

"I think we should all go back to the dining room and sleep together," Xander said. "These bungalows aren't safe." Justice was already shaking her head and backing away from them.

"I'm not staying with you," she said. "I'm not staying with any of you. One of you just poisoned a sixteen-year-old girl." She paused, as if waiting for one of them to deny it. "Murderer," she said, louder this time. "Murderers!" And then she turned and ran back to her bungalow.

CHAPTER NINE

Damien was here, just one bungalow over. He was waving and smiling, his T-shirt rippling in the wind. He had a huge grin on his face, but he wouldn't answer Xander.

"Come over here!" Xander yelled from his bungalow. "Come here!"

But Damien wouldn't answer, just kept smiling and waving. If Damien wouldn't come to him, then he would go to Damien. He climbed up on the railing of his balcony and perched on top of it. He could swim, it wasn't that far. But as he looked down into the sea, the perfect blue water became darker and darker, until it was black and swirling and bubbling. Xander recoiled, but Damien was still on the other side, smiling and waving.

The water grew even darker, and now there were creatures in it. Xander couldn't see what they were. They were shapes that slithered under the surface, amorphous and undistinguished, but still, he had to go. He owed Damien that much but he wouldn't swim it. Xander started to climb back down the railing when he lost his grip and slipped. He woke up right when he hit the water.

He sat up in bed, his heart racing. The lamp was lying on the other pillow. Damien wasn't here, of course, because Damien was dead. But there was sun. It was morning. Xander had made it through the night.

He hadn't expected to sleep. He'd planned to just lie on the bed and stay vigilant, but at some point, his body must have given in. As his heart slowed, last night came back to him. The sad fire, and Emma Jane falling down the cliff. Celia's awful end. Xander sat and listened. The island was awfully quiet. Too quiet, a quiet that gave him chills. He forced himself out of bed and walked to the bathroom, where he saw himself in the mirror. He looked haunted, the dark circles under his eyes like dugouts. How did he get here? To this place where his whole life was a lie? If he got off this island—no, *when* he got off this island, he was going to change everything.

He left the bathroom, grabbed the lamp, and headed out the door. Outside, he paused and made himself look at the water. He breathed a sigh of relief when he saw that it was clear and bright blue, with no black things swimming in it. He looked around, half expecting to see the creatures slithering through the air.

He remembered which bungalow was Manny's and used the base of the lamp to knock on the door. The sound was loud and rang out across the island. There was no way anyone could sleep through it, and Xander held his breath, growing more anxious as each second ticked by. He had the lamp up, ready to knock again, when Manny finally opened the door.

"Shit!" he yelled, jumping back, and Xander immediately realized that it looked like he'd been about to bludgeon him.

"No, no, sorry, sorry!" he said, dropping the lamp onto the boardwalk. "I'm cool, it's cool, I was just trying to wake you up."

Manny blinked, his chest heaving. He stepped out of the bungalow and caught his breath. After a few seconds, he looked around.

"Where are Frankie and Justice?" he asked.

"You're the first one I tried," Xander said. "Did you sleep?"

Manny shook his head, and then nodded. "I wouldn't call it sleep, but I was unconscious for a while," he said. "What time is it?"

Xander shrugged. "No idea." He looked out over the horizon. The sun was getting higher in the sky, and the only clouds visible were innocent wisps. The storm clouds had vanished overnight. "It doesn't look like it's going to rain," he said. "You think maybe someone will come for us today?" He looked back at Manny. A couple of locks of hair had fallen over his forehead and into his eyes, but he didn't brush them away as he squinted out over the water. Manny didn't answer his question.

"That one is Frankie's, right?" Xander asked, pointing to a bungalow. Manny nodded, and Xander walked over to it, Manny following a few steps behind. This time, he knocked with his knuckles, and Frankie answered quickly.

"What's going on? What happened?" She looked like she might cry, and Xander felt relief flood through him again. She, too, was still here.

"Nothing," he said, resisting the urge to add, *Not yet.* "We were, uh, just checking on everyone. I think we should go see what we can find to eat." Frankie nodded. She stepped back into her room to pull on a pair of shorts and then came out.

"Where's Justice?" she asked.

"We were just going to get her," Xander said, and then the three of them walked over to Justice's bungalow. Frankie did the knocking this time, and Xander thought maybe she hadn't knocked loud enough, because Justice didn't answer. Xander could feel the black things circling, in the water, in the air, and inside him, as he stepped forward and pounded on Justice's door as hard as he could, sharp pain shooting through his knuckles with each knock. There was still no answer. No way Justice could sleep through this.

"Oh no," Frankie said as Xander reached out and turned the knob. It was unlocked, and he was surprised by how easily the door swung open. He flinched with expectation. He hadn't prepared himself for whatever he was about to find. Except, there was nothing. No stench, no body, nothing in Justice's room seemed out of place. Xander walked in and looked around, and after a moment of hesitation, Frankie and Manny followed. Xander felt his pulse speed up, and he took a few steps toward the bathroom and peered in. Justice wasn't in there either.

"Where did she go?" he said, spinning back toward the other two. "This is sketchy. You don't just get up and go off by yourself."

"She might have," Frankie said. "She really seemed like she wanted to get away from us last night."

Xander walked over to the bed and looked down at the tangled sheets. He picked up a pillow and tossed it aside, and something flew out, hit the floor, and then rolled. Plastic, he could tell by the sound it made when it had landed on the floor.

"What's that?" Frankie said. Her voice had chilled. Xander walked over and stared down at it.

"A syringe," he said. Manny and Frankie were right behind him, and they all stared in silence.

"It's Margot's EpiPen," Manny said.

"No way," Xander said, but when he bent down and looked closer, sure enough, Margot's name was visible on the prescription label.

"Why would Justice have Margot's EpiPen?" Frankie asked. "She was the one who was looking for it when . . ." She trailed off. "Do you think she had it all this time?" Her voice was small.

"If she did . . . ," Manny started, but none of them seemed to be able to put the words together to make what they were thinking into a complete thought. If Justice had stolen Margot's EpiPen, then what else had she done?

Manny was shaking his head. "We have to find her," he said. "And quickly. Whatever it is she's up to, I don't want to give her any more time to pull it together."

"It just doesn't make sense," Frankie said. "Why would Justice want to kill everyone? There's no way she set this whole thing up."

"I doubt she did," Manny said. "But whatever part she did play in all of it, she needs to confess. And now."

Xander felt dizzy. He hadn't been able to believe that one of them was the killer, but one of them helping the killer, that could work. Justice had seemed so nice, so honest, but then she was here, right? And being on this island meant she wasn't who she seemed to be. None of them were.

"You're right," he agreed. "We need to find her ASAP."

Manny and Frankie stepped out onto the boardwalk, and Xander started to follow, but then he stopped and went back into the room. He picked up the EpiPen and closed his fist around it. At least it was sharp. It might be good to have.

They each got what they needed from their rooms, then walked down the boardwalk and to the beach, all three of them silent as they trudged through the sand. Xander found himself looking around, his eyes automatically drawn to any movement. A bird here, a falling palm frond there. It was already hot out, but he felt cold. No matter where he went, he couldn't shake the feeling that he was being watched.

"Should we climb to the top of the cliff again?" Frankie asked.

"Sure," Xander said. He felt like he'd agree to anything right now, just to keep moving, busy, one step ahead of being swallowed by despair.

They picked their way across the beach and through the trees to the mountain. As they climbed to the top, sweat poured off Xander and he struggled to catch his breath. His body, which normally thrived on physical activity, was now rebelling against it. It didn't want to run on adrenaline anymore, and neither did he.

At the top of the cliff, the remnants of their fire made him want to laugh—it was so pathetic. To think that they could have ignited a flame any bigger than a candle was a joke. No one spoke as they peered over the edge of the cliff and saw what it had been too dark to see the night before: Emma Jane's body, twisted and turned on itself like a doll tossed out a car window on the highway. Xander was the first to turn away. The hike was pointless. Justice was nowhere to be found.

They were walking back toward the hotel when something by the boathouse caught Manny's eye.

"What's that?" he said, pointing.

He altered course and headed toward the boathouse, with Xander and Frankie right behind him. As they got closer, they could see what it was: a Hydro Flask. Not just any Hydro Flask, but Justice's bright yellow one with a BLM sticker. Manny picked it up and dusted the sand off it.

"Do you think she tried to swim for it?" he asked, turning back toward Frankie and Xander.

Xander hopped up onto the boardwalk and peered into the boathouse, which smelled rank and was swarming with flies. He held his breath, trying not to look at the oozing mess that was Graham, and glanced around. On the other side of the boathouse, several life jackets had been tossed on the floor like someone was trying to find one that fit.

"Holy crap," he whispered, then took a step back out of the boathouse. "I think you're right. It looks like she took a life jacket." He thought about what the driver of the boat had told him on the way over, and then he tried to remember if Justice had been close enough to hear. Big waves, currents, one way in and one way out, even for boats. It was certain death. If she had decided to swim for it, then she was desperate. He walked down and joined Manny and Frankie, and the three of them stared out at the water, the path Justice had surely taken if she'd swum for her life. Maybe that had been her plan the whole time, maybe there was someone out there who would pick her up.

Xander had always had a fear of drowning. He couldn't imagine anything worse. But give him one more day here, he thought, and he might change his mind. One more day here, and drowning would be the easy way out.

There was only one thing left to do. Manny didn't say it out loud, but he could tell by the way that Frankie and Xander followed him wordlessly they knew where he was going. They hadn't looked at the screen, their personal oracle of doom, since before they had climbed up the cliff to build the fire last night. Before Emma Jane had gone tumbling down that same cliff, before Celia had . . . exploded.

In the dining room, flies were swarming around the dirty dishes and glasses that had been sitting there since yesterday morning's brunch. If Unknown Island ever wanted to redo its branding to reflect the true nightmarish experience, a swarm of flies would be a good option for the logo. Pools of blood, bits of brain, and insects that feast on decay.

Sure enough, there were two new posts, which wasn't a surprise. The surprise would have been if the account had gone dormant. Dormancy would have been a relief, but instead, it continued to taunt them. The new picture of Emma Jane sitting by the pool, silhouetted against the sunset. Manny tapped on the photo to enlarge it, and Frankie read the caption out loud. "'Emma Jane was more than just a pretty face, so she had to be put in her place. Rich girls don't go down without a fight, but what if this rich girl was right?'"

"This one is different," Manny said. "It doesn't hint at anything about how Celia died."

"It's almost like it knew we weren't going to see it until after she was dead," Xander said. "So it didn't bother dropping hints."

Manny felt his body move as if of its own accord as he took a step to place some distance between himself and Frankie and Xander. Ever since it had been suggested that the killer was one of the ten people on the island, Manny had resisted. It was too wrong, too odd. These people had their faults, but they weren't killers. That was what he had thought. But now he wasn't so sure. The cold truth was that there weren't really any other options; Emma Jane had seemed so sure of it. What if, as the caption suggested, she was right?

If either Xander or Frankie were thinking similar thoughts, they didn't say anything. Frankie tapped the screen and moved onto the next post. Sure enough, it was a picture of Celia.

They were all strange pictures, but this one especially so. It had been taken yesterday morning, when they were just sitting down to breakfast, and in it, Celia was beaming. Not at the camera or at any of them, but at the plate of biscuits and gravy in front of her.

"She looks so happy," Frankie said. Manny thought he heard a catch in her voice. "One of you read it," she said, "I can't."

Xander cleared his throat and read, "'Celia Young won many games, including the one that brought her shame; when she came here, she had no fear, but now her winning streak will disappear.'" Manny took a slow breath. *Disappear*—a reference to Justice? Manny got a feeling, dark and heavy, in the pit of his stomach. He doubted that Justice had tried to swim for it, but he was almost certain they would never see her again.

He jumped back as something hit the screen and shattered.

Shards of green glass rained down on his feet. Frankie had picked up a champagne bottle and hurled it at the screen. She had another bottle in her hand, gripping the neck as she geared up to swing it like a baseball bat.

"I hate this thing!" she screamed. "It's awful, it's evil. It's all evil." It took Manny and Xander both an instant for the shock to wear off, and then Xander reached out, trying to stop Frankie, but he was a split second too late. Frankie swung right at the center of the screen, and the bottle broke into hundreds of pieces. Xander and Manny both flinched, squeezing their eyes shut and turning their faces away to protect themselves from the flying shards. As soon as Manny looked back, he could see that Frankie's hand was bleeding. She started to shake and sob.

They were all barefoot. As Manny took a few careful steps toward Frankie, he stepped on a piece of glass and sharp pain bit into his toe. He picked Frankie up, and she wrapped her hands around his neck and sobbed into it. He carried her to the other side of the room and set her down on the floor, up against the wall. When he looked down, he saw that his shoulder and chest were smeared with Frankie's blood and that he'd left a trail of bloody footprints across the floor.

"Here," he said, grabbing what looked to be a relatively clean napkin from the table and twisting it. "Give me your hand."

She held her hand out obediently, blood dripping onto the floor. He tied the napkin tight around the cut and then moved her hand so it rested on the top of her head.

"Keep it above your head," he said. She sniffled and nodded.

"I'm sorry," she said. "I'm not normally . . . I bled all over you. . . ." She stopped, and her shoulders sagged. Her whole body sagged. "I just don't know what to do anymore." Manny nodded. He knew the feeling. Xander picked his way through the glass to come stand beside them.

"It's behind some sort of reinforced pane," he said, pointing at the screen. "It's way more protected than we are."

Frankie nodded. "I just don't ever want to see it again," she said.

"I don't either," Xander agreed. "So let's not look. We know it's not going to tell us anything good, so it can post all it wants, and we just won't look at it."

Frankie wiped her eyes with the hand that wasn't on top of her head. "Let's agree to never come back in here again."

"Agreed," Manny and Xander said at the same time.

"And agree to all stay together this time," Manny said. Xander and Frankie nodded.

"What else can we do?" Xander asked.

"I guess we just wait," Manny answered.

So they did. They waited. And waited. Everything they did, they did together. They took group trips to the bathroom, Xander and Manny going in with Frankie and turning their backs when she peed. They got snacks from the kitchen, even though Xander was the only one who could manage to eat. They always returned to the pool. It was the place most out in the open, with the longest views and the fewest places to hide.

For a while, the sun was right above them, barely casting any shadows, and then it was moving closer and closer to the horizon. Each hour that passed, each movement of the sun, made it harder to believe that anyone was coming for them. They still waited.

Frankie hadn't moved in over an hour. She might have been asleep, or she might have just been very quiet, the skin on her back and shoulders getting redder and redder as the day wore on. Xander couldn't sit still, so he paced and swam, getting in and out of the pool over and over again. At one point, Manny looked over and Xander was doing push-ups and crying. The sky turned orange. They had passed another day on Unknown Island, another day in paradise. Manny couldn't remember the last time any of them had spoken, and then Xander turned to Manny and broke the silence.

"Dude," he said. "So are you a drug dealer?" Manny was so shocked by the question that it took him a second to realize it had been addressed to him.

"What?" he sputtered, and Xander shrugged.

"Sorry," he said. "It's just what I thought when I went through your phone. You've got more unread texts and messages than anyone I've ever seen."

Manny was quiet. "Drug dealer." The words pinballed around in his head. They sounded ridiculous. Like something straight out of *Miami Vice*. He'd never thought of himself as one. In fact, he tried to think of it as little as possible. When he did, he thought of himself as someone who just helped people out, who got people what they wanted when they couldn't get it for themselves. As Lindsey had put it on the phone when she was inviting him to Unknown Island, he was a person who helped people have fun.

Manny reached into the pocket of his backpack and took out a plastic bottle of pills and set it on the table. Xander came over so he could get a closer look at the label, his face twisted in confusion as he read it.

"You have the runs?" he said. Manny shook his head.

"It's MDMA," he said. "A hundred pills. I thought I was going to have a heart attack getting through customs, but that was a breeze. I haven't let them out of my sight since I got on the island, though."

"Why'd you bring it with you?" Frankie asked. "And that much?"

"I thought it was why I was invited," Manny said. "When Unknown Island first reached out, the person I talked to kept telling me how she wanted me along to make sure that everyone had a good time."

Xander and Frankie were both watching him. They didn't say anything, so Manny kept talking.

"I guess it all started a year and a half, two years ago maybe," he said, thinking back to the beginning of what he had assumed had gotten him here. "This promoter I know asked me to help him out because he had a big-time rapper in town for the weekend, and the guy was notorious for going hard. The promoter wanted to make sure he had everything he could want lined up and ready to go. He was having a tough time, though, so he asked me if I could hook him up." Manny stopped and swallowed. "I hit up a few people I knew from growing up, and was able to find everything he wanted, so I took it to the club. I thought I'd just be in and out, but the next thing I knew, I was in the VIP hanging out with everyone. This dude started following me, tagged me in a couple of stories, and I got like fifteen thousand followers overnight." Manny stopped and shook his head.

Saying it out loud, it sounded so stupid, but he could remember how he'd felt that morning. Hungover as he'd ever been but high on hope, looking at his new numbers and thinking that something big was happening.

"After that, I started getting more calls from different promoters, and I was doing it a lot, and every time, it was almost the same story," he said. "People like you when you show up with a bunch of shit, and I started to make a lot of friends. Or I started to think I made a lot of friends, but yeah. You're right." He stopped and looked up at Xander. "I guess somewhere along the way I became a drug dealer. I just thought that I was . . ." Oh god, was he really going to say this out loud? In front of someone like Frankie? But he took a deep breath and said it anyway. "It sounds so idiotic, but I thought that I was building my brand."

"It's not idiotic," Frankie said, sitting up and shifting. "Aligning yourself with celebrities is a good strategy." But Manny continued shaking his head. He wasn't going to let her make him feel good about this.

"I just always thought that if I kept posting pics of me with some rapper, or some producer, or some singer, and kept getting followers, that would help me get my music out there, make people listen to it, make people care about it. I was kidding myself, that those numbers meant something, that it meant I was successful." He laughed.

"Yeah, I know," Xander said. "Those numbers really fuck with you. They go up, you feel good. They go down, you start to wonder what you did wrong." A loud thud made all of them jump, but it was just a coconut falling off a tree. Xander picked up the prescription bottle and rolled it between his palms.

"What's this stuff do, anyway?" he asked. "I've never even smoked weed."

"People call it ecstasy for a reason," Manny said. "It makes you feel good."

"You feel like you're one with the universe," Frankie said, wistfully, "and that all is right with the world."

"I could use some of that right now," Xander said.

Frankie cracked a smile. "Yeah," she said, "we all could."

"Help yourself," Manny said. "I have plenty." He meant it as a joke, but the next thing he knew, Xander was unscrewing the lid and popping a pill in his mouth.

"How many do I take?" he asked.

"Just one," Frankie said, holding out her hand. "For now. Gimme."

Xander shook one of the pills into her palm, and she put it in her mouth and swallowed.

Manny took a deep breath. This was not what he had expected to happen. "Oh, what the hell," he said, and swallowed one himself. He looked up and met Frankie's eyes, then looked at Xander. At the same time, the three of them grinned. The wolves had circled long ago. Why not go ahead and let them close in?

"What do we do now?" Xander asked.

"Watch the sky," Frankie said, leaning back. "Give in."

"Hey," Manny said, thinking of something. "What's your real name, anyway? It can't be Frankie Russh."

Frankie grinned. "It's not," she said. "It's Dolores Frances Rosinski."

"And now I understand why you changed it," Manny said.

Xander found this uncontrollably funny.

• • •

Xander kept his eyes trained on the sky, just like Frankie had told him to. He was watching for a sign. First, that the drugs were kicking in, and second, that it was all pink skies ahead. He looked over at the hot tub, a small circle of water that everyone had ignored because who wanted to sit in hot water on a tropical island? But now he got up, walked over to it, and dipped his foot in. It was the same temperature as the pool. He pressed a button on the side, and it came alive with bubbles. He climbed in and, by how good it felt, he guessed that the pill was starting to work.

"Is it hot?" Frankie called out, and Xander shook his head.

"Nah," he called back. "It feels good."

A few seconds later, she was sliding into the hot tub, and Manny was right behind her. Frankie held her hands out and skimmed them across the top of the bubbles.

"Feels like ten million tiny kisses," she said. Xander just nodded. He didn't want to speak, didn't want to do anything to jeopardize the feeling that was coming on. He slid down so that the water was up to his chin, and then he leaned his head back and closed his eyes. Xander couldn't believe he'd lived eighteen, almost nineteen years without ever trying drugs. Drugs weren't bad, they were glorious. He felt like he could hear everything, the rustle of individual leaves, the fish darting around in the sea, the very beginning of the birds' chirps, before the sound even came out, when the song was just barely a vibration in their tiny, feathered chests. He felt alive, pure, free, for maybe the first time in his entire life. Then Frankie spoke.

"Hey," she said. "So are you gay?"

He sat up so quickly that he gulped in some water. But the

look on Frankie's face wasn't confrontational. It was gentle, almost concerned. "Since we're talking about what we saw on people's phones," she explained.

"What'd you see?" he asked her.

"It was more like what I didn't see," she said. "Everything had been scrubbed. You'd have like one browser window open, so you were clearly looking at something you didn't want people to see. And then there were your DMs."

Xander had no idea what she was talking about. His DMs were just as clean, if not cleaner.

"You have literally thousands of unread messages from girls," she went on. "Some really hot girls, too. I mean, I've gone through some phones in my day, and usually, even if a guy has a girlfriend and is super loyal to her, he still opens the message, just to check and see if the girl sent nudes."

It was none of her business, Xander knew that, and he knew he didn't have to answer her question. But he wanted to, because Xander had been praying for someone to ask him that very question so that he could answer. So that he could finally talk about it as opposed to just turning it around and around in his head.

"I don't know," Xander said, and saying it out loud made him feel like he'd just sprouted wings. "I honestly don't know." From across the hot tub, Frankie gave his knee a reassuring tap with her own.

"That is totally okay," she said. "It's not a yes-or-no question."

Xander nodded, then licked his lips and swallowed. Frankie had settled back so that her head was resting on Manny's shoulder, his arm around her. Looking across at them, Xander was momentarily struck by how beautiful they both were, how the tangled worry that had taken over their faces earlier in the day had been replaced by a look of dark-eyed bliss. Since they were on the subject, Xander figured he might as well go ahead and tell them everything.

"Damien Richards was a kid in my calculus class in high school," Xander started. "I was failing, so the teacher asked him to tutor me. At first we'd meet at school, and then we started going to his house. He was really cool; it was the first time I felt like I could let my guard down. I was the quarter-back on the football team, and most of my friends were also on the team and I always felt like everyone was watching me, that all these people were depending on me not just when we were on the field but all the time. Like I couldn't just go out there and throw the ball. I had to be the quarterback, like I had to play the role." He sank down again so that the bubbles burst on his chin. "I don't know if that makes any sense," he said.

"Yeah, it does," Manny said. "I could never play sports, because I couldn't handle the pressure."

Xander nodded and continued. "But Damien didn't give a shit about football, or that I was the quarterback, and so we never talked about it, and the less we talked about it, the more I felt like myself. I stopped pretending. And then one day, it just kind of happened, we hooked up. And I liked it, and it kept happening, and it started to feel like he was the only person who knew the real me and the only person I wanted to be around."

Xander paused and squeezed his eyes shut, trying to blink

back tears. "I left my phone open in the locker room," he went on, "and someone saw our texts. I panicked. I didn't know what to do, and so I pretended like it was all a joke and that I'd just been texting him to like, I don't know, make fun of him or something."

"What happened to him?" Manny asked.

Xander drew in a big breath and let it out. Just thinking about it made his chest tight. "Shit got really bad for him, I guess. He was getting bullied. It spread way beyond the football team, and then he stopped coming to school."

"Did you ever talk to him again?" Frankie asked, and Xander shook his head.

"I never got a chance," he said. "He killed himself before graduation."

"I'm sorry," Manny said softly. "And now you're here." Xander nodded miserably. He was almost relieved when neither Manny nor Frankie tried to make him believe that it wasn't his fault.

"Did you ever tell anyone?" Frankie asked.

Xander started to shake his head, then reconsidered.

"Not in person," he said. "But I used to go on this forum, and I told a couple of people on there. I was freaking out; I needed to talk to someone and I figured it was safe, because it was all anonymous. Or so I thought . . ."

He looked up and Frankie was holding out her arms. It took Xander a second, but then he realized that she wanted him to come over there. He moved around the side of the hot tub, and she wrapped her arm around him, pulling him close so that his head rested on her shoulder. Xander settled in, feeling her skin against his. Aside from a high five, he couldn't remember the last time he had touched someone. It felt good, like maybe he could be a human again.

"One way or another," Frankie said. "It's going to be different now."

Sandwiched between the two of them, with her head on Manny's shoulder and Xander's head on hers, Frankie felt safe. Protected. Almost. She sighed, and then she wasn't sure if she had sighed, or maybe it had been Manny, or Xander. They were all one now, and every time she breathed, it filled their lungs with air.

This was the first time Frankie had taken anything stronger than a vitamin in a year, and she was remembering why she liked drugs so much in the first place. It was like hitting pause on your brain, muting the voices that talked all the time, saying the same things over and over and over. Things that made you feel bad. Without drugs, she was forced to listen to those voices. The voices told her she was trash, talentless, cruel, unworthy, a has-been destined to die alone. They told her that she should have been the one to die, not Hannah. Hannah was good and Frankie was awful, an embodiment of self-interest that happened to pick up on choreography and look good in a crop top.

The voices were right. Now, with the drugs, the voices had taken the night off, but they'd be back tomorrow. Working even harder, clocking overtime, to make sure Frankie never felt a moment's peace. But now, she wondered if this was what babies felt like when they were in the womb, before the world rushed in and flogged them raw.

"Okay," Manny said, his voice slow and dripping with color, "say you're trapped on a desert island . . ."

"So hard to imagine," Frankie said, and she felt his chest rise as he laughed.

"So you're trapped on a desert island," he started again, "and you can only listen to one album. What album?"

"Easy," Frankie said. "Fleetwood Mac, *Rumours!*"

Manny laughed, and Frankie pinched his leg. "Why is that funny?" she demanded.

"Because girls love Stevie Nicks!" he said.

"Are you serious?" she said. "Of course girls love Stevie Nicks! She's a badass with great clothes who writes amazing songs. Why *wouldn't* girls love Stevie Nicks?"

"I'm just messing with you," he said. "I, too, love Stevie Nicks." He started to sing. " 'Thunder only happens when it's raining, players only love you when they're playing . . .' "

Frankie raised her eyebrows in surprise. His voice wasn't half bad.

"I'd bring some Whitney Houston," Xander said.

"Ha!" Now Frankie was the one laughing. "How do you even know about Whitney Houston?"

"She's my mom's favorite," Xander said. "No joke, when Whitney died, my mom put her photo up in the living room, right there with all our family portraits."

Frankie nodded. "Whitney's a freakin' legend, for sure," she said, then turned to Manny. "What about you?"

"Easy," he said. "*Purple Rain.*"

"Damn," Frankie said, "that's a good one. I would one hundred percent listen to Prince right now." Frankie felt momentary panic as Manny twisted away from her and climbed out of the hot tub. She didn't want him to leave, ever. The few yards between them were too much. What if the air froze, became solid, and he could never make his way back to her again?

She watched in fear as he walked over to his backpack and dug something out of it. When he stood back up, he was holding his phone and smiling.

"Fortunately for you, I have it right here," Manny said.

Frankie relaxed. The air was still air. He was coming back. He hit a few buttons and then, to Frankie's relief, Manny climbed back into the hot tub and she settled back into his shoulder right as the first few notes came through the phone's speaker. She felt the music enter her bloodstream and start to course through her veins.

"I never meant to cause you any sorrow," Prince sang. "I never meant to cause you any pain . . ."

"Oh my god," Frankie said as the tears started to gather in her eyes, "it's so sad."

"It's a song about the end of the world," Manny said.

The tears started to stream. Frankie was crying for all of them. Her tears would wash them clean. She wondered if she would ever again feel as close to anyone as she felt to Xander and Manny right now. After all they had been through, after what they had survived, how could the three of them ever be apart?

"It's such a shame our friendship had to end," Prince sang.

"Do you think we're bad people?" Xander asked.

His question pierced Frankie like an arrow, and she answered immediately. "Yes," she said.

"What do you mean?" Manny asked.

"We're here because we did something bad," Xander said. "All of us. What was in that letter was true for me, and it was true for you, so it was probably true for everyone else too. Was it true for you, Frankie?"

He shifted, pulled away from her slightly so that he could look at her, but Frankie couldn't meet his eyes. She felt like she had just been about to step off a ledge, but then had pulled her foot back. She would stick to her story.

"Hannah Carrington was my best friend," she said. "She died of a drug overdose when she was with me in LA. We'd been out partying that night and went back to our hotel. I was just a few doors down from her"—Frankie stopped and swallowed—"but I didn't know what she was doing. If I had, I would have helped her."

Frankie's face twisted in grief. "Hannah was the person I cared about more than anything in the world, and she died just two doors down from me, and I slept through the whole thing. I never tried to stop her, I never tried to make her get help, and I knew . . . I knew . . . I'm not just bad, I'm awful. I couldn't even save my best friend."

"You're not," Manny said, wrapping his arms around her and pulling her toward him. "We all made mistakes, but that doesn't define us. We're not bad people."

"You're not," Frankie said. "Out of all of us, you were the only one who admitted to what you did."

"Chelsea did, too," Xander said.

"Okay," Manny said, taking one arm away so that he could

push his hair out of his face, "so we're all bad people. But everyone is a bad person, and everyone is a good person. Good people do bad things, and bad people do good things. We're all here because we fucked up. But, you guys," he pleaded, "every single person on this planet will fuck up, and it doesn't mean they deserve to die."

Manny was intrinsically good, Frankie knew that, just like she knew she was intrinsically bad, and she pressed herself harder against him, as if she could absorb some of his goodness through her skin. She tried to think of words that would explain how she felt.

"I know I'm bad," she said, "because no matter what I get, I want more."

"That doesn't mean you're a bad person," Manny said. "It just means you're ambitious." But Frankie shook her head.

"Nothing makes me happy," she said. "Good people are happy, they don't think about themselves all the time. I analyze and overanalyze every single thought I have and every single thing I do."

"I don't understand," he said, his words a breeze in her ear. "How does that make you a bad person?"

"Because a good person wouldn't think so much!" she said. "They'd just live and be happy and tell people happy birthday because they wanted to, not because they wanted people to like them." Frankie flushed under her sunburn. "Hannah was like that," she went on. "She was good because she was good, not because she wanted people to think she was good."

Manny was shaking his head. "Everybody thinks a lot," he said. "If you ever got a chance to be inside someone else's head, you'd probably find out that it's a lot like your own.

None of us are as different as we think. No matter what we're going through, we're never going through it alone. The world is just set up to make us feel that way, to make us feel like we can't be ourselves and that no one will ever understand us, and that's all a lie."

Xander rolled his head back and forth, stretching the muscles of his neck. "Sometimes I think I hate myself, but then I realize I just hate my brain," he said. "It won't shut off or shut up. I'm so wrapped up in my head that sometimes a whole day will go by and I can barely remember where I went or what I did. I'm in a fog all the time." He stopped and looked up at the palm trees and the sky, and waved a hand at some birds flying overhead.

"Being here has been hell, but at least trying to survive has shut my brain off." He laughed. "It's fight or flight because I'm worried someone might kill me, not because I'm worried someone might look at my phone. In a way, it *has* been a vacation."

"I feel the same way about my brain," Frankie said. "It's a feedback loop that won't stop. Sometimes it feels like no matter what changes, where I am or who I'm with, I'm still living the same experience over and over because my brain is running the same script."

She rolled her head like Xander, and it felt like her muscles were breathing, exhaling and inhaling through her skin.

"I used to be like that," Manny said.

"How'd you stop?" Xander asked, and Frankie could feel Manny shrug in response.

"I just stopped," he said. "I realized that if I ever wanted to get up off the couch and do something with my life, with who I was, I had to control my mind, and not the other way around. So, when I'd catch myself starting to go down that path, where

I blamed myself for everything and kept telling myself that I was a fuckup, I'd tell myself to stop. I'm not proud of my past, but no amount of shame is going to change that. It just is what it is. After a while, my brain got the message and it stopped trying to go there at all. Your brain is a tool. It is *one* part of what makes you *you*, but it's not the whole thing."

Frankie took his hand and laced her fingers through his.

"You're a good person, Manny de La Cruz," she said, and he shrugged again.

"All you have to do is try," he said. "Trying to be a good person is what makes you a good person."

Frankie didn't respond, because she wasn't so sure it was that easy.

The sky grew dark, hours passed, and they continued to wait. Xander and Manny had both fallen asleep on the beach. Xander lay on his back, sprawled out like a king, while Manny lay on his stomach, arms tucked under his head, his cheek on his hands.

Frankie was starting to come down. She no longer felt radiant; in just her swimsuit, she felt cold. It was a clear night, the sky exploding with stars, and as she looked out at the ocean, she couldn't see the light of a single boat. She was no longer surprised by how isolated this sliver of an island was. She wasn't sure that she'd ever be surprised by anything again.

Frankie had a hoodie in her room. It was soft and oversize, and wearing it felt like a hug. It was exactly what she wanted right now, the only thing she wanted. If she had it, she was pretty sure she could fall asleep on the beach too. She could see her bungalow from where they were. She and Xander and Manny had promised that none of them would go off alone, but she didn't want to wake either of them. They both looked so peaceful. They were both good people, and maybe Manny was right, maybe she was good, too. Even after all of this.

Frankie decided to make a run for it. She stood up and sprinted across the beach, jumping up onto the boardwalk. There, she ran on her toes so that the pounding of her feet wouldn't echo on the wood. She went into her room, leaving the door open. The hoodie was on the back of a chair, and she tossed it onto the bed. Then she went into the bathroom, brushed her teeth, and slathered some after-sun lotion on her arms and shoulders. It wouldn't do much good. She was so burned that she was going to be in major pain as soon as the pill wore off, but the lotion felt good and made her smell like jasmine and coconut.

She filled a large glass with water and took her supplements, adding an extra vitamin B in the hopes that maybe she wouldn't feel totally awful later. She squirted a vitamin C packet into the last inch of water and then downed it like a shot.

Then she walked over to her bed and grabbed the hoodie. She pulled it on over her head, and when she saw what was lying on the bed, hard and black amid the soft pillows and wrinkled sheets, she didn't even scream. It was the gun.

Frankie felt her ears ringing and the room starting to tilt. She forced herself to breathe. How could she have missed it when she entered the room? She hadn't missed it, right? There was no way she could have. But if the gun hadn't been there . . .

Frankie reached out and picked it up. Her hands were shaking. "Hello?" she said softly. "Who's there?"

The only sound was the light rustle of the curtains, stirred by a breeze blowing in through the open door. Before she could think too much, Frankie tucked the gun in her swimsuit, making sure it wasn't visible underneath the sweatshirt, and then ran back out of the room.

CHAPTER TEN

It was dawn. The sun was sherbet-colored and the birds were starting to sing. It took Xander a second to realize where he was and what had happened. Blinking, he pushed himself up to sitting. He had sand in his mouth. His head felt like he had been bashed with a hammer, from the inside. He opened his mouth to spit out the sand and his jaw popped. Every movement felt like metal rubbing against broken glass. His stomach felt hollow and hot. He wasn't hungry, but he was pretty sure he had never been this thirsty in his life.

Manny and Frankie were still asleep. At some point, Frankie had put on a pale blue hoodie. She had the sleeves pulled down over her hands and the hood up over her head. She and Manny were curled up, back to back, their feet intertwined. Xander had known he was the third wheel, but he didn't mind. They were good people. They had a future together.

He tried to decide what to do. Last night, the three of them had promised they would stay together, that no one was going to go off on their own, but he didn't want to wake them. They were breathing in unison.

Xander stood up quietly and brushed himself off. It had been at least twenty-four hours since Justice had left the island. A whole day had passed and nothing had happened. Maybe this was all there was, and now they just had to wait it out and someone would come for them, eventually. As much as Xander wanted to leave, though, he wasn't quite looking forward to going home.

Xander sighed. He'd made a mess of his life and he had caused someone else to take their own. Or, if he hadn't caused it, he'd at least given Damien the final shove. In that moment, even with the headache and the cottonmouth and the body that ached all over, Xander had a flash of insight.

He needed to make things right for Damien—as right as he could at least—and he couldn't do that on his own. He needed help. He needed his mom. Sure, she was so conservative that she wouldn't even watch *Grey's Anatomy*, but she was also tough. She loved her son, fiercely, and she loved God, and if there was one thing Xander's mom had taught him, it was that God understands, God forgives. Xander had to start to ask for forgiveness. Eventually he had to forgive himself, but for now, God was a good place to start.

Xander made his way to the main buildings. His head hurt so much that he kept his gaze down, his eyes on the ground in front of him. His body winced with each step. He didn't want to go in the kitchen and see Robby's body, and he didn't want to go in the dining room and see the screen. In the lobby, he found a vase on the check-in desk, tossed the flowers on the floor, and then rinsed the vase out and filled it with water from the bathroom sink. He took a long chug—he could feel the cool water running down his throat and into his stomach—and then set the vase down. Taking careful steps, he walked back outside, and decided to sit by the pool for a minute. Then he'd go back down to the beach and wait for Manny and Frankie to wake up.

At some point in the night, Frankie had put on a hoodie, and Manny shuddered to think how she'd gotten it—running across the island in the dark, alone, after they'd promised to stick together. But then, Manny was apparently the only one taking that promise seriously. Xander was gone too.

Frankie was curled up in a ball, cuddling a beach towel like a teddy bear, and in a parallel universe, one where he wasn't worried about getting murdered, Manny could have watched her sleep forever, but now he reached out and touched her shoulder, giving her a gentle shake.

"Frankie! Frankie, wake up," he said, his voice low.

Frankie gasped, and bolted upright, her chest heaving as she tried to catch her breath.

"Is the boat here?" she asked.

Manny shook his head. "No," he said. "It's still just us, but Xander's gone."

Frankie looked at him, and their eyes transmitted thoughts they wouldn't say out loud.

"He probably just went to get a drink of water," she said, and then swallowed. She pulled the sleeves of her hoodie down over her hands.

"I've been up for a while," Manny said. "At least ten minutes."

Frankie nodded and stood up, brushing herself off. They both scanned the beach and the horizon. They'd made angels in the wet sand last night, and somehow they hadn't been washed away. They'd written their names underneath them. Under hers, Frankie had written *Dolores*.

She looked at Manny again, and he could see the demons behind her eyes. He was sure he looked the same.

"Xander!" Frankie called toward the bungalows.

Manny yelled toward the kitchen. There was no response.

"We have to look for him." Manny reached out and took Frankie's hand and started pulling her toward the hotel lobby. She shook her head. She didn't want to go.

"I want to stay here," she said, fear in her voice. "He'll come back to us."

"We can't stay on the beach all day again," Manny said. "We need to eat. We need water. You need to get out of the sun." Her cheeks were bright red, and small blisters were starting to appear on her nose. "We have to find Xander. I'm sure he's fine, but we still have to find him."

That was a lie. There was no way that Xander was fine, and they both knew it, but Frankie nodded and let herself be pulled along. She gripped Manny's fingers so hard that his knuckles were crushed; she kept her other arm wrapped around her, as if she was trying to give herself a hug.

They walked across the beach, toward the bungalows, and then down the boardwalk, still calling Xander's name. And then they stopped to listen. Silence and sunshine and chirping birds.

"I never want to hear a bird chirp again," Frankie said. "Ever."

"Should we look in the rooms?" Manny asked, but Frankie

shook her head. Manny didn't really want to look either. It was hard to remember which room had a dead body and which one didn't. They turned and walked back down the beach, then up the little sand path that wound through the palm trees and flowering hibiscus to the pool.

The first thing Manny noticed was the sound. Bubbling. The jets were on in the hot tub, which meant that someone had pressed the button within the last thirty minutes. The pool came into view as he stepped out from the trees. The surface was calm, glassy and red. The color of the hibiscus flowers, the color of beet juice, the color of blood.

Instinctively, Manny grabbed Frankie and shoved her behind him. "Stay here and don't look," he said.

"No," she said. "What is it?"

She pushed him out of the way, gasping when she saw the pool. Before Manny could stop her, she was running toward it. She made it to the edge a split second before he did, and they simultaneously registered what they were looking at. Xander, lying on the bottom, a large spear protruding from his back. Neither of them even bothered to scream.

Manny spun in a circle, looking in every direction. He could hear his heartbeat. "Justice is still on the island," he said. "She has to be. We were right by the dock all last night. We know there's no one else here."

"She can't be, though," Frankie insisted. "We looked everywhere!"

Manny couldn't believe it himself, but it had to be true. "She must be good at hiding. We have to look for her again." He stopped himself. "Wait, no, that's what she wants. She wants us to come find her. We have to make her find us."

Frankie nodded silently. She stood at the edge of the pool watching the water grow redder and redder, her arms still wrapped tight around her.

"We have to go someplace where we can see her coming," Manny said. "She's gone crazy. She's snapped."

Manny felt something in him harden, a part of his soul turn to steel. He knew in that moment that if Justice tried to hurt him, or Frankie, he would kill her. It was that simple. The realization made him feel better. Made him feel calmer. They would get where they could see her coming, and when she came, it wouldn't be easy, but it wouldn't be hard either.

"Where do we go?" Frankie asked.

Manny walked around the pool and looked out over the beach. He stood there for a few seconds, and when he turned back around, his mouth was set in a grim line.

"The end of the dock," he decided. "We'll wait there. We'll be able to see the whole beach, the pool, the path from the bungalows. We can see everything from there, and there will be no way she can sneak up on us."

Manny grabbed a vase off the registration desk and dragged Frankie to the bathroom with him, where he filled the vase with water. It would have to do.

He took two of the straw hats that hung behind the desk and put one on himself and put the other on Frankie. Then they started their walk to the dock. Manny didn't like being empty-handed. He wished they hadn't burned all the wood in the bonfire. He would give almost anything to get his hands on that gun they'd locked in the safe last night. Or was it two nights ago? He couldn't keep track of anything anymore.

"What's that?" Frankie said.

"What?" Manny asked.

"There," she said, pointing, "in the sand, by the boat-house."

Manny followed her gaze, and then he saw it too. Something bright red sticking out of the sand that hadn't been there when they'd walked by just a few minutes before.

"It's Justice's scarf!" Frankie said as they got closer. "The one she was looking for." She started to run, Manny right behind her. When she got to the scarf, she fell to the sand on her knees, grabbed it with both hands, and pulled.

Frankie tugged and it didn't come loose. As the sand fell away it became clear why. The scarf was tied around Justice's neck, her body buried in the sand. There was no doubt that she had been dead awhile. Her eyes and tongue bulged and ants crawled in and out of her nose and mouth. Frankie screamed and fell backward, and both she and Manny scrambled to get away.

They were in a movie. What was happening wasn't happening to them, but to actors, people who looked like them. The movie was beginning—no, it was over. The scene went on too long. The actors' silence had made the director's point. The audience knew, they got it. One of these two people was a killer. It was time to see what happened next.

"Ha." Manny said it, rather than actually laughing. "Ha ha ha ha ha. I guess I was wrong. Sure had me fooled."

Frankie didn't look at him. "It's just us now," she said. "You and me. I guess it's been just you and me all along."

"Maybe it has," Manny said. He should have known. The

hoodie should have tipped him off. She'd left him in the middle of the night and come back, and he'd been none the wiser.

"Aren't you going to say something?" he asked. "Explain what this is all about? I think you owe me that much. At least."

Panic was rising in Manny, and he could hear the note of pleading in his voice. He wanted Frankie to tell him why she'd done it. More than wanted, he *needed* her to. He needed a reason, even if it was a bad reason. If he was ever going to believe in people ever again, he needed her to explain. Then, as soon as she did, he was going to drag her into the ocean and hold her under the water. He wasn't going to go out like that. Not for a girl. Not even for her.

Frankie looked at him, and it felt like she was seeing him for the first time. His tattoos, his scars, the hollows under his eyes. People tell us who they are from the beginning, it's just that most of the time, we don't believe them. Manny was a killer. He'd never denied it. He'd told her, told them all, that first night, what he had done. Frankie felt dirty, vile. To think that she'd respected his honesty, that she'd thought he was noble. Good, even. What a fucking joke. But he wasn't fooling her anymore, and he wasn't going to get her either. Frankie was a survivor. No matter what life threw at her, Frankie survived. She always had, she always would. She reached inside her sweatshirt and closed her hand around the gun tucked in the waistband of her swimsuit. She pulled it out and pointed it at him.

• • •

Manny laughed. For real this time. Threw his head back and looked up at the heavens and laughed. He wasn't even surprised. What did surprise him was that Frankie's hand was shaking. Manny doubted she had held a gun before, much less shot one. Poison, stabbing, strangulation were more her style.

He held his hand out. He doubted she even knew how to take the safety off.

"Give it to me," he said.

"And why on earth would I do that?" she asked. Her voice was cool, composed. It was only her body that betrayed her, her hand continuing to shake like she had palsy.

Manny sighed and debated taking a step closer. He decided not to, not right now. "Because I care about you," he said. "Not you, Frankie Russh, but the real you. The Dolores you. And I want to help you, as much as I can. I know you think it's too late, but it's not. It's never too late." Manny was lying. She'd killed eight people. Of course it was too late. "Please," he begged, "just give me the gun so we can both get out of here."

Frankie shook her head. She knew what he would do if she gave him the gun. He was going to shoot her. He was going to kill her, just like he'd killed the others. No way in hell was she going to give him the gun.

Manny lunged at her, and Frankie jumped back, squeezing the trigger. The gun went off with a crack and Manny crumpled to the ground. She'd done what she had to do to survive, and so she'd shot him right through the heart.

She dropped the gun onto the sand, and it made a tiny *thud* when it landed. Then Frankie walked into the ocean and looked at the sun sparkling on the surface. A curious fish, black-and-white striped with a banana-yellow tail, swam over to check out her toes.

Frankie thought that she, too, would like to go swimming. Now that she was alone, she could do whatever she wanted. She walked to the boathouse dock, avoiding Manny's body on the way, and opened the door. It swung open easily, and the stench and the flies from Graham's body barely bothered her.

She stepped over his body and found a snorkel and a mask quick enough and then walked back out. She didn't bother to shut the door behind her as she left. She put the mask and snorkel down, pulled her hoodie off, and let it drop onto the boardwalk. Then she picked the mask and snorkel up and walked down to the beach.

She should put on some sunscreen. She should get some sleep, should get something to eat, should drink some water. Should, should, should. There was plenty of time to do what she should, but all the shoulds could wait. Frankie waded out into the water, and the deeper she got, the more at peace she felt.

Frankie couldn't remember the last time she had been alone, and now she was alone on a beautiful, tropical island. Just her, and the fish. A speck of red flashed in the corner of her eye. Justice. Frankie grimaced and turned away. Just her, and the fish, and nine dead bodies, yes, but Frankie didn't care.

It was glorious. She had won a game she hadn't even signed up to play.

She pulled the mask and snorkel on and plunged into the water. She floated on her stomach, not moving a limb, and let herself be gently tossed by the waves, this way and that way. It felt like the ocean was cradling her, rocking her to soothe her, to let her know that everything was going to be okay now.

A fish darted past, one of the most beautiful creatures Frankie had ever seen. It had neon stripes, pink and blue with a little bit of green and yellow, as bright and loud as Manny's swim trunks. She paddled her arms a bit so that she turned. There were electric-blue fish and tiny rays, barely bigger than her hand. If she hadn't had the snorkel in her mouth, practically choking her, she would have giggled.

A shark swam by. It wasn't that big, hardly dangerous, but Frankie congratulated herself on not freaking out, not even a little. Manny had a tattoo of a shark. It ran down the back of his left bicep. A reminder to keep moving or you sink, he had told her. Frankie kicked her feet and started to swim.

She swam and swam, and saw so many things she had never seen before. Life was beautiful, this earth was beautiful, and Manny was right, she was a good person. No, she would stop thinking about Manny. She had stopped him, and that was what made her good.

She kicked a little farther, and all of a sudden, the bottom dropped out. She could no longer see it, and the water was cold. Snorkeling wasn't fun anymore. It felt ominous, like something big was going to come along any minute now and swallow her right up. She turned and swam back to the beach.

When the water was shallow enough, she stood up and pulled off the snorkel and the mask, and walked ashore. She dropped the snorkel and mask right there on the sand.

Frankie didn't feel alone anymore. She felt like someone was watching her, taking her picture, but she shook it off. It was old paranoia. Wherever she went, someone was taking her picture. And they could go right on doing it. Hadn't there always been stories of people who believed that a picture stole part of your soul? Surely that wasn't true, or Frankie would have no soul left. She would go back to her bungalow and lie down, but she wanted to check something first.

She walked up to the hotel and into the dining room. The screen was what she was looking for, and there it was, glowing, like an old friend. Frankie crossed the room to it. Several new pics had been posted: Justice swimming under the waterfall, Xander hiking up the cliff, and one of her and Manny walking down the beach, holding hands.

Frankie was wearing the hoodie, which meant the pic had been taken that morning. Had she and Manny been holding hands when they'd gone looking for Xander? Frankie couldn't remember. She didn't bother to read the captions. Clues and riddles meant nothing to her now.

Then, as she was watching, another post popped up, the one she had been waiting for. It was a grainy video, security camera footage of a hotel hallway. The time stamp at the bottom read 3:52 a.m. A few seconds later, Frankie appeared, hurriedly coming out of a room and closing the door behind her. She looked up and down the hallway, her face panicked, before sprinting down the hall.

She read the caption. No rhymes this time, just a straight-forward sentence. "On July 6, 2021, Hannah Carrington overdosed at the Sunset Marquis Hotel in West Hollywood, California. Authorities place her time of death between four and six a.m. Her body was discovered the next morning, when she did not check out of her room. Hannah was alone when she died."

Frankie had seen the video before. She knew it well. She and Roger had paid a lot of money to make it go away. Or so they had thought. But things like that never really went away, did they? She remembered that night so clearly: goading Hannah to drink more, pushing the pills on her, guilt-tripping Hannah when she resisted. Then, hours later, waking up with a start, Hannah, lips blue, barely breathing in the bed next to her. Frankie had panicked and run away, back to her hotel room to pretend like she'd had no part of it, to wait for Hannah to wake up. Hannah, of course, had never woken up.

Frankie double-tapped the screen to like the video and then turned and walked away.

The sun was hot as Frankie walked across the beach, and when she opened the door to her bungalow, the cool darkness and the sight of her bed greeted her like a warm welcome. She shouldn't have been so hard on the accommodations at Unknown Island. Not every place could be as comfortable as the Sunset Marquis. She was tired, so tired, bone-tired. She would crawl in that bed and sleep until someone came to find her. But first, she needed a shower. Just a quick rinse. Her skin felt like it was on fire, and the salt water wasn't helping.

When she walked into the bathroom, she didn't even gasp.

All her supplements, the bottles that she had lined up under the mirror, were gone, and in their place was one orange prescription bottle. Frankie picked it up and read the label.

It said Hannah Carrington.

Of course, Frankie thought. These were Hannah's pills. They were pills for Hannah. It all made so much sense now. Being a survivor was lonely, and Frankie didn't have to be alone. She could be with Hannah. She should have been with Hannah all along. She and Manny . . . no, no, she and Hannah were meant to be together. They were all meant to be together. Life didn't have to be so lonely.

She opened the bottle, shook half the pills into her hand, and swallowed them. When they were all down, she took the other half, then screwed the lid back on the empty bottle and put it where she had found it. Then she climbed into bed and settled back into the pillows. A shower could wait after all. For now, she was going to sleep and wait for Hannah to come get her. She was about to doze off when she heard a click. The door opening. Frankie turned her head to see Hannah coming into the room, bringing Frankie an extra pillow. Frankie smiled. This was how it was meant to be. She was a bad person, but that didn't mean she had to be alone.

A Survivor's Homecoming

The only person who lived through the world's most infamous unsolved murder now finds herself very, very famous—whether she wants it or not.

BY CHRISTIE MILLER

Originally published on the-slice.com

If this was a profile of anyone else, I would begin with a breezy description of where I was meeting my subject. Maybe a restaurant, the reservation made by a publicist who requested a booth in the back. Or a miniature golf course, if the subject wanted to come across as quirky and fun, an art gallery if they want to be taken seriously, or drinks by the hotel pool (though, inevitably, this is the kind of activity suggested only by those who are newly famous).

But here, all I can and will say is that I met Celia Young. Both her parents were there, plus the family's publicist and their lawyer. All other details are off the record, because since April 18, 2022, when Celia was found unconscious and severely dehydrated, the victim of arsenic poisoning on Unknown Island, the Young family has been keeping a low profile.

Except, of course, for agreeing to this article, which will be a cover story. And their Oprah interview, which will air this weekend. And then, of course, there's the seven-figure book deal that they just inked with Random House. And the life rights that were sold to Reese Witherspoon's production company, also for seven figures, and the Netflix documentary, which Celia's father, Robert, executive-produced. And then of course, there's her mother Celeste's Instagram account, which is up to 8 million followers and where she recently urged people to also follow her on TikTok.

I want to write something about how the Youngs seem to be ardent followers of Winston Churchill's advice to never let a good crisis go to waste. But then, the events that happened at Unknown Island weren't so much a crisis as a tragedy. A gripping, unbelievable one at that, and maybe, when a family has been to hell and back, maybe the only thing they can do is try to make some money off it. Empathy, people. Remember empathy?

On January 15, 2022, Unknown Island achieved something rare: it launched a marketing campaign that went viral and truly set everyone talking. A private tropical locale in an undisclosed location in the South Pacific, Unknown Island entered the social media smackdown arena with a slick YouTube video that featured some of the world's biggest models and influencers cavorting on beaches, laughing in pools, snorkeling, splashing, and generally being sun-drenched, beautiful, and aspirational.

The campaign was conceived and executed by NothingBurger Media, the agency offshoot of the popular NothingBurger meme account, and while the video was good, it alone wasn't enough to go viral. No, it took the promise to do that, because Unknown Island wasn't just any old resort. First, there was the age limit—21 and under. And the real kicker was the price: everything at Unknown Island was absolutely free.

Unknown Island billed itself as a destination where the brightest minds of the next generation could come together for inspiration, relaxation, and relationship building. People under 21 could apply online and also, of course, follow all of Unknown's socials. From there, the island would select groups of travelers to come for a weeklong, all-expenses-paid trip. It sounded too good to be true, but amazingly enough, it also seemed legit.

The big question, of course, was who was behind it. Nothing-Burger dodged questions, releasing a statement that concealed more than it revealed: "While they are flattered by the attention and inquiries, the owners of Unknown Island wish to remain anonymous so that their mission, not their identities, is the focus of this project. What we can say is this: They are a group of wealthy angel investors and philanthropists who have combined experience in tech, hospitality, and media. The idea for Unknown Island came to them in the middle of 2020, and with the launch of this new concept in travel, they hope to give Gen Z a reason to be excited again." Less than a week after posting the video, Unknown Island's Instagram account had more than 11 million followers, and was a top trend on TikTok with the hashtag #unknownpickme (which was not conceived by NothingBurger, but rather sprang up organically), with people posting plea videos about why they deserved a week on the island.

A few weeks later, Unknown Island announced they would be doing a soft launch with a curated group of ten "influencers and high-profile people" before picking the first group from the public pool of applicants. This created even more buzz and speculation around the island, as commenters everywhere debated about who would be chosen. Unknown Island was incredibly tight-lipped about who would be in the inaugural group, and in what seemed at first like a brilliant PR move, announced the guests' identities only the day before they were to depart on the trip by following them on Instagram. This was also the first day that Unknown Island began to seem like anything less than a perfectly polished utopia.

"I remember thinking it seemed weird," recalls my 17-year-old cousin Sofia, who, like hundreds of thousands of others, applied to go to Unknown Island. "Here was this resort that literally everyone in the world was talking about, and the people they selected to go were mostly people no one had ever heard of. There was so much buzz about it that it kind of seemed like a letdown."

The first ten were Emma Jane Ohana, the 18-year-old daughter of billionaire financier Noah Ohana, from Los Angeles; Justice Wilson, a 17-year-old environmental activist from Mission Hills, Kansas; Robby Wade, a 17-year-old restaurateur, chef, and YouTuber from Atlanta; Xander Lee, a 19-year-old college football player turned social media personality from Carrollton, Texas; Chelsea Quinn, a 19-year-old beauty YouTuber from Los Angeles; Margot Bryant, the 20-year-old, New York–based CEO of the now-defunct SHEmail; Graham Hoffman, an 18-year-old political organizer from Minneapolis; Manny de La Cruz, a 19-year-old DJ and producer from Miami; Frankie Russh, an 18-year-old social media megastar from New York; and Celia Young, a 16-year-old video gamer from Alameda, California.

On March 22, all ten posted videos about how excited they were to be traveling to the island and what they were most looking forward to about the trip. On the evening of March 24, local authorities arrived on the island, believing they were there for a facilities and safety tour that had been scheduled weeks before. There, they found Celia Young, dehydrated and comatose, but alive. The other nine were dead. Frankie Russh and Manny de La Cruz appeared to have been dead for only a few hours.

But today, almost a year later, Celia Young is not here to talk about Unknown Island. In fact, I have signed a statement that I will not ask about it, and that if I do, the interview will be terminated immediately. I have no doubt that the Youngs' lawyer will remind me if I should happen to forget that I signed the document. No, today Celia Young is here to talk about her new project, a collaboration with Entertainment Arts to release a series of video games for girls. When I press her to elaborate on what will make these games more female friendly, Celia squirms in her seat. "They'll be more accessible, I guess?" she says finally.

Her mother jumps in. "A lot of women find the world of video games to be very intimidating. The games are violent and individualistic, and these games will be more focused on community building. You won't get points for blowing someone's brain out."

Celia Young, however, never played video games for girls, and she was, and is, very good at blowing brains out. Celia began streaming on Twitch at age 12, and quickly amassed a following due to her skill at *Fortnite* and *Counter Strike: Global-Offensive*. Her age, gender, and mastery of the headshot made her a fan favorite in the male-dominated world of gaming. It also, of course, made her the target of a fair amount of sexism and harassment. But even at such a young age, Celia was undaunted.

"It just felt like a challenge," she says now. "I wasn't intimidated when people insulted me, because they had just revealed themselves to be pathetic humans and it made me want to beat them even more." She smiles. "I still take a lot of joy in ruining a grown man's day."

Celeste Young jumps in again. "Obviously, we would never have let Celia go on these platforms if we had known what went on there," she says. "Caroline was always so bubbly and social; Celia was happier alone in her room. So when Celia found video games, we were thrilled that she had something she liked and was good at."

"But that changed after the World Cup," Robert adds. "Then we saw that it was more than just a hobby; it was a career." He is referring to the inaugural *Fortnite* World Cup in 2019, at which Celia placed third and took home $1.2 million in prize money.

"I didn't really care about the money," she tells me. "It was just cool to win." It's true that Celia might not have cared about the money, but her parents sure did.

By 2019, Celeste and Robert Young had already spent two years and an estimated $150,000 trying to launch the influencer career of their eldest daughter, Caroline. (This figure came from an anonymous source familiar with the Young family's business dealings.) Robert is a serial entrepreneur whose previous, mostly failed business ventures were a gym franchise, a supplements company, and what he describes vaguely as "lifestyle technology." Celeste, a former catalog model, was an Arbonne sales rep and stay-at-home mother when Caroline's Instagram began to take off when she was just 16.

Celeste's voice cracks when she talks about her older daughter. "Seeing Caroline put so much effort into styling outfits and taking photos, it reminded me of my own modeling days," she says. "Girls now have so many more opportunities than I did back then, and so I really wanted to help Caroline make the most of them." By the end of 2018, Caroline had amassed a following of just over 1 million, which, to the Youngs, seemed like a lot at the time.

"A million followers, it seemed huge, you know?" Robert recalls. "We thought she was really going to take off. I never had anywhere near a million people like anything that I did." And in a lot of ways, Robert is correct. In almost everything else, a million is a lot. In the world of influencers, however, it's barely a drop in the bucket, and the Youngs soon found out how hard it was to keep that number growing.

"We were posting two to three times a day and had branched out into YouTube and TikTok as well," Celeste recalls. "But the numbers started to plateau. The platforms were becoming more and more crowded, and Instagram kept changing its algorithm, and it started to seem like we weren't even going to make it to 2 million. It had nothing to do with what we were posting. Caroline's photos were gorgeous, her outfits were very stylish, and she always stayed on top of the trends. She was working really hard." Celeste stops and dabs her eyes. "Still, when her growth started to slow, she took it very personally."

At the end of 2018, Caroline was diagnosed with Hashimoto's disease. For several months, she had been feeling tired and sluggish, but she and her parents had chalked it up to her increasingly strenuous work schedule. She was also, in spite of an increase in calorie monitoring, gaining weight, a fact which her followers and random commenters were quick to point out. Her younger sister, trigger fingers honed on Twitch, was one of Caroline's biggest defenders and would lash out with blistering, highly personal retorts to anyone who left negative comments on Caroline's photos.

"It was crazy to me that someone who was a grandma with a Bible verse in her bio would think it was okay to comment on a teenage girl's photo and call her a fat slut, or something like that," Celia said. "I just liked to remind people that the internet wasn't as anonymous as they thought." To do so, she would often decipher the commenters' identities, and then ask them if their coworkers at, say, the Des Moines Jamba Juice, or their friends at Calvary Bible Church in Springfield, Illinois, knew they talked like that. "It was my favorite thing to reply to someone and then see that they'd deleted their account the next day," Celia says, a sly smile playing on her lips.

"We've been portrayed as stage parents," Celeste says, her eyes wet with tears, "but we always told Caroline that she could delete her accounts whenever she wanted. We never forced her to do social media. It was her choice. It was her dream, and we weren't going to keep her from her dream."

While Caroline struggled to grow her following, Celia's grew seemingly on its own. "I never cared about followers," she says. "I just liked to win. I posted whatever I felt like, and I guess people responded to that." Celia's Instagram and Twitter feeds were a mix of shit-talking other gamers, gaming tips, memes, and the occasional cute animal photo, always posted without a caption. It was one of those funny, random accounts that seemed like a glimpse directly into someone's head. In early 2020, @spork _attack was named by BuzzFeed as one of the top accounts to follow. Caroline commented on almost every one of her little sister's posts, usually something like "STOP," the laughing-so-hard-I'm-crying emoji, or the occasional "I'm telling mom."

By all accounts, the Young sisters were close. Celia is so petite she's mouselike, with dark hair, a smattering of acne scars across her cheeks, glasses, and a heavy fringe of bangs. Blond, blue-eyed Caroline had the look of a Miss USA contestant. It was the kind of odd-couple pairing that has carried a million movies, and after Celia's *Fortnite* World Cup win, the Youngs were in talks to star in their own YouTube–based reality show. Then the unthinkable happened.

In addition to the standard lip-synching and dance routines on TikTok and the beauty shots on Instagram, Caroline had started posting short confessional videos to TikTok in the spring of 2019. Some of them were emotional and personal, like her explaining her decision to go on antidepressants, and others were comical and self-deprecating, like a dissection of why she never asked for no tomatoes on her sandwiches, even though she hated tomatoes and knew she would inevitably pick them off. These types of videos did fairly well.

On October 12, Caroline uploaded a TikTok that was a rant about her perceived mistreatment at the hands of a Dairy Queen employee. Perhaps taking a misguided cue from her sister's personal attacks on commenters, Caroline delivered a diatribe mocking the employee's economic status and employment opportunities over what she believed was his offensive reaction to her order. Shortly after posting the video from her car, Caroline went home and, as she often did in the afternoon because of her condition, took a long nap.

By the time she woke up, approximately two hours later, the video had gone viral, and not in a good way. Caroline immediately deleted it, but it had already been Stitched and Dueted thousands of times. Even with the video deleted, the hate continued to flood the comments sections on her other posts. The next night, the Youngs called an emergency family meeting. YouTube had reached out and definitively passed on the reality show. Caroline, the family decided, would post an apology video, and then Caroline and Celia would both go quiet on social media while they waited for the storm to blow over.

Caroline was inconsolable. "I think she felt like her world was ending," Celia says. At this point in our interview, both Celeste and Robert are crying openly, but Celia's face remains etched in stone. "I think she truly felt like she'd ruined her life, that no

285

one would ever forget, and that there was no way she could ever move on. She thought she'd spend the rest of her life known as the 'Blizzard Bitch.'" Caroline never posted an apology video.

The next morning, Celia found Caroline dead in bed. She had overdosed on a combination of antianxiety and pain medications. Her parents believe that Caroline did not intend to kill herself but rather was probably trying to fall asleep. I ask Celia what she thinks, and she is silent for a minute.

"I'm done," she says, finally. I ask her to clarify. Does she mean that she's done trying to guess what was going on in Caroline's mind? "No," she says, "I'm done with this." Then she gets up and walks out of the room.

Her parents, the publicist, and the lawyer all follow her. I sit there for five minutes, ten minutes, and then the lawyer comes back alone. The interview is over, he tells me. If I have any follow-up questions about Celia's new games, and the games only, I can email them. He shows me to the door. I'm Ubering back to my office when the Youngs' publicist emails me to ask if this will still be a cover story.

Obviously, the answer is yes. With or without her consent, the saga of Celia Young is too compelling, too twisty and contradictory to ignore. And, if I am being transparent, it is easier to tell Celia's story without her involvement. Because . . . it's complicated. While Celia is the only survivor of the Unknown Island murders, she is also its only suspect, though she has never been officially named a person of interest. As our previous conversation—which started, innocently, with video games, and traveled, through no steering of mine, into the territory of her sister's suicide—indicated, Celia Young is having a hard time controlling her own narrative. Or any narrative at all, for that matter. In various corners of the internet, Celia is a victim, a villain, a hero, or all three. I would be interested to know how she sees herself, but it's clear I won't get the chance to ask.

If the first cracks in the facade of Unknown Island appeared with the release of the guest list, those cracks became canyons as soon as those guests arrived. Instead of a flood of content from happy influencers, all of the guests went dark and the main Instagram account for Unknown Island released only a trickle. There were no stories posted, just photos, and each image was accompanied by a cryptic, poorly written couplet as a caption.

"I remember thinking it was stupid, but we also weren't sure," recalls Sabrina, a 24-year-old social media coordinator in Santa Monica. "Like, we all know at this point how hard it is to actually be disruptive with social media, so my coworkers and I were like, okay, maybe this is just genius. Like maybe being crappy and weird is the only way to get people to pay attention these days."

If getting people to pay attention was indeed Unknown's goal, it succeeded. With each successive post—usually an image of a single guest, with a cryptic couplet about that guest—Unknown's following grew, and the comments rolled in.

Sabrina chokes back a sob as she remembers how she and her coworkers were totally absorbed in Unknown's posts. "The posts felt like they were leading up to something," she says. "And in those two days, we were constantly debating what it was going to be. Our guesses got more and more outlandish, because we were just making a joke of it, and I think at one point someone even said, 'They're all going to die!'" She takes a deep breath. "If we had known, we would have never . . . We had no idea what was really going on." The truth is, no one did. What was going on at Unknown Island might have seemed weird from the outside, but for those who were actually there, it was terrifying.

Through Celia Young's own testimony, cell phone notes and video diaries made by the guests at Unknown Island, and through official investigations, authorities have been able to piece together a bizarre and horrific picture of ten people trapped in a paradise that quickly became hell.

The guests found themselves alone on the island almost immediately upon their arrival. They were also shocked to discover that the luxury accommodations that Unknown Island had been touting and promoting across its various social media profiles were little more than a lie. They couldn't connect to Wi-Fi and there was no cell service, so there was no way to communicate with the outside world. The resort staff was MIA, there was no hot water, and the bungalows were rustic and barely finished. Celia's memory has been spotty and is coming back to her only in bits, but she repeatedly told investigators that there were snakes in the pool.

The guests dined on a beachside brunch of biscuits and gravy. Shortly afterward, they were presented with ten identical envelopes. The letters inside accused them all of having gotten away with murder, and it wasn't long after this that the guests began to die. Just a little over 48 hours after their arrival, everyone on the island—except for Celia, who miraculously survived—was dead. In spite of the very public nature of the murders, and the intense scrutiny they have received from authorities, both official and self-appointed, the world over, the murders at Unknown Island remain unsolved. A vague picture has emerged about how the murders were orchestrated, but there is still very little known about why, how, or, most importantly, who is responsible.

In the middle of 2021, a local businessman named Victor Boucher initiated a one-year lease of a small island called Toto Motu. The island had been purchased in 2008 by a multinational hotel chain for the purpose of developing a luxury resort, but the project never got off the ground due to a series of setbacks and unforeseen challenges. For one, the island proved to be too remote. Toto Motu is surrounded by a chain of reefs and atolls that leaves the island approachable by boat on only one side, via one route. In bad weather and rough waters, this route becomes virtually impassable, which is not exactly a selling point for most guests, who tend to chafe at the thought of not being able to get away from their getaway.

There was also the island's reputation. During the 1700s and 1800s (with some reports dating as late as the 1930s), Toto Motu's remoteness made it an ideal location for a prison. Criminals, or those alleged to be criminals, were deposited on the island and left to fend for themselves, as there were few ways to escape and no hope of swimming to another island. It was during this period that the island earned its name (roughly translated as "Blood Island") because the prisoners frequently fought, with some even resorting to cannibalism. Many locals insist that the island is haunted to this day, and many local boats give it a wide berth.

In short, Victor Boucher was able to rent the island for a song, and his doing so raised few eyebrows. Boucher had a reputation as a hustler and a con man who frequently skirted the law. He had previously run a short-lived hotel on the mainland and had owned and operated various nightclubs over the years. Boucher's main business, though, was money laundering, and he dabbled in drugs and human trafficking on the side. His clubs were known to be frequented by tourists looking for entertainment in the form of underage girls, and Boucher was known to provide. During the course of my investigation, I spoke with several locals who said that opening a resort on Toto Motu was exactly the kind of business venture Boucher would undertake.

"He talked a big game. Told everyone he had these rich foreign partners who were going to put up all this money, and that it was going to be this big-deal hot spot for celebrities and models," one local, who wished to remain anonymous, told me. "No one believed him, of course. We were surprised when he actually started building out there, but it made sense. He was the kind of guy who could make anything happen, because he didn't care about the law or screwing people over."

Boucher was good at being a bad apple. Previous investigations into fraud, money laundering, and tax evasion hadn't turned up enough evidence to convict him, and there has been little found in his business records to prove where the money for Unknown Island came from.

The final arrangements Boucher made for Unknown Island, in the week prior to its opening, were, by any account, odd ones. He hired a temporary skeleton staff and paid them handsomely to work for just one day. They were told that other employees, ones more skilled at dealing with high-profile guests, would be brought in to actually run the resort.

He also installed a ring of security cameras in the waterways around the island and hired two security boats to patrol the perimeter and make sure no other boats attempted to get in. The security firm he contracted was told that the guests would be shooting a reality show similar to *I'm a Celebrity . . . Get Me Out of Here!* and that they were to ignore any distress signals that might come from the island, so as not to interrupt filming. The operators of one of the security boats reported seeing a fire the first night the guests were on Unknown Island, but, as they had been told to do, they did not investigate.

Boucher himself is unavailable for comment, as the night before the guests were to arrive on Unknown Island, he was found dead in his Mercedes, which was parked outside one of his nightclubs, a bullet through his left temple. Not surprisingly, his murder remains unsolved. "The timing makes us think it has something to do with what happened on the island," a local police chief told me, "but we can't be sure. There were dozens, probably even hundreds, of people who would have liked to see the guy dead. It could have been a business deal gone bad, or someone seeking revenge. He had no shortage of enemies." Thus, when it comes to solving the Unknown Island murders, Victor Boucher is quite literally a dead end.

This is where the conspiracy theories (or "evidence," as some like to call it) about Celia Young start to get really wild. In late 2019, Celia changed her gamer name to Nemesis. All traces of humor vanished from her social media profiles, and Celia seemed to get serious in other ways as well. She streamed incessantly and competed in tournaments around the world. Her profile grew even more during the 2020 pandemic, and her clapbacks at trolls and negative commenters became more and more vitriolic. "Nemesis went too far a lot of the time when it came to trash talk," one gamer told me. "But a lot of us knew what she'd just gone through with her sister. Plus, many of us guys who were really trying to move gaming forward respected her playing and were stoked to see a girl, especially one so young, climbing the ranks. If out-trolling the trolls was something she thought she needed to do, then we thought she should do it."

During this time, Nemesis also became a favorite of esports gamblers, especially on the dark web, where anonymous gamblers placed bets in cryptocurrency and were paid out in kind. Several gamblers won big after predicting, within just a few points, what Nemesis's final score would be. This led to speculation whether Celia herself was watching the bets be placed and controlling her scoring to help specific people win. This speculation spun off into the idea that Celia herself was the one placing these bets and pocketing the winnings.

These sites were only accessible via encrypted browsers, such as Tor, and a winner would process their payout through a cryptocurrency mixer such as Dark Wallet, which combined a user's own bitcoins with that of other random users' to render the origins of the currency, and its owner, untraceable. To complicate things even more, the people who frequent these types of places on the internet, and who understand how they work, are unlikely to come forward to volunteer information in a murder investigation. Still, in spite of this, various leaks and sources have estimated that between late 2019 and early 2022, online gamblers amassed a payout of close to $20 million in cryptocurrency by betting on Nemesis. And $20 million is more than enough to lease a small island in the South Pacific, construct a shoddy hotel, arrange a few flights, and run a marketing campaign. (Shortly after the discovery of the bodies, NothingBurger Media released a statement saying it was just as shocked as everyone else about what had gone on at Unknown Island. The company had been engaged for the social media campaign only, and had never met, or even talked to, its clients in person. NothingBurger Media disbanded shortly after.)

Further speculation about Celia as the mastermind behind Unknown Island rests on the fact that she survived. Unknown Island's security boats reported that no one arrived on or departed from Unknown Island during the time frame that the murders took place. Security camera footage, which does not appear to have been doctored, backs this up. Frankie Russh was the last person active on the island, yet when she was found dead from an apparent overdose of prescription drugs, the doors and windows on her bungalow were locked from the outside, suggesting that someone else had locked them.

Thus, it seems both impossible that Celia Young committed these murders and impossible that she did not. The FBI has repeatedly said that Celia is not a suspect in the deaths on Unknown Island or the murder of Victor Boucher. The internet isn't so sure, and that's understandable. At least to me.

Not from anything I picked up during my brief interaction with her, nor from anything that I discovered in my research. Just from what I know about human nature. Celia Young committing these murders, in the public eye, and getting away with it may be improbable, but it is also the safe bet. After all, if Celia didn't do it, then who did? The only answer to that question is someone who is still out there. Someone who might do it again. Celia Young's first video game for girls hits consoles this fall. Play it if you dare.

The Netflix doc was a waste of time.

Posted by u/LikeAVagrant

I feel like I watched a 90-minute commercial for Celia's video games. What a fucking bummer. I was really hoping it would shed some light on the case, but nah. Buy Celia's stuff!

grassshoppper

Ugh, dude, her dad was a producer on it. Back when I first read about it, I knew it was gonna be a bunch of BS. There's no way it was gonna really look at what happened. I'm really disappointed that Netflix bought into a bunch of propaganda, and that Celia's family is making even more money off this whole thing.

Bert_Macklin_4_Prez

Look, nothing, I repeat, nothing from the mainstream media will ever look at this case fairly. Celia Young killed nine people—ten if you count the promoter who helped get the resort built—and she's getting away with it. Celia Young is also a 16-year-old girl who was found barely alive on an island full of murder victims. She got massive amounts of public sympathy and even if there is massive amounts of evidence pointing to her, no one in their right mind is going to go after her, because if it does turn out that they are wrong, they will be crucified publicly for putting her through more hell.

Mom_jeans_whale_tail

New to this thread. I came here after watching the doc because I was disappointed. I'm still struggling to understand what really went on. What evidence points to Celia?

Bert_Macklin_4_Prez

Here's what I know, which makes me think (know) that Celia did it.

One: Celia was the only one on Unknown Island who didn't belong there. All of the accusations that were leveled at the Unknown Ten were proven to be true, but no one has ever been able to find anything that conclusively links Celia Young to Stacia Lindstrom's death. If she wasn't really responsible for someone's death, like everyone else was, then the only other reason for her to be there was if she was the killer.

Two: Celia had a motive. Celia's gamer name was Nemesis. Nemesis was also the Greek goddess of revenge. Celia didn't start using that name until after her older sister Caroline committed suicide. Caroline was a low-level influencer, and she and Frankie Russh had been friends at one point, but then Frankie's career took off and Caroline's didn't. If Celia blamed Frankie for her sister's death, this was her way of taking revenge.

Three: Celia had the cash, and she knew how to hide it. That article in the Slice estimated someone, or some*ones,* made almost $20 mil betting on Nemesis. Seems like enough to pull this off, if you ask me. And then the pandemic got everyone so used to doing everything online that people didn't think twice about going into business with people they never met in real life. With a few forged papers, one girl became an entire multimillion-dollar corporation.

FreeBritneyBitch

I think you're right on the money here. I have a cousin who was a pretty successful gamer for a while, and he met Celia a couple of times. He told me that she was so smart it was almost scary, and that the only reason she wasn't winning tournaments was because she didn't want to. He thinks that she was a good enough player that she could control what score she got. That's not impossible, just really hard to do.

Eat_a_Bag_of_Ducks

I have a coworker whose nephew lived in Alameda and their neighbor's son used to be friends with her. This kid told his dad who told his neighbor who told his aunt who told me that Celia was obsessed with the idea that her sister's death wasn't suicide, but murder. She really thought that anyone who had ever left a negative comment on one of her sister's posts had helped murder her, and she was obsessed with the idea that people got away with murder all the time.

VeganGurl2006

How do you know that everything that the FirstTen were accused of was true?

Bert_Macklin_4_Prez

There wasn't anything in the doc, but various people here and on Websleuths have pieced it together. The deaths that Chelsea Quinn, Margot Bryant, and Manny de La Cruz caused were all public knowledge, so those three are easy enough.

Frankie Russh's manager admitted to helping her cover up her role in Hannah Carrington's death, and that they paid a hotel security guard a lot of money for the surveillance footage that was posted on Unknown Island's account. However, this guy apparently made a copy of it, which he was trying to blackmail Frankie with by leaving comments on her Instagram posts saying he'd keep quiet if Frankie followed him back!!! Her manager says they blocked the guy of course, but if Celia was paying close attention to Frankie's account, she could have easily seen these posts and then done a little investigation to find out who the guy was and what he had on Frankie.

Xander's, Justice's, and Graham's crimes were all posted about right here on Reddit. Xander himself posted about his relationship with Damien Richards in r/confession. Justice's sister posted on that same thread that she had seen her older sister do something that killed someone and hadn't told anyone. Finally, someone witnessed Graham push Tommy Bledsoe down the stairs at that party. The witness had some pretty lame reasons about why he didn't come forward at the time, but he seemed to change his mind later and was asking a lot of questions in r/legaladvice about how he could come forward now and if he would get in trouble. My guess is that Celia paid close attention to these threads and then did a little investigating when something seemed interesting. It's not all that hard to find out who an anonymous account belongs to if you know what you're looking for. Xander, for example, used the same username on Reddit that he had used on a fantasy football account he'd had in junior high and never deleted!

Emma Jane's and Robby's stories both came through a now-deleted Discord server that someone, possibly Celia, created about people who got away with murder. Someone claimed to have seen Emma Jane steal the jewelry at the party but didn't come forward because they were scared of Emma Jane's father. Someone else said that his or her dad was a line cook at a restaurant where the chef deliberately put something in someone's food and they died. The people left out all identifying details—or so they thought—but again, you can find anything on the internet if you're patient and know what you're looking for.

I also heard from several sources, none official of course, that authorities found a letter in Emma Jane's stuff. It looked like she had written it while she was on the island, and it was addressed to Sergio Ramirez's mother. In the letter, Emma Jane admitted she was the one who stole the jewelry and that she let Sergio take the rap for her. Look, I'm not going to go as far as saying these people got what they deserved, but I'm also not going to be all boo-hoo about their deaths either. Celia picked her people carefully.

Gymnast4Jesus @Bert_Macklin_4_Prez
That is an awful thing to say!!! No one deserves what happened to these people! They had friends and families, and people don't deserve to die just because they did one bad thing.

Terd_Furgeson
Excuse me while I go delete my accounts, including this one.

TheBigSalad @Bert_Macklin_4_Prez
Ok, so let's say Celia did do it and that your three points are correct. She didn't belong, she had the funds, and the motive—that's still a long shot that she actually did the killing.

Throwaway6666
If I were Celia, here is how I would have done it, based on the Slice article and the documentary. Chelsea Quinn was

murdered with a dose of cyanide. Justice Wilson's video diary and Emma Jane Ohana's notes both said that everyone was in the room the whole time, but surely no one was paying attention to someone else's glass. With the accusations, there was a lot going on, and it would have been easy for Celia to drop the cyanide in Chelsea's glass so that it was there when she poured her own drink.

jpaulw3789 @Throwaway6666

Yeah, but where does a 16-year-old girl get cyanide? You can't just buy that stuff at Walgreens!

ItsOctober3rd

I love how 99 percent of the arguments for Celia's innocence come down to "But she's a 16-year-old girl!" stfu

Throwaway6666 @jpaulw3789

Lol. You don't know much about the internet, do you? Ok, so on to Margot Bryant, who was killed by bees. The driver who was supposed to pick Celia up at the airport reported that she never showed, and the helicopter pilot who took the group to the island said that Celia was late getting to the helipad. That leaves about an hour of her time unaccounted for. We already know that an exotic-bee seller overnighted a special order of Africanized bees—also known as killer bees due to their tendency to swarm and inflict hundreds of stings—to the airport, and that someone picked up the package that morning. We also know that a now-deleted TaskRabbit account hired someone to pick up a small package at the airport that same day and deposit it in a rental locker, and that they paid handsomely. Easy-peasy. Celia orders bees, has someone pick them up for her and stash them in a locker, and as soon as her plane lands, she retrieves them and gets to the helicopter late. She knows it won't leave without her, because she's the one who booked it in the first place.

TheBigSalad @Throwaway6666

Ok, color me intrigued. Keep going. Graham Hoffman's death dissected, please.

Throwaway6666 @TheBigSalad

The boathouse was built to kill, and those scuba tanks were lined up in a spot where it wouldn't take much for them to fall off the balcony. Place them right above the button that opens the door, and construct the boathouse in a way so that the opening of the garage door shakes the whole building, and voilà. The murder happens on its own. Robby Wade was a different story, though. Celia had to actually sneak up on and stab him.

jb4k_09 @Throwaway6666

No way. You've seen pictures of Celia, right? She weighs like 85 lbs, max, and looks like she's been in a basement her whole life.

ItsOctober3rd @jb4k_09

You forgot to add "bUt sHe's A 16-yEAr-OLd gUrL!"

Throwaway6666 @jb4k_09

You'd be surprised at how little force it takes to stab someone. With a knife, it really only takes about two to four pounds of force, and once the blade penetrates the skin, it will keep going until it hits something hard, like bone. Robby was stabbed with one of his own knives, a 9.4" Masamoto VG-10 chef's knife that he kept very sharp. He had talked about his love for this knife in interviews, and he frequently used it on his YouTube show, so Celia would have known way in advance what her murder weapon would be. She could have bought that exact knife and would have had plenty of time to practice on a pig leg to get the force and angle just right. Then all she had to do was sneak up on Robby, and he would go down with one stroke.

TheBigSalad @Throwaway6666
A pig leg?

Throwaway6666 @TheBigSalad
Forensic scientists often use pig legs because stabbing them closely resembles stabbing a human body.

TheBigSalad @Throwaway6666
I think I just threw up in my mouth a little, but thanks for clarifying.

Throwaway6666
We know from Celia's own testimony and from Justice's video diary that Emma Jane Ohana's death was an accident, that she fell down the side of the cliff all on her own. Celia just had to fake her own death, and this is where it gets really genius, IMO. It's easy enough to induce vomiting and diarrhea, like with ipecac syrup, and by doing so, Celia made it so that no

one would want to get close to her body, much less move it, so people wouldn't see that she wasn't really dead.

OnlyAfterM1dn1ght @Throwaway6666
Yeah, but in one of Xander Lee's video diaries, he says that Justice took Celia's pulse and confirmed that she was dead.

Throwaway6666 @OnlyAfterM1dn1ght
Yep, so clearly Justice was in on it by that point. Imagine that Celia told Justice she had a plan to catch the murderer. She'd fake her own death, Justice would confirm it, and then the real murderer would be caught off guard and reveal themselves. This would also make it easy for Celia to get Justice in a vulnerable position, like alone and away from the others, so that she could strangle and bury her in the middle of the night. Again—because I know someone is going to try to be all like "But Celia's a scrawny teenage girl, she couldn't have strangled anyone!"—people can be stronger than they look. A lot stronger. Now we're down to Celia's—I mean, the Unknown Island Murderer's—last three victims. So indulge me and let me finish. Xander was shot with a spearfishing gun, which is straightforward enough. The gun could have been buried in the sand, so no one would have found it and all Celia had to do was dig it up when she needed it. Manny de La Cruz was shot with a gun that had only Frankie Russh's fingerprints on it, so we can assume Frankie shot him, right before she was suffocated in her hotel room. And, The End. So, by my tally, Celia Young is actually only responsible for eight murders, since Emma Jane died accidentally and Frankie shot Manny.

Celia's heart was already pounding when a light tap on the bathroom door almost made her jump out of her skin. She quickly shut her laptop and shoved it between two of the plush hotel towels folded under the sink. Her parents had decided that she should go computer-free ("Not forever, sweetheart, just for a while. Until all of this blows over. And people forget so quickly") and smuggling one in was one of the harder things she'd done in recent years. She made sure the laptop was completely concealed and then opened the door a crack, her toothbrush hanging out of her mouth.

"Hey," she said to her mother's concerned face.

"You feeling okay, honey?" her mom asked. "You've been in there for a while."

Celia groaned. "Since when are you the toilet police?" she asked, causing a wrinkle to appear on her mother's forehead.

"I was just checking on you, Celia," she said, scowling. "This launch is a big deal. A huge deal. And we have to be there at eight in the morning. You need to finish up getting ready for bed and get some sleep."

"Okay," Celia said, making her voice softer this time, "I will."

As soon as her mother shut the door, Celia grabbed the laptop and deleted the throwaway account she'd been using to post. There was nothing on the laptop that could be traced to her, and she'd used a VPN, but she started the process to wipe it anyway, just to be on the safe side. Tomorrow, she'd ditch it someplace random, or maybe give it to a homeless person.

Then she brushed her teeth, for real this time, staring at her face in the mirror while she did so. She was disappointed in herself. She'd let her ego get carried away and done something stupid. She couldn't screw up like that again. She, of all people, should know better, but the hardest secrets to keep are your own.

ACKNOWLEDGMENTS

My editor, Krista Marino: What else is there to say other than "you're a beautiful genius and I love you"? My agent, Kerry Sparks: Five years ago, you decided to rep me because of a boner joke (well, probably not entirely because of that, but it did play a role), and now here we are! Thank you for being a friend, and for being in my corner. To Lydia Gregovic, my other editor: You helped shape this book in so many ways. Thank you for your invaluable input. To Beverly Horowitz, publisher extraordinaire; Josh Redlich, publicist extraordinaire; and the whole team at Delacorte Press: I couldn't be happier to be working with all of you and feel incredibly honored to be in your tribe of writers. To Regina Flath: This book is bonkers beautiful, thank you! To the entire team at Levine Greenberg Rostan: Thank you for everything you do, and for just being awesome in general. To copyeditors Colleen Fellingham and Heather Lockwood Hughes: Thank you for dotting the t's and crossing the i's—or is it the other way around?—and basically keeping me from looking like an idiot. To sensitivity readers Ashley Lauren Rogers and Jasmine Walls: Thank you for your incredible, thoughtful insight, which helped shape these characters and this story. To Carolyn: For your friendship, and for actually listening to me when I started to ramble about this book again. To my family, Diane, Joe, Molly, and Poppy: Thank you for a lifetime of support and putting up with me. I love you all so much. To dude one and dude two: You are the best people on the planet. We had a lot of adventures while I was writing this book, and I'm so excited to have many more. I love you to the moon and back (and to the moon again, and back again, and to the moon . . . you get it). To every bookseller, librarian, reviewer, and poster: Thank you for helping to spread the word. We authors could not do this without you. To my readers: You keep me young. Oh, I love you so much.

ABOUT THE AUTHOR

Kate Williams is a ghostwriter and celebrity journalist whose work has appeared in *Cosmopolitan, Elle, Seventeen, NYLON,* and more. She is also the author of the Babysitters Coven trilogy, and lives in Kansas with her family.

HEYKATEWILLIAMS.COM